DEVILS DON'T LIE

BOOK 7 OF THE VALKYRIE BESTIARY SERIES

KIM MCDOUGALL

ABOUT THIS BOOK

Critter wrangler rule eighteen: if wrangling isn't messy, you're doing it wrong.

The forest is whispering to Kyra that something's coming. The creatures are restless. Smoke and ash fall on their homestead. And the shanty towns outside the ward are bursting with refugees.

But Kyra doesn't need omens. She has a direct line to Terra, the god who put humankind in their place once before and won't hesitate to do it again.

Unless Kyra finds a weapon called a "world killer." Finds it and destroys it. The only problem is, that weapon is now in the hands of Montreal's oldest enemy, the vampires.

Kyra and Mason have fought vampires before, but with Mason's demonic magic threatening to push him over the edge, this time, the risk might be too high.

Can Kyra appease an angry god, face off against the vampires and protect her growing family?

It turns out that being a working mom chosen to save the world is going to take practice, courage, and a whole crew of creature companions as backup.

Devils Don't Lie is book 7 of the Valkyrie Bestiary Series.

This one's for my brother, Loch, who put my first fantasy book in my hands and began my life-long love for dragons and their kin.

C H A P T E R

———————

1

March 2084

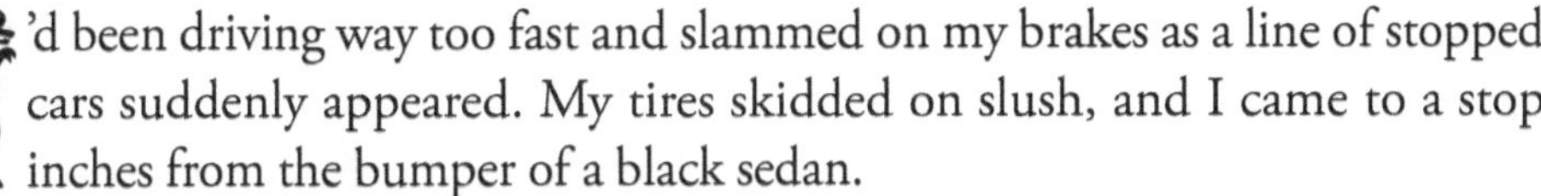

'd been driving way too fast and slammed on my brakes as a line of stopped cars suddenly appeared. My tires skidded on slush, and I came to a stop inches from the bumper of a black sedan.

As far ahead as I could see, nothing moved.

The discarded bones of Montreal's rapid transit train cast sharp shadows across my windshield. I glowered at the ancient structure as if it were to blame for the traffic snarl. I pounded my fists lightly on the steering wheel and leaned back against my seat. A headache was blossoming nicely inside my skull.

The call from Raven's school had come over an hour ago, but I'd been across town on my last job of the day—an infestation of scarab beetles, of all things. The beetles weren't so bad, but panicked godlings of the Pharaoh Sect had camped outside the temple. Having their inner sanctum overrun by the sacred creatures was taken as a very bad sign.

I had to agree. Seeing the ornate walls and sculpted columns covered in chitinous bodies had been unsettling, and I couldn't shake the feeling of foreboding it left in me.

Now I was parked on Highway 40 and that feeling wouldn't leave me. Why does traffic never run smoothly when you're in a hurry? I switched the van to auto-drive so I wouldn't be tempted to zoom up the shoulder.

Mason had been in Parliament all day, but I called to let him know that Raven was in trouble again. The call went to voice mail. I hung up, not wanting

5

to leave that kind of message. He'd learn all about Raven's latest dust-up when we got home.

Tail lights blinked out, and the line of cars finally snaked along the old road. Twenty minutes later, I turned into the parking lot of Bremmer Academy. It was nearly empty. Classes ended hours ago, but Raven had stayed for Alchemy Club.

I waited to be buzzed in at the front doors, then headed toward the main office, suppressing the shiver that schools always gave me. Some people dislike hospitals. Me? I hate schools. They all had that stale smell that I equated with old paste and sweat. To my sensitive keening, the walls seemed to vibrate with adolescent emotion—and not the carefree kind. I keened years of angst over pop quizzes, acne outbreaks, hurt feelings and broken hearts.

My boots squeaked against the gray industrial floors as I hurried down the hall.

Raven was slumped on a bench outside the main office. He was in trouble again. Must be Tuesday.

Mason and I had adopted Raven after finding him on the prison island of Grandill. He'd been born there, but it was no place to raise a child, especially one as magically gifted as Raven. His mother had been a kelpie. His father was either a deadly nuckelavee or a thunderbird. We'd find out which when Raven came into his full power. He'd grown by leaps and bounds once away from the stifling null magic of Grandill, but at fourteen, he was still small for his age.

When he saw me, he straightened. I resisted the urge to brush hair from his eyes. It was too long, as usual—a shaggy black mane with the one shocking streak of white.

"I'm sorry," he said.

I nodded. He was always sorry.

From the vice-principal's irate phone message, I understood that Raven had punched another boy in the science lab. A fight had ensued. A terrarium was smashed in the melee, and the science club's valuable specimen escaped. I wanted to throttle the kid. This wasn't the first fight. It wasn't even the tenth fight. Nothing we said to him on the subject seemed to register.

My son looked up at me with a miserable expression, and all thought of punishment drained away. Poor kid.

"They called me a nuckelavee. Said I'm evil." His voice was barely above a whisper and it rasped with unshed tears. "I'm not!" His hands were clenched into fists, and they shook as if he held them back from violence.

"I know." I gave in and smoothed down that one white lock. "We'll sort it out."

The office door opened and Vice Principal Ferdinanda Cohn marched out. She insisted that parents call her "Ferdy," but students addressed her as "Vice Principal Cohn." She stood over six-feet tall and was as thin and rigid as a flagpole. She wore her hair cut short to accentuate the pointed ears that hinted at her fae ancestry. Perhaps she thought that would intimidate most parents.

I wasn't most parents.

"Ms. Greene, what are we going to do about this situation?" She spoke to me like I was one of her students, with one hand on her hip and an eyebrow raised in a peak.

"I don't know what you're going to do, but I'm going to make sure my son is okay first. Then I'm going to find out if this 'situation' has anything to do with the bullying that we have repeatedly reported to your office. The bullying that you have done nothing about. And if I find out it does, then I'm going over your head to the school board. That would be Mr. Sommors, wouldn't it? I believe my husband is having dinner with Mr. Sommors and all the school district heads later this week." I smiled sweetly. I wasn't above a bit of name dropping, not when it came to protecting my kid.

Cohn didn't faint away or beg for my understanding. Hmm. I'd have to work on my threats. But her eyes shifted from me to Raven and back again. She was unnerved at least.

"We take bullying very seriously at Bremmer Academy, Ms. Greene."

Sure you do. If she *Miz Greened* me one more time, I was going to show her some real bullying.

"But allegations aside, Raven's actions caused damage to the lab. The science club will be very upset when they find Blondi is missing."

Blondi? I glanced at Raven.

"Spider," he mouthed silently and held his hands about two feet apart.

I sighed. Of course. It couldn't have been a hamster. It had to be a spider the size of a cat.

"Fine," I said. "Show me the lab and I'll try to catch…Blondi."

"I should expect nothing less, considering this sort of thing is your specialty. It's the least you can do." Cohn whirled on her heel, assuming I would follow.

Raven grinned and rose to join us. I pointed a finger at him.

"You stay right there. And don't look so smug. We're not done talking about this."

He frowned and slumped back on the bench.

I followed the Ferdy down the hall to the science lab. She stopped in the doorway, and her lips pressed into a thin line.

"Look at this mess. Who's going to clean it up?"

I studied the science lab as if it were a crime scene. Broken glass littered the floor along with a Bunsen burner that thankfully wasn't connected to a gas line. Chairs from two lab tables were toppled. One was broken.

"I'm sure Raven will clean it up. But those other boys should help." I wanted to teach Raven responsibility, but that only worked if everyone involved owned up to it.

"Those boys have done enough damage," Ferdy said. "All I need is for one of them to cut himself on broken glass. I'll have irate parents blowing up my phone line." Then she seemed to remember that she was speaking to one of those parents. "Yes, well. Just find that creature. I'll get the custodian for the rest."

"Aye, aye, captain." I saluted. She made a face as if the air smelled bad and left.

I carefully stepped around the broken glass. The worst mess was the shattered terrarium in the corner. That had to be the home of Blondi, the mammoth rat-eater spider and the science club's mascot.

I closed my eyes and took a deep breath, wondering why the gods didn't like me.

Then I took out my widget and called my office.

"Hey." Emil answered on the first ring. "What's up?"

"I need you to move tomorrow's morning appointments. I have to go back to the Pharaoh Temple."

"Beetles proving too much for the mighty critter wrangler? I never thought I'd see the day."

"Don't be a smart ass or I'll make you take the temple job."

"Not in a million. Beetles are too creepy-crawly."

"How do you feel about spiders?"

"Creepy-crawly too, but at least they have fangs. I can relate."

Emil was my vampire office-assistant. He knew almost as much about vermin as I did. He was usually kind of broody. His playful tone could only mean one thing. Gabe was there.

Emil had been crushing on Gabe, my former office assistant, for years. But Gabe was complicated, and even though I always felt he returned the feelings, he'd rebuffed Emil's advances until last month when they finally got together. And then promptly broke up over some imagined slight.

Emil had been as grumpy as a phoenix about to go up in flames ever since. And yet today there was banter. I took that as a good sign.

"Great," I said. "Meet me at Raven's school and bring a net. I tore my last one this afternoon with Mrs. Trudel's wart-bats."

"And what exactly are we trapping?"

"Mammoth rat-eater."

I heard a muffling sound as if Emil was covering the phone mic, and then an impressive array of curses. I waited for him to recover.

"You're kidding, right?"

"Just meet me at the school." I hung up.

While I waited for Emil, I assessed the situation. Ferdy insisted that the emergency protocols had been initiated within minutes of the fight and Blondi's escape. That meant every exit was locked, windows automatically shut and even air vents sealed.

No wonder it's so hot in here. I took off my jacket and set it on a desk.

The protocols meant the missing critter had to be in the school somewhere. If we were lucky, she was still in the science wing.

Critter wrangler rule number twenty-two: never underestimate a creature's ability to flee.

So with my luck, she probably wasn't in the science wing, but I started there. I searched every cubby hole, looked under counters and behind the specimen fridge. Nothing. I found the air vent slightly askew and pulled it aside to peer inside. Still nothing. But I'd recommend a good air duct cleaner to Ferdy. Dust-draped cobwebs were strung like garlands along the shaft.

But there…the silky webs were broken along the right side. Something bigger than a rat had stampeded through there not long ago.

Emil found me crouched by the open vent.

"Found it already?" He held two nets and handed one to me. I pushed it back to him.

"Not yet. She's in the basement. You'll need that."

"Me? You want me to catch a giant spider?"

I nodded. "I have to go take care of Raven."

"Fine. Good thing I brought backup." He grinned and nodded over his shoulder.

I did a double-take when I saw Gabe Devi stride through the door. I hadn't seen him in months, and he'd changed. He'd put in some time at the gym and was brawnier than usual. His face was ashen, not as in sickly, but almost like he'd powdered it. It was a startling effect against his black hair—hair that was now dreadlocked, attached in a topknot and hanging past his shoulders.

"Hey Kyra." He peered at me over his designer sunglasses and grinned. "Emil said you've got some little beastie that needs catching." He flexed his fingers on empty air to mimic catching something and muscles rippled up his bare arms and under his too-tight t-shirt.

Wow. And I mean, wow!

My very married self shut my jaw that had been hanging open.

"Hey, Gabe. You're looking…fit."

"I feel great."

"So things are better with your parents?"

Gabe's father wanted him to join the family business, but Gabe had been resisting, mostly because the family business, while ostensibly in the insurance field, also meant taking over leadership of the Saivites, one of the most powerful godling pantheons in the ward. And Gabe didn't see eye-to-eye with their militant views. They tended to blow things up and ask questions later. Though they weren't quite as trigger happy as the Olympian godlings who'd bombed the train last year just for the media attention.

Gabe hated clan politics. He'd refused to be a pawn for his family. That was how he'd ended up as my assistant. It was a minor rebellion. He'd eventually gone back to his family, but tensions had been running high—tensions that spilled over into his relationship with Emil.

Gabe walked over and squeezed Emil's hand. The vamp blushed. With his mop of brown curls and eyes that would make an anime character jealous, Emil looked like a kid with his first crush. I felt my toes curl at the sweetness of the gesture. It was the first time I'd seen a public display of affection from Gabe.

Emil cleared his throat but didn't pull his hand away. "Looks like the beastie is in the basement. Fancy a bit of a chase?"

Gabe grinned. "I thought you'd never ask." Emil blushed even harder.

I rolled my eyes. "Just be careful. Blondi is expected to win the blue ribbon at the ward-wide science fair next month. If you hurt her, you'll have to answer to a bunch of angry teen science buffs."

Gabe saluted me and grabbed a net. Emil followed him out the door, still wearing a dopey grin.

I had complete faith in my critter wrangling assistants. That meant I could face a creature even more scary that a mammoth rat-eating spider—my own angst-riddled teen.

SPIDERS ARE PEOPLE TOO

March 14, 2084

I have nothing against spiders. Actually, I think they're kind of cute with their fuzzy faces and multiple eyes. And they eat a lot of other pests, so if I find one at home, I try to gently relocate it.

I don't have any spiders in captivity at the moment because I only keep animals in need, except for the vampire slugs that I find highly useful in the field. But I've never come across a spider that needed a home. For the most part, they do just fine on their own.

Take my recent encounter with a mammoth rat-eater. This spider does its name justice! Blondi is the mascot of the science club at a local school. She got loose during a minor scuffle, and immediately took off.

Not only can these spiders run as fast as a cat, they can fly! Not exactly like birds. They can't launch into the sky, but if they start from a high perch, they can glide as well as any flying squirrel.

Now imagine a spider the size of a dinner plate soaring through a dark hallway toward you. I'm pleased to say that my two assistants handled the situation with courage and Blondi is now safely back in her classroom terrarium. Well done boys!

COMMENTS (5)

Make sure you check for eggs. Nothing worse than finding a surprise clutch of mammoth eggs. I speak from experience :o
ScienceGuyForHire (March 14, 2084)

> Yikes! Since Blondi is a lone captive female, this shouldn't be a problem. I hope.
> *Valkyrie367 (March 14, 2084)*

If you slow roast them, mammoth legs taste just like lobster.
HungryHomesteader (March 14, 2084)

> **blocks sender**
> *Valkyrie367 (March 14, 2084)*

How do you "gently relocate" a spider that size?
Bluebeard46 (March 15, 2084)

> Very carefully.
> *Valkyrie367 (March 17, 2084)*

CHAPTER

2

fter sitting through Ferdy's practiced tirade about the school's policy of zero tolerance for violence, I accepted Raven's fate—a two day suspension. He could use the downtime anyway.

I'd enjoyed a few suspensions in my time at middle school, and I never understood why they thought two days away from class was a good punishment. Seemed like a holiday to me.

"Come on." I tugged Raven out of the chair by his shirt sleeve. He followed me out the front door and through the parking lot with his head down, feet scuffing through the slush.

Raven had issues. He was small for his age, and the All-father knew bullies loved to pick on the little guy. But until last year, he'd been the only child in his world. He'd had to learn the delicate art of social interaction fast. And for the most part, he'd done a good job. He had a small group of close friends from the alchemy club. He did well in school, and seemed to enjoy it.

If only he could avoid confrontations like today.

"You can wait for explanations until we're home and then tell Mason and me at the same time. Until then, I want you to truly evaluate your actions and decide if you had any other option than fighting."

"But…"

I whirled on him and held up a hand. I must have looked fierce because he backed up a step. I took a deep breath and forced down my frustrations. Lectures hadn't worked in the past.

"When I say seek out alternatives, I mean for you. Bullies are gonna bully.

14

You can't change them. You can only do you. And if you do turn into a nuckelavee, so what? You'll still be you. I'll love you no matter what. Mason? He's crazy about you. He wouldn't care if you turned into a rhinoceros in a tutu." I gripped his shoulders and forced him to meet my eye. "We love you, Raven. Screw the bullies."

He smiled, but his chin wobbled a bit. "Yeah, screw the bullies."

Maybe not my finest parenting advice, but I meant it. I slung my arm around his shoulder and gave him a squeeze before we headed to the van.

Emil and Gabe were already there, leaning against the driver side door. Emil's head rested on Gabe's shoulder and Gabe's head was tilted against Emil's curly hair.

They looked like a couple. Finally.

"Did you catch it?" I asked.

Emil stretched. "Sure did. Blondi is back in the lab. In a somewhat smaller terrarium, but she'll be fine."

"Did she give you any trouble?"

"Nah! Gabe sacrificed himself for the cause. Once she bit him, she went all gooey eyed."

"Gabe has that effect on females," I said.

"Even spider females, apparently." Emil grinned.

Gabe frowned. "That was no spider. It was a monster. With wings! No one mentioned wings!"

"Buck up." Emil patted his chest. "You're just out of practice."

"Out of practice? Look at me!" He held up his arm. A trickle of blood had dried in a line down his wrist. "Kyra, tell me I'm not going to turn into some kind of super-spider guy now. It doesn't have radioactive venom or anything like that, right?"

"Don't be such a baby." I examined his wound. It was already scabbing over. "Mammoths barely have enough venom to subdue a rat. I'm sure you put more poison in your body every Friday night at the clubs. Does it hurt?"

"It tingles a bit."

"Let me have a better look. There's a first aid kit in the back."

I left Emil quizzing Raven about the fight in the science lab and opened the back of the van to rummage in the bins.

"You guys look happy." I shot a glance at Gabe.

"Yeah. We are." He grinned that thousand-watt Gabe grin.

"So things are better with your family?"

"Things are good."

"And Sai?" Sai was ostensibly his nephew. Only a few people knew he was really Gabe's son, conceived because his sister-in-law snuck into his bed when he was sixteen. Her husband, Gabe's brother, had failed to produce an heir yet, so Uma decided to take matters into her own hands.

"He's amazing," Gabe said. "I never thought I could feel this way about another human. He's just an amazing kid, you know?"

"I know." I smiled at him and we shared one of those private moments between parents—me, thinking about how I couldn't remember life without Raven or Holly anymore, and Gabe probably still marveling at the fact that he had made a perfect small human.

I cleaned his wound and bandaged it.

He patted the bandage. "Feels kind of numb."

"That's the venom. Be thankful for it. Once it wears off, it's going to hurt."

I packed away my kit. Gabe lingered by the back of the van. He wanted to ask me something, and I waited for a cringe-worthy question about Emil. Instead, he said, "Can we have lunch together this week? I have a new project in the works, and I'd like to hear your thoughts about it."

I squinted up at him. "New project?" Considering he was a major player in the godling revolution, his "project" could be anything from blowing up a train to storming Parliament.

"Don't look so suspicious. It's nothing dangerous. Just a side-hustle I'm considering."

"Okay. How's Thursday?"

"Perfect." He typed the meeting into his calendar then tapped his widget to mine to send me the info. "See you then."

ON THE WAY HOME, Raven answered my questions with grunts and sighs until I left him to sulk and play games on his widget. I switched the van to manual drive as we left the highway for the dirt road that ran through Dorion Park. A recent storm had left the road pitted with potholes, and I preferred to keep control while driving.

Something large and hairy ran in front of the van. I didn't even have time to press the brakes and it was gone.

"Did you see that?"

"Huh?" Raven glanced up too late, shrugged and turned back to the game on his widget.

I peered through the windshield. The light was fading to inky gray, dissolving colors and blending shadows. Had I imagined it?

"Probably just a deer," I said.

Raven grunted.

When I turned onto the long driveway that led to our homestead, I thought I saw more shadows running through the trees, but by the time the house came into view, we were driving alone again. I parked and peered into the darkness before turning off the engine. My fingers gripped the steering wheel tight enough to hurt.

A hand tapped on the window beside me, and I yelped.

Raven glanced at me. "Geez. Stressed much?" He got out of the van, and I turned to find Mason peering through the window.

I took a deep breath to calm my heart and opened the door. He leaned in and kissed me. As far as kisses go, it wasn't one that rocked my world, but it wasn't meant to. It was meant to greet and reconnect. I loved that we were in a place where Mason and I could kiss each other hello, goodbye, how-are-you, and I-missed-you. I'd been alone for so long, I never took those for granted.

"You're home early." I admired his country squire look. He was dressed in work clothes—jeans, quilted flannel jacket and boots. A crowbar was slung over his shoulder, and he held a shovel in his other hand.

"Parliament adjourned early, and I needed a break."

"So you decided to what?" I pointed at the shovel. "Bury some bodies?"

He kissed me again and grinned. "Don't be silly. You know I'd wait for you to bury bodies."

I let out a weak laugh and his eyes narrowed. "You okay?"

"Fine. Just a hectic day. I'll tell you about it later. But have you noticed anything weird going on? I swear I saw something on the road just now. Several somethings actually. The wildlife seems overactive tonight."

"No kidding. Take a look at the gate."

We walked over to the tall cedar hedge that separated our yard from the old cemetery. The evening had grown cold and I shivered inside my thin jacket. An arched gateway broke the line of the hedge. Usually a wooden gate closed it off. Now the gate hung by one bent hinge.

Raven ambled over to join us while we inspected the damage.

"Coy-bears?" I asked.

"Maybe." Mason turned to Raven. "Have you been stirring up their den again?" It was a valid question. Raven had been known to tease the pack of coy-bears living nearby. But, of course, Raven saw the question through adolescent-tinted glasses.

He straightened and his eyes went dark. "Sure. It's always my fault, right?" He stalked off toward the house.

Mason raised one eyebrow. "A little touchy tonight?"

I sighed and pinched the muscle in the hollow between my neck and shoulder where I seemed to hold all my tension.

"He had a bad day at school. The bullies have been at it again."

"Hmm." He watched as Raven mounted the steps to the house, disappeared inside, and slammed the door behind him. "I'll talk to him later. Why don't you go inside? Gita has Holly in the bath, so you have about half an hour to unwind. Have a glass of wine."

It was a tempting thought. Instead, I watched Mason work for a few minutes. The gate hinge was too bent to salvage and the fence post had splintered. He pried the gate from the post and put it aside, then started digging out the post.

In the fading light, his face was hidden in shadows and his shoulders flexed like the withers of some magnificent coursing beast.

"Can't this wait until morning?" I asked. "It's almost dark."

He glanced up and a bit of stray light caught his eyes.

"Is it? I hadn't noticed." He shrugged. "Old habits, I guess."

Mason had spent most of the last three hundred years in the dark. He rarely spoke of what it was like to make that switch from a nocturnal creature to a diurnal one, but once in a while I caught him standing in the light with his face tilted toward the sun.

He leaned the shovel and crowbar beside the discarded gate, then draped an arm over my shoulder and pulled me in close. He smelled outdoorsy—like fresh water and loamy earth.

He breathed into my hair and said, "Let's go see about that glass of—"

A figure burst through the open gate. Hooves clattered over the discarded wood. The beast was taller than me at the shoulder and crowned in a black shaggy mane. It reared and pawed at the sky, then took off toward the house, veering before it reached the porch and galloping into the trees.

Mason and I watched in silent awe.

"What was that?" he finally said.

"Dunno. Shagamaw, I think. Or maybe a hugag." It was too dark and the intrusion had happened so fast, I didn't get a good look.

"Dangerous?"

"Only if you get in their way." Shagamaws were in the deer family, though closer to the moose side than the white-tails. They had claws on their front hooves and could eviscerate a man, but mostly they kept to themselves. Hugags were like the hummingbirds of the deer clan. They never sat still and were notorious for trampling gardens in their frenzy to eat wildflowers, berries or anything sweet.

I turned to look up the driveway. The wards around our house were pretty solid. Errol boosted them every month. They were keyed to keep out humanoids and highly magical creatures. Forest creatures could come and go as they pleased, but they usually avoided the homestead, preferring to stay clear of our family bustle.

"Should we be worried about a shagamaw invasion?" He pointed to the path the creature had fled down. I gripped his fingers tightly in mine, needing the comfort of solid contact.

"No. We wanted to live with the forest, not apart from it." Mason nodded his agreement. "That means respecting creatures and not driving them away for stomping on our wildflowers or breaking our gates. That's just a shagamaw doing its thing, but..." I hesitated.

"But..." Mason prompted.

I thought of the shadows running beside the van on our way in and shivered.

"I don't know. Something feels off. The forest is restless and that makes me nervous."

Fat flakes started to fall from the sky. I groaned.

"More snow. Just what we need." We were well into March and my usual childish delight at seeing snow fall had worn off months ago.

Mason tipped his face to the sky and scowled. "That's not snow."

I caught a flake on my hand. I didn't melt.

"It's ash."

The flakes fell thick and fast, enough to dust the branches of the hedge.

I turned into the wind coming from the north. Somewhere up there, the Inbetween was burning.

C H A P T E R

3

breeze brushed my cheek and stirred my loose hair. It was a gentle, warm wind, and I felt safe in its embrace. I stood on the edge of a cliff, looking over a landscape dressed in greenery as far as my eye could see. Only inches from my toes, the land dropped away. Hundreds of feet below, a stream burbled through the early morning shadows. It would be a killing fall. The wind whispered comforting words. Words I forgot even as I heard them.

I turned. Between me and the forest stood a giant bird. It had the beak of an eagle, golden and curved into a wicked point, but its head hung low between hunched shoulders. Yellow eyes watched me without blinking.

"Who are you?" I asked, but the bird only cawed. It flexed massive wings and they burst into flame. Fire licked at the trees and in moments, the entire forest burned.

The bird melted into the flames.

"No!" I cried, reaching out, as if I could somehow smother the inferno. "No. Stop it!"

"Kyra, wake up." The hand on my shoulder was relentless. I fought against it, wanting to catch the wind.

"Kyra, you need to get up."

I opened one eye to find Mason peering at me in the dark. I groaned and rolled over, but he wasn't giving up. He turned on a light and I flung an arm over my eyes.

"You were talking in your sleep again."

"Oh, gods. What did I say this time?"

"Mumbles mostly." He traced the line of my jaw with a finger. "And not the sexy, inviting kind."

"Hmmm." The dream was already slipping away, but it left me with a shaky feeling of unease.

I pulled my pillow over my head.

Mason poked me again. "Time to get up."

I groaned. "No way. What time is it?" I peeked at the window which was still dark.

"Early. Not quite four. But Raol is here."

"Raol?" I was suddenly wide awake. "Is something wrong."

"Don't know. I haven't seen him yet. You coming?"

I thought of the ash fall last night and sat straight up, flinging blankets and pillow aside.

Raol was the ratatosk who'd been our guide in Asgard over a year ago. He'd returned to Terra with us and spent the months since trekking through the Inbetween. Already, he was making a name for himself as a valuable guide for Montrealers who needed to travel through the dangerous terrain outside the ward. He looped around to our homestead every three months or so, but he was early this time, and that could only mean the news was bad.

Mason left me to get dressed. I swung my legs out of bed. The morning was chilly. I decided to forego slippers and a robe and went straight for boots, jeans and a warm shirt.

Downstairs, Angus was pulling food from the fridge for an early breakfast, or a late dinner by gargoyle standards. Since Mason had become Prime Minister, Angus had taken over as Captain of the Guardians. He was a green-man gargoyle, about a head shorter than me but twice as broad across the shoulder. His hair was a brambly mess of twigs and leaves.

"Found our wee friend here lurking on the road. Thought it was a bright and shiny idea to bring him in," Angus said.

"I didn't want to wake anyone." Raol was perched on a kitchen chair. As a descendant of the great Ratatoskr, he looked like a three-foot squirrel dressed in hunting leathers. His tail curled into a question mark above the rim of the chair. Tiny, nimble hands snatched up the oat clusters that Angus had put on the table and stuffed them into his mouth. He ate with quick efficiency, and his eyes never stopped scanning the kitchen. When they landed on Grim, the night jaguar disguised as a Maine Coon, his gaze stopped. Whiskers twitched. Tail spiked.

Grim gave him a slow blink. He wouldn't attack a guest in our home, no matter how fluttery that guest's tail was. Raol went back to his breakfast, but his tail jerked in agitation.

"You shouldn't worry about waking us." I sat beside him at the table. Mason already had coffee brewing, and he handed me a mug. After the godling riots last year left us short of the priceless beans, I cherished every cup. I let its velvety heat soothe my soul before asking the question I knew would irrevocably change my day, and not for the better.

"So what's up? You weren't due back here for another month."

"Opji. They're everywhere." Raol clasped his clawed hands against his chest, almost like a prayer. It was a pose that I'd seen wild squirrels take when scenting danger on the air.

"Aye, we've heard from others that the vamps are on the move," Angus said. "Can you tell us where you've seen them, laddie?"

"Close." Raol's eyes were so dark brown, they were almost black. They made reading his emotions difficult, but his body language told me he was nervous, if not scared.

"How close?" Mason asked. He still wore cotton pajama pants and a plain white t-shirt. Yesterday's beard gave him a dark, roguish look.

"There's smoke over the Hewitt homestead," Raol said.

"John Hewitt?" I asked.

Raol twitched a nod.

That wasn't good. The Hewitts were our nearest neighbor. Their homestead was twenty kilometers to the west, less than a two-hour ride on a fast horse.

"What happened?" I asked.

"Couldn't get close enough to see. The opji roam freely now."

"This far east?" I shot a glance at Mason. He wore a deep frown that creased the space between his brows. He was thinking the same thing as me. The opji always raided homesteads, but rarely this close to Montreal. Hub's militia kept the forests around the ward fairly safe, if only to protect their valuable farms.

"Farther east than that. The camp towns are full," Raol said.

Angus rubbed a hand across his chest. "That's too close for comfort."

Montreal boasted three bridges with gates into the ward. They were the only way onto the island. The alchemists guarded the western gate. They didn't allow settlers to squat on their land, but shanty towns had grown up outside the human and fae gates. Normally, they were way stations for people coming and going from Montreal. But the exaggerated opji activity had them bursting with homesteader refugees—people who'd been driven out by the opji or who'd grown tired of living in fear of attack. They had good reason.

The opji kept pens of humans like livestock—their krowa. Some of the humans were for breeding, others were food, and the most unlucky were turned into wojaks, mindless undead soldiers that the opji deployed with ruthless efficiency.

For over a year now, I'd heard rumors of an illness in their krowa pens. It was the same flu that was ravaging the shanty towns. The illness must have been taking its toll if the opji were raiding this far east. They were desperate. There was no other reason for them to risk running into Hub's militia.

The kitchen was silent as we all considered these ramifications in the light of Raol's news. Angus pushed his chair back and stood, breaking the bubble of worry that surrounded us.

"It's a right bit of sore news you bring us, laddie. But the sun is coming and I cannae help until it's done." Angus's brogue always intensified when he was tired or stressed. Right now, he seemed to be both.

Mason nodded as the green man shuffled out the back door. The Guardians had their own house on the property, near the front gate. Angus would likely perch on the eaves and watch the road for intruders until sunset. For a fleeting instant, I wondered if Mason missed his stone days. But then the image of the Hewitt's homestead in flames brought me back to the problem at hand.

"We should go to them," I said.

Mason rubbed the back of his neck. "It's a long hike. By the time we get there it could be too late."

"John is a stubborn old goat. He won't go down without a fight. Or they could be hiding until the opji leave." I glanced at the bay windows in the living room. The sky was already lightening. "If we're going, we should go now."

Mason gulped the last of his coffee and nodded. "I'll tack the horses." He turned to Raol. "Are you coming too?"

The ratatosk nodded. "If you have another mount for me. I rode Betsy all night."

They headed out to the new barn, the one that we'd built over the summer to house the few horses we'd acquired. I buzzed Dutch's widget to let him know we were leaving.

Holly was, thankfully, a good sleeper, but she rose with the sun. I'd have to wake Gita to care for her. And there was Raven to consider. His suspension from school meant that I didn't have to worry about driving him into the city. But I didn't want him lounging around all day.

Sigh. Going on an adventure was so much more trouble when you had kids.

I snuck into Raven's room. Princess, who slept on the end of his bed, raised her nose and gave a quiet "woof."

"Shhh. It's just me." I shook Raven awake, told him I was taking Princess for the day and that Arriz, our goblin estate manager, was expecting him for work in an hour. That was the deal for fighting. Getting suspended wasn't going to be a holiday. Raven grumbled a response and went back to sleep. I didn't worry. Arriz wouldn't let him squirm out of his duties.

I hadn't seen Jacoby all morning. He liked to find nooks and crannies to sleep in—a throwback to his days living in random chimneys. I didn't need or want an apprentice this morning, so I tip-toed back to my room to grab my jacket and travel kit.

When I emerged into the cool morning air, the sleepy-eyed dervish was waiting for me.

"Kyra-lady needs 'prentice today?"

"No. We're just going to visit John Hewitt. Go back inside and sleep," I said.

"Okays." Jacoby yawned and followed me to the barn.

NO MORE ASH FELL, but the air had a sooty tang to it. My roan was a sweet gelding named Spencer. He was a solid ride as long as his girlfriend Hedy, an assertive chestnut, was in the lead. Mason rode Hedy with the confident seat of a man who'd grown up riding. Valkyries, of course, were known for their horses, and to any layman, I would seem to be an excellent rider. But like all my Valkyrie training, I'd come to riding later in life and could never quite shrug off the feeling that I was less than competent. Sweet, steady Spencer was just my speed.

Raol took the lead on our ornery pony, Sammy. Princess trotted along beside him, zipping into the woods every time she caught an interesting scent.

Jacoby rode on a special padded seat that I'd added to my saddle, even though I'd told him repeatedly to stay home. His hands gripped the waistband of my jacket and his head had fallen against my back as he dozed through the early morning ride.

The morning was turning crisp and clear. This part of the Inbetween had a healthy mix of pine, cedar and white birch. Sunrise turned the leafless birches pink. Mist hovered at ground level like smoke.

A deer burst from the trees and crossed our path in one bound. His rack had at least eight points to it, and they seemed tipped in gold in the morning light.

Princess let out a bark and took off after it.

Unflappable Hedy stood her ground, but Spencer shied, and I took a moment to get him under control. I called to Princess and she reluctantly left off her chase.

We continued down the mist-shrouded road.

Mason scanned the shadows between the trees. I glanced at Raol, whose back and tail were stiff and straight. He felt what I felt—uneasy.

"There's something out there." My breath steamed as I spoke. My toes were turning to ice, and I wiggled them inside my boots.

"Something's watching us." Mason's gaze was sharper now as he tried to make out shapes moving in the shadows between trees.

"Not watching," I said. "Traveling. I don't know how to explain it, but I keen movement. Lots of movement. Like a great migration."

Raol turned in his saddle and Sammy took the opportunity to wander off the trail toward some saplings that were showing signs of spring growth. Raol hauled hard on the reins. He might be small and slight, but he was tough as old leather and Sammy wouldn't get far with his usual tricks.

"The beasts have been on the move all week," Raol said. "Something has them stirred up."

"The opji?" Mason asked.

Raol stared into the distance. "Could be the opji pushing them east. Or the fires but…"

Raol didn't finish the sentence, but I understood. The restless movement of the forest critters seemed too…*organized* to be panicked flight.

We continued in nervous silence. From the shadows, the cracking sounds of branches had Princess swiveling her head. Several times I commanded her to stay close. The last time, I laced the command with a bit of magic to make it stick. She trotted beside Spencer, but the tense line of her body proved she was ready to leap into the trees.

Jacoby's tiny hand slithered around my waist as he pressed himself closer to my back.

We saw no other creature activity until we turned off the main road for a dirt packed trail that led north into the hills.

A raucous scream alerted us seconds before a giant bird dropped from the trees and landed on the ground with a scrabbling of claws. It flexed three-foot featherless wings, like batwings with bony thorns at each joint. Its face was like the nightmare child of a Komodo dragon and a vulture. It hissed at us for blocking the road.

Then the wings burst into flames.

I had a moment of utter disorientation, as if my horse had stumbled into my dream world.

Mountain devils were once thought to be a hoax, but the Flood Wars had a funny way of making the unbelievable believable. Stories from early settlers of the Appalachian Mountains were mixed. Some feared the mountain devil as an omen of impending disaster. Others believed it was a watchdog of gods. Most stories agreed on one aspect though: mountain devils punished those who didn't respect the essence of the land, often by plucking out their eyes. Fun stuff, those mythologies.

The flaming bird let out a shrill caw. Spencer snorted and huffed and back-paced. I yanked the reins right to make him circle until he calmed down.

The mountain devil didn't seem aggressive, just annoyed. It hissed again, then hopped along as if it owned the road before launching into the trees.

The moment of silence after its departure didn't last.

A frenzied charge of critters followed. Large, small, furred and feathered. They bolted across our path like all the demons of hell were after them, stirring up dust and leaves, cawing, screaming, kicking and stomping. Taller hugags lumbered after scampering weasels. A late-season snow wasset slunk by. It was hard to pick out individuals while trying to keep Spencer from fleeing, but I spotted fox, coy-bear, deer, and a gumberoo. Higher up, owls, bats and squirrels filled the branches.

Spencer reared and tried to throw me off. Jacoby tumbled to the ground and rolled away from trampling hooves. By the time I brought Spencer under control, the stampede had faded away, leaving the road ahead a churned-up mess of mud.

Princess was barking madly. My magic-laced command held. She stayed close, but I saw her quivering with the need to chase.

We were headed in a westerly direction and the stampede had cut across our trail. The road would soon veer north and take us right into the path of whatever the forest creatures were fleeing.

Mason turned in his saddle. Even Hedy was spooked. The mare's eyes were white all around and she pranced sideways. Mason calmed her with a hand on her neck and soothing words.

"Critter wrangler rule number two," I muttered.

"Which one was that again?" Mason asked

"When scary things run away, something scarier is coming."

Sammy had taken off, and I worried for Raol until a few minutes later, when the pony came trotting back with the ratatosk perched on his saddle.

"I thought he'd run me all the way home before I got control." Raol didn't talk much and he joked even less, but there was a glint of humor in his eyes.

He was such an adventure hound.

The rest of the journey was uneventful, but that didn't stop us from jumping at every cracking branch or blowing leaf.

We knew something was really wrong at the Hewitt's long before we reached the homestead. The sharp scent of woodsmoke grew as we approached, too much for a simple kitchen hearth. When we turned down the road that led to the Hewitt's, we found the first real evidence of a raid.

A mule cart was overturned in the road. The mule's throat had been savaged, and it bled out in the snow. Someone had tried to burn the cart. The fire hadn't taken, but one wheel and the canvas awning were badly scorched.

Mason hopped off Hedy and threw me her reins. The horses were too nervous to let her roam free while he inspected the cart. He avoided the wheel that still smoked and peered into the cart. Then he bent and laid a hand on the dead mule's neck.

"It's cold." His eyes narrowed as he looked down the road toward the homestead.

That didn't bode well for the Hewitts. We were probably too late.

Mason mounted up and we rode on. A few minutes later, the main house came into view. Or what was left of it. Only a chimney and smoking debris remained. Several other buildings had once filled the yard—barn, sheds, cottages—but only one badly singed cottage still stood. As we watched, its roof collapsed, sending smoke and sparks rocketing into the sky.

A scorched table, broken chairs and other furniture littered the yard. Clothes were strewn about and stamped into the mud. The body of a dog lay by the remains of the front door. Scanning the rest of the yard, I spotted more carcasses—pigs, goats and horses—but no humans. Even the small kitchen garden had been torn up. The opji didn't need pigs or salad greens. Even if they took the humans, they could have left the livestock. There seemed no reason for this destruction other than the joy of killing and destroying.

"Place is deserted," Mason said. "Either the opji got to them or they fled. Can you sense anyone alive?"

I shook my head. "It's too big an area for me to be sure." The homestead stretched over several acres. My keening wouldn't reach that far. We'd have to search the buildings. I worried for the Hewitts, but I didn't like the idea of blundering around the homestead blind. The opji didn't like to travel by day but they could still be hiding among the smoking ruins.

"Let me try something else."

We backtracked along the path and tied the horses to a tree, loosely so they could break free if attacked. It would be a long walk home without them, but I'd rather walk than let the horses come to harm.

I knelt and placed my palms flat on the ground. Jacoby mimicked my action, though as far as I knew, he had no green magic.

"Like this? Kyra-lady?"

"Yes. Now hush."

I closed my eyes. I'd been working with Errol, my bodach magic instructor, to link my keening to my green magic. That was easier to do under Errol's watchful eye in our backyard. Now, I had trouble focusing my magic. The wind shifted, bringing the smell of smoke again. Princess growled, low and steady. She hadn't let up since we spotted the burning cart. The horses stamped in the cold. And I could feel Mason and Raol's attention on me.

I had to block it all out. I had to pretend it was just another afternoon of magic class with Errol.

I searched for the power inside me and felt it humming along my veins.

I scratched at the mud and dug my fingers deeper into the earth, connecting us as one. Once I found my keening, it was easy to sink it into the ground. It floundered for a moment, until it found the mycelium, the system of fibrous tissue that linked fungus to tree and tree to fungus in a vast underground network. My magic snapped along these connections like synapses, ranging farther and farther sensing nothing living until…

…I tasted ash in my throat. Heat tingled along my skin. My keening had reached the far end of homestead, where the hay barn was still blazing. This deep into the magic, I could no longer distinguish myself from my keening sense. I choked on the acrid smoke.

My magic had been attracted to the flames. Fire was its own kind of life, but not the kind I was looking for, so I pushed farther and found death. A lot of death. I swallowed down bile. I couldn't be sure the deaths I keened weren't the Hewitt family, but I suspected the opji had slaughtered the small herd of cattle that had been John Hewitt's pride and joy.

I kept pushing my keening and found the opji.

They were huddled nearby. It was easy to miss opji magic altogether. Their spirits were dull, like lanterns shuttered against a storm, so I couldn't be sure, but I thought there were more than three vampires, maybe as many as six. I didn't sense any humans with them. Either they'd killed the Hewitts, or they'd taken them away already, and these remaining opji were left…for what reason? In case some of the Hewitts had escaped? In case someone came to help?

That was more likely. If the opji were raiding for captives, they would lay a trap for any rescuers too.

Snapping off my magic at this point would have been the easiest thing to do, but I'd learned from experience that this would leave me feeling disoriented for hours. So I started to reel my magic in when I suddenly sensed someone else. Not the dull undead magic of the opji, but a candle flame burning bright with life. Two flames!

My keening didn't have eyes, exactly, so I couldn't see them, but someone was definitely hiding near the hay barn. Hiding or too injured to move.

Painstakingly, I spun my magic back along the organic network, snaking past the burning barn and through the ruined buildings. It came back to me with a jolt that tumbled me onto my butt. I jumped up.

"Someone's alive out there."

I was sure of it. Not all of John Hewitt's family had been taken or killed. I pointed to the far end of the yard, where another forested path led to the winter pasture and the burning hay barn.

Mason and Raol followed my gaze. There was no sign of my survivor.

"Someone's there. I'm sure of it. Past that tree line it opens up again. It's another pasture. There's a barn on fire. And someone is hiding nearby."

Mason was already heading down the slope, but I grabbed his sleeve.

"That's not all. The opji are there too." I shielded my eyes from the sun, looking toward the smoke through the trees. "They may be using the smoke to mask their scent from predators while they sleep."

The vamps wouldn't burn up in the sun like in the old myths, but daylight made them sluggish and it affected their eyesight. Usually, they went into a kind of stasis during the day. Left undisturbed, they wouldn't leave their hideout before dusk.

"Should we wait them out?" I didn't relish the long cold hours until dark. And even then, we had no guarantee the opji would leave.

"No." Mason wore his determined face, the one that reminded me of his gargoyle days. "We go now. If anyone is alive down there, we can't leave them for the opji."

I shuddered at the thought. Some things were worse than death. Life as a krowa was one of them.

The sun had risen enough to warm the snow to slush, and we half slid, half walked down the sloping drive toward the winter pasture. I kept Jacoby and Princess close and admonished them to be quiet. We needed to get in and out without waking the opji.

At the head of the pasture we found cover and examined the scene. Flames still flickered around the fallen roof of the hay barn but the rest of the pasture was quiet. A pall of smoke hung in the air. Dozens of cows lay dead in the field. My last remaining hope of finding John Hewitt alive winked out. John would have died fighting for his cattle.

I pointed to the one remaining shed and mouthed "Opji." Mason nodded. Then I pointed to a stack of firewood covered by a tarp. That's where I'd sensed the survivors.

Princess was still growling low in her throat and I hissed at her to be quiet. The opji had keen hearing, even in their daytime stasis.

We crept through soggy undergrowth slowly, making as little noise a possible, stopping when we had a good view of the far side of the woodpile. I expected to find bodies, hiding or maybe unconscious.

Nothing.

A light rain started to fall and the dying fires spit and hissed. The wind shifted. Smoke blew over us, and I held in a cough. Mason motioned for me to follow as he crept toward the woodpile. I didn't understand why. Clearly, I'd been wrong. There was no one alive here. But I trusted him, and I had his back, just like he always had mine.

The weak daylight filled the space behind the woodpile with shadows. Mason stopped and crouched. A shovel with a broken handle lay in the dirt. Mason picked up the splintered shaft with the metal shovel blade attached and examined it. He pointed to the dark stain on the blade. Blood.

He leaned the shovel against the woodpile.

His gaze swept the ground. Mine was fixed on the shed where the opji were hiding. At the first sight of movement, we'd be gone.

Raol pointed into the trees. A trail led away from the pasture. It looked like nothing more than a deer path, but Raol was motioning us to follow it.

I threw a glance over my shoulder at the small shed and the sleeping opji and followed the ratatosk.

Jacoby tucked his hand into mine. My brave little dervish. I gave him what comfort I could.

The bare trees offered little protection against the rain, and soon I was wiping water from my eyes.

Raol stopped. "Trail ends here," he whispered.

I looked around the small clearing no wider than my outstretched arms. Early spring snow mingled with a mess of rotting leaves and fallen branches. The ground didn't look any different than the rest of the forest, except for small footprints that joined the clearing from the other direction—footprints that were quickly disappearing in the rain.

The prints seemed to end for no reason. I looked at the muddy clearing. It made no sense. Then I remembered that many homesteaders had bunkers for storing food and waiting out storms. Mason had the same thought, and we bent to inspect the ground at the same time.

If there was a bunker, it was well hidden. But I knew we were close—so close that someone's energy pinged my keening.

I dug my fingers into the dirt and found the lip of a steel door. Digging around this base, I unearthed an indented handle and pulled upward.

A dim light shone from a root cellar, illuminating a young woman and the point of a crossbow.

"I won't go!" she shouted.

"Hush!" I held my hands in front of me to show I was unarmed. "You'll wake the vamps."

The crossbow dropped an inch, revealing a dirty, scared face.

"Soolea?" I said. The girl dropped the crossbow even farther. Her hands were shaking from cold or fear. She wasn't dressed for the weather, as if she'd run into the night in a hurry. And she probably had. The opji didn't announce themselves before they attacked. They swooped down on a homestead, usually in the dead of night, lighted fires to smoke out their victims, killed those who resisted and took the rest captive.

Soolea was John Hewitt's daughter-in-law, newly married to his only son. We traded with the Hewitt's every spring and fall, and she'd joined their homestead last year. I'd only met her once, but her striking features weren't easily forgotten.

She was tall and sturdy with long black hair that was usually glossy and hanging free to her waist. Now it was tied back in a tangled pony tail. Her high cheekbones were smudged with soot and her eyes were big and glassy.

How long had she been hiding in the cold and the dark?

"Ms. Greene? Mr. Mason?" Her voice rasped.

"It's us." Mason held out his hand. "Come on now. Before those opji wake up."

Soolea dropped the crossbow and reached for him. As Mason pulled her up, I peered into the small cold storage chamber.

"Are you alone?" I'd been sure I sensed two survivors.

Then I got a good look at Soolea. She was very pregnant. That's why I'd keened two life forces.

Soolea winced and held a hand to her belly. "Jeremy told me to hide. Said he'd be right behind me." She gazed into the empty forest as if her husband might suddenly appear.

Mason took off his coat and draped it over the shivering girl. Despite her height, she looked like a scared kid.

"Jeremy and father John?" she asked.

"I'm sorry." Mason shook his head. "We haven't seen them."

Soolea's eyes filled with tears. "Why? Why would they come here and take everything?" The last word was lost in a sob.

I held her hand. I had no words of comfort. We all knew why the opji took captives, but that would only bring her more pain.

"We have to hurry," I said. "We have a long way to go before sunset." Before the opji woke up and started tracking us.

The girl sniffled and wiped her nose on her shirt sleeve, but she nodded.

Another sob escaped her lips when we dashed through the burning yard. She stopped to gape at the smoking remains of the house, but I tugged her forward. We would come back another day to salvage what we could once the opji were gone.

The horses were waiting right where we'd left them.

A shrill cry pierced the air. I knew that sound. It was the call of a wojak, the opji's undead soldiers.

The vamps were awake.

"Raol, take Soolea and the horses and go!" Raol nodded. I liked that about him. He never countermanded a good order. Soolea hesitated, her feet locked in fear. Raol stood no taller than her waist, but he grabbed her hand and dragged her away. "Jacoby, go with him and take Princess. You don't stop until you get home. Tell Dutch where we are. Understood?"

Jacoby's eyes were wide with fear, but for once he didn't argue.

"Princess, *guard*!" I sent magic into the command and pointed at Raol who was already leading Soolea to my horse. Princess yipped and went after them. It would be a bumpy ride for the pregnant woman, but that couldn't be helped now.

I unsheathed my knife and my sword, balancing one in each hand. The sword vibrated with anticipation.

Then Mason and I turned to face the vampires.

5

'd underestimated the numbers. We faced three opji and a dozen of their wojak minions. They fanned out with one opji standing a few paces in front of the others.

Way to announce who's in charge.

I flung my knife at his undead heart.

The opji's hand snapped up and batted away the blade before it struck him. His lips rolled back to show white fangs.

"You missssssed." He drew out the word in a hiss. "I won't."

He didn't move, didn't blink or twitch a finger, but the wojaks leapt forward. Strangled shouts emanated from their withered throats, something halfway between a war cry and a gorilla's challenge.

The first wojak met Mason's stone fist. He fell with a thud and didn't get up. Others were already jumping past him to get at us.

A wojak lunged forward with grasping claws to seize my throat. I sheared off his arms. My sword sang. I swallowed down fear in the face of the wojak's crazy red eyes and landed a kick in the middle of his chest. He stumbled back, severed arms flailing.

I slashed at the next wojak, a female who ducked under my blade. I chopped down as her fangs sank into my leg.

I screamed and slashed until she finally went limp and let go of my calf. She sprawled in the mud, jaws still grappling to bite empty air.

I fell backward and caught myself on a fence post. Pain shot through my calf and knee, but this wasn't my first vamp bite. I'd learned the hard way that wojaks had no venom. Unlike their opji overlords, they had no need for venom that would paralyze their victims so they could more easily feed. They were blunt instruments that the opji used to keep their hands clean.

Once I was sure the wojak was dead, I took a precious few seconds to wrap my bandanna around my calf. My jeans were already soaked with blood. I had no time to fuss over a wound. I gulped down pain and spun to face the next attack. And the next.

My hands grew slick. My boots churned up mud. My sword sang with evil glee. So much blood—mine and the wojaks—already spilled.

I had no chance to look for Mason. I'd taken down four vamps, but they kept coming.

This wasn't a normal sword fight. The wojaks had no weapons—they were weapons. Their filthy claws and fangs could take down a bull. They had no fear, no sense of self-preservation, and their wasted, sinewy bodies were agile and unnaturally strong. The perfect killing machines. I could only keep my blade moving to fend off their constant assaults.

They pushed me backward, step by step along the fence line. My arm was tiring. My feet found no traction in the mud. I bumped up against Mason who was fighting his own battle. I knew it was him straight away. His magic was sizzling hot and dark as thunder.

A wojak leapt past me. Mason flung up his stone arm and screamed when the vamp bit down on it. It was a scream of rage, not pain. I dove sideways, slipping in the slush and mud and slashed down. My blade bit into the wojak's neck, nearly severing his head. Mason flung the creature aside.

I spotted two more corpses lying in the mud. That was seven down by my count.

By some silent communication, the opji called off the others. The wojaks loped away like good dogs to encircle their overlords who stood by the driveway, watching the fight. I hoped we'd given a good performance.

Mason straightened and drew his sword along his stone arm, as if to sharpen it. The metal screeched. His hair, normally neat, had curled with humidity and sweat. His eyes were tinged black with demon magic. He grinned at me and looked like a madman. But he was my madman.

I gave him a nod and turned to face the opji, waiting for their final attack. It never came.

Mason pointed his sword at the vamps. I felt the current of magic pulse down his arm and through the blade. It shot forward like a bolt of black lightning, ensnaring the lead opji. He convulsed as if he'd been electrocuted. The lightning branched off, jolting through opji and wojaks. One by one, they seized and collapsed.

Mason laughed as the last one fell with a thud. It was a sharp, deep laugh on the edge of hysteria.

And then he toppled face-first into the mud.

I dropped my blade and crouched at his side. My arms shook with fatigue, and I struggled to turn him over before he suffocated. His face was caked with mud and ice. I wiped it with my bare hand, mumbling incoherent gibberish about how he'd be okay and how well he'd done against the vamps. I believed almost half of it.

His breathing was shallow, eyes closed. I rested my head on his chest and listened to the slow chiming of his heart. I was numb. From cold or excess adrenaline, I didn't know. I didn't care. Minutes went by. Maybe longer. I would freeze to death before I'd leave Mason.

Nothing moved. The wind shifted, bringing back the scent of woodsmoke and the stench of dead—truly dead—wojaks.

Mason sucked in a long shuddering breath. I raised my head. His eyes were open and still shrouded in black magic. He lifted a trembling hand to caress my hair. I grabbed it and kissed his palm. Then I turned it over. A new black tattoo snaked across the back of his hand.

Mason had been learning to master his dark magic, to test its limits and finesse his control. Too many times, he'd been overwhelmed by it. Each time, I'd thought I'd lost him. And each time, the magic marked him with a new tattoo. They now wound around his wrist and up his forearm.

We had no idea what they meant, but in my heart I knew it was nothing good.

Tears blurred my eyes.

"Hey!" Mason sat up and pulled me close. "It's okay. We beat them."

I shoved him back with a fist.

"You dumb ass! You did it again!" My words were choked by sobs. My chest felt raw with worry and fear. I pounded his shoulder again. "You promised you wouldn't go too far again."

"Come on now. I'm fine. Look at me." He tipped my chin up, forcing me to meet his eyes. The blackness had retreated. They were his normal silver-gray with a hint of amber around the iris.

"You're not fine." I sniffled and raised his hand. "Look."

Mason dropped his gaze to the new tattoo and shrugged. "Some people pay money for good ink."

"It's not funny. Your magic overwhelmed you." He started to protest and I grabbed his muddy shirt by the collar. "Don't deny it. You can't lie to me, remember? I *know* when you've used too much magic."

He dragged a muddy hand through his muddy hair.

"The opji are dead. You're safe. That's all that matters."

"Not all!" I stood and he followed me to his feet. "We could have taken them without magic. We killed seven without breaking a sweat."

Mason pressed his lips into a thin line. "You could have been hurt."

"Maybe. Maybe not. But I know for certain that this magic is taking a toll." I gripped him hard, my hand squeezing until the skin under his new tattoo turned white. "You have to stop."

He pulled his hand away and turned his back. I was losing the argument. It was one I'd lost before. Mason thought he was invincible, thought my safety was more precious than his own. And nothing I could say would change that.

I sighed and laid my hand on his back. I felt his muscles twitch, like a cat who wasn't sure if he'd accept the caress or turn and bite.

"Just promise me you'll tell Kester. About the tattoos and the blackouts. See what he has to say."

Kester Owens was a senator from Manhattan and the only other demon hybrid we knew. He'd been mentoring Mason as he navigated this new power.

Mason's shoulders slumped. "I'll talk to him. Let's just get this mess cleaned up and go home."

I agreed.

We didn't take any chances with the vamps. They seemed dead. But the only reason that Mason's magic had affected them was because they were undead to begin with. We had no idea what the effect of his magic would be long-term. So we decapitated the opji and the wojaks and dragged their bodies to the still burning barn. Once they were piled on top of the fallen wall, we added more kindling and logs until the barn was ablaze again.

I looked around the homestead. Last spring we'd visited to trade. It had been bustling with life and color. Now it was desolate. Lifeless. The capricious weather had shifted again. Snow was falling and would soon cover the remains of the homestead like a shroud.

I shuddered, thinking how fast life can change.

Raol had done as we asked and taken the horses. I knew he'd send someone back for us as soon as he got Soolea to safety, but we weren't waiting around for rescue. It was well past noon. We'd be lucky if we made it home before dark.

Before heading out, I slit my left pant leg from ankle to knee. The wojak bite was ugly and oozing dark blood. I prodded the tender flesh around the punctures. It was already red and inflamed. Wojak mouths were cesspools of bacteria. I cleaned it and bandaged it as best I could.

"Can you walk?" Mason handed me a walking stick he'd pulled from the underbrush.

"Of course. It's just a scratch." I leaned on the stick and took a tentative step. The tight bandage only added to the intense pain in my leg.

Mason eyed me with a frown and I bucked up. If he thought I couldn't walk, he'd carry me, and I wasn't going to make him hike twenty kilometers with an extra sixty-plus kilos on his back.

I smiled and indicated that he should lead the way.

We decided to stay off the main roads in case there were more opji in the area. Most likely they'd be inactive during the day, but as we'd already seen, that didn't mean they couldn't put up a good fight.

I limped along, trying to think of anything but my throbbing leg. With nothing else to look at, I watched Mason's back for long minutes. His shoulders flexed as he pulled himself up a short incline, using a sapling as leverage. He reached back to help me up and our eyes met.

We hadn't spoken since leaving the Hewitt's, and the unresolved argument over his use of the demon magic hung in the air like an unfinished question.

"Careful, it's slippery," he said.

"Thank you." I took his hand. Courtesy had always been Mason's shield. When things got rough, he hid behind his old-world manners. Sometimes I found that endearing. Other times it made me want to shake him until his teeth rattled.

We topped a ridge and Mason stopped to drink from his canteen. I bent to check my bandage. It held but was already soaked in blood. Until I could rest and put that leg up, there would be no stopping it.

"Does it hurt?" Mason asked.

"Not much," I lied.

I heard the worry in his voice and keened the nervous magic buzzing around him. I decided to defuse the situation. I couldn't do anything about my leg, but I could keep Mason from wigging out and going dark again. Without turning, I scooped up a handful of mushy snow and packed it into a missile. I whirled around and launched it in the same motion. It smacked Mason right in the middle of his chest.

With the canteen halfway to his lips, he looked down at the wet splotch on his jacket and raised both eyebrows. A tiny smile quivered at the edge of his lips.

Uh-oh.

He carefully put the cap back on his canteen and stowed it in his pack. Then he bent, scooped and flung a wedge of snow as fast as old Thor could throw lightning.

A white soggy blanket hit me. I sputtered and cleared snow from my eyes. Mason was already armed with another ice missile. I laughed and ducked as he launched it. The snowball hit a tree behind me with a wet slap. I gathered up more snow, not bothering to pack it, and threw, aiming for his smug face. But my aim was off because he was suddenly right there, close enough to circle me with his arms and trap me against the tree.

Snow dripped in my eyes, but I couldn't look away from the intensity in his gaze. He licked drops from his lips and gently wiped slush off my cheek. Then leaned in and kissed me. The tip of my cold nose butted against his warm cheek. Ice melted between us, dripping down my chin as his kiss deepened. His tongue lightly brushed mine, making me wish there weren't so many layers of clothing between us.

My hands roved up his arms to the soft place where his hair curled at his nape, so I felt it when he suddenly stiffened.

He pulled away and cocked his head.

"Do you hear that?"

Still caught up in the heat of his kiss, I heard nothing but the rushing of my own blood.

Mason stood back. Something rumbled in the distance, too steady to be thunder.

"Avalanche?" I said.

Mason shook his head, not in denial, but in perplexity. We weren't in the mountains, so an avalanche was absurd, but that's what it sounded like, and this was the Inbetween. Anything was possible.

Then I keened the rush of magic coming our way like a flash flood barreling through a dry culvert. Hundreds, maybe thousands, of souls on the run all at once.

I saw the moment realization hit Mason too.

"Stampede." He was already dragging me up another small ridge. The noise grew until the forest trembled.

"Quick! In there!" Mason pointed to a jumble of boulders that had sheared off the ridge line. Behind them, a narrow fissure in the rocks would provide some safety. We climbed over the boulders and squeezed into it. After a few feet, the cave opened enough that we could stand side by side.

A caterwauling of snarls, squawks and screams came from the trees along with the pounding of feet. I peered out in wonder as creatures of every sort sprinted by, toppling young trees and tearing up wet ground. It was breathtaking and terrifying at once.

Finally, the rush of fur and feather dwindled. The last stragglers—some kind of deer with golden horns and a jackrabbit the size of a cow—lumbered by.

Then silence fell as if the spectacle had never been.

"Wow." It was the most inadequate thing I'd ever uttered, but words failed me. That was the second stampede today. "You think they're running from the opji?"

Mason shook his head. "We can only hope so. The opji are a threat we understand. I hate to think of what else could cause such panic."

Something bumped against my boot. I looked down to find two bright eyes shining in the dim light.

"Oh, hello."

The creature blinked.

My first thought was that it was a platypus, which was ridiculous. The only marsupials native to this area were possums. But it had that chimera-like look of a platypus—a beaver's body with the webbed feet of a Labrador retriever and a duck bill, which it opened to say, "Chip!"

"It can't be," I said.

"You know this creature?" Mason had his knife out, ready to skewer it.

"Only from some of my blog readers. I think it's a peyochip."

The creature said, "Chip!"

"Very rare," I added, "and usually found in southern swamps."

"Dangerous?"

"I don't think so."

The peyochip rubbed the side of its bill on my boot like a cat marking its territory. It seemed agitated and I realized we were blocking the only way out of the cave. I moved my legs to make room, but it only spun in confused circles.

"Come on, fella. Door's this way." I reached down, meaning to shoo it outside. The critter gripped my arm with all four legs and hung there, big eyes gazing at me with total trust.

"Look. How cute!"

"I suppose you want to bring it home." Mason lowered his blade. His grin told me he already knew the answer.

"We could leave it here, but I think it's too cold. Look how it's cuddling me for warmth."

"Chip!" Hanging upside-down, it crawled up my arm like a sloth hanging from a branch. I stroked the soft fur on its head. It made a purring sound and another "Chip!"

Something bit my wrist, the pain sharp and hot.

Too late, I remembered the rest of the blog post about peyochips and the venomous spur on their back legs. A buzzing sound filled my ears. Mason called my name. He seemed far away.

And then the world spun to black.

PEYOCHIPS AND THE MANY WORLDS THEORY

March 15, 2084

So, funny story. I got stung by a peyochip. Okay, not ha-ha funny, but certainly bizarre. If you're not familiar with this little critter, it looks very much like a platypus, but with a smaller beak and a more golden hue to its fur.

Fun fact about peyochips: just before the Flood Wars, the state of Louisiana in the old republic of USA was infested with the little critters. No one knew where they came from. At the time, biologists suspected they were an unknown variant of the Australian platypus that someone had kept as a pet and let loose in the wild. It was a pretty flimsy theory. This new variant took to the brackish waters of the bayou like a native, even though the platypus normally fishes in freshwater creeks. As I said, flimsy theory. But in those days, any suggestion of real magic could mean loss of respect by the scientific community.

The peyochips thrived in the bayous and soon pushed out other local fauna like otters and turtles. A hunt was proposed to cull the infestation, and a local man, Joachim Bledel, decided to profit from the whole business. He started raiding peyochip dens for eggs. He raised the puggles (Yes, that's the term for a baby platypus. Have your moment to squeal at the cuteness.) and started a whole new pet industry.

In Mr. Bledel's defense, peyochips are terribly cute. Their little rubbery beaks are almost like big noses. They have soft brown eyes and ridiculously pudgy feet. The name peyochip may be partly derived from the only sound it makes which is a sharp *chip-chip*, a bit like an angry red squirrel.

Bledel's cottage industry never took off, however. Three years later, the first demon was spotted in Kentucky and the gates of the Flood Wars opened.

This is where my many worlds theory comes in. What if the peyochip wasn't an unknown Terran variant of the platypus? What if the veils between worlds had been tearing for years or even decades before the wars? Not great gaping holes big enough to let in demons. Those came later. I'm talking about tiny tears. A little rip here, a microscopic hole there. Just enough to let through creatures from alternate dimensions. Most wouldn't have survived in our world, and so we never learned of them. But in the infinite worlds theory, it stands to reason that at least one of those worlds would have a creature suited to our environment.

Maybe the peyochip came through the veil years before alchemists first detected any dimensional rifts.

That might explain how a peyochip ended up in a boreal forest outside of Montreal Ward. Poor little guy. Spring is coming, so he should make it through the next few months, but then what? Winters are hard this far north. I have a mind to go on a peyochip hunt and take him in before next fall.

Oh, and did I mention that peyochip males have a venomous spur on their back feet just like the platypus? While no deaths have ever been reported from platypus venom, I can attest to the unbearable pain of such a sting. It's like nothing I have ever experienced. Even childbirth doesn't come close.

Joachim Bledel removed the spurs from the baby males before delivering them to his customers. That sounds too much like declawing a cat for my comfort, and I would suggest leaving peyochips alone if you come across any.

Yes, I know. I should take my own advice. But I can't rest knowing that poor critter won't survive the winter, even if he did wallop me a good one with his little sack of venom.

I'm just wondering if there have been any other peyochip sightings in the north?

Comments (7)

I know it's hard for you to resist helping a creature in distress. Please use caution (and maybe some thick leather gloves?) if you seek out the peyochip again.

cchedgewitch (March 15, 2084)

> Thanks! I'll be careful.
>
> *Valkyrie367 (March 15, 2084)*

I migrated to Montreal from a ward down south. Peyochips are still thriving in the bayous. Not much likes to eat them. Too much fur and beak. They're great for target practice though.

Colt45-4Ever (March 15, 2084)

The many worlds theory is as old as Socrates. Older even. But it has never been more relevant than today. I have studied what you call tears in the veil for many years. And yes, I believe the first tears predated the Flood Wars by decades, maybe even more. In fact, once you start reading our mythologies with an open mind, you can see evidence of these portals all through history. Where did Rip Van Winkle go? Where do the stories of dragons come from, and why don't we find any of their fossilized remains? I could go on with hundreds of examples, but to what purpose? The Flood Wars came. They changed everything. And to think that all the tears between worlds have been closed would be naive.

Dr-Salazar (March 15, 2084)

> I'm fascinated by the many worlds theories. Do you think there are actually an infinite number of worlds, all variations of this one?
>
> *Valkyrie367 (March 15, 2084)*

> > 5000 years ago the philosopher Chrysippus suggested that the world died and was reborn for all eternity with many of those

incarnations overlapping. Who's to say he was wrong? I love to chat about all things multiverse. Perhaps we could meet for coffee one day, on a purely professional level, of course.
Dr-Salazar (March 16, 2084)

If you've got coffee, I'm game.
Valkyrie367 (March 16, 2084)

C H A P T E R

7

hat I know of the next hours comes mostly from what others told me. I remember only pain, not in my arm, but all around me, like I was swaddled in a cocoon of pain that was growing tighter with every passing minute. And nausea. At one point, I came to heaving so hard I thought I'd turned my stomach inside out.

Mason was there. He held me by the shoulders while I rattled and heaved into a pile of dead leaves. I was shaking badly with no control of my limbs. I couldn't remember why I was puking my guts out. Then the pain washed over me again, a hot wave radiating from my arm through my whole body.

My breath came in huffs as if I couldn't suck in enough air. I tried to ask him what happened, but my words came out in a whimper.

Mason picked me up and I blissfully lost consciousness again.

I don't know how long he carried me. I woke up several times. My head banged painfully against his collarbone as he ran. I remember that the light was dim and we were still in the forest, but little else.

Later, I woke briefly from the darkness to find he'd slung me over his shoulder in a fireman's carry. My hair had come loose and hung around me like a curtain. The jostling, the pain, and the weight on my stomach made me retch and I blacked out again.

The next time I woke to arguing.

"Dammit, man! Let Berto take her!" It was Angus, angrier than I'd ever heard him. Behind him I saw the blurry outline of Berto, the duck-faced gargoyle with wings.

A wild animal snarled. No. Not an animal. Mason in a rage.

And that's when I knew I was dying. Nothing else would put Mason over the edge. He crouched over me like a wolf protecting its kill.

It was dark. How long had he been dragging me through the Inbetween all alone? Now, it seemed, the Guardians had found us, but Mason was too far gone into his magic to see reason and give me over into their care. I tried to make some reassuring noise, but the wave of pain hit me again, and I gurgled incomprehensibly. Mason growled and scooped me closer.

"Let her go!" Angus again.

Mason snarled. Angus shouted. A cat hissed. Grim? What was he doing here? I had no time to wonder at that. I felt myself being lifted. I struggled, weak as a day old pup. Berto's deep voice told me not to fight him. I must have passed out again. I had one more brief moment of lucidity where I felt like I was flying. The wind on my face was bitingly cold, but I could do nothing for it. Pain wracked my body again. I lost my faint grip on reality and fell into a nightmare of blackness.

I WAS LEANING ON the window sill in my bedroom. A brilliant sun shone on me, but it was neither warm nor too bright for my eyes.

How had I gotten there? The last thing I remembered was flying home in Berto's arms. I'd been hurt. Badly. It was all coming back. The peyochip's poison had burned like wildfire in my veins. I glanced at the bed, wondering how long I'd been out.

A body lay there with blankets pulled up to hide everything but the pale, sleeping face. My body. My face, cleaned of dirt, but pale and lifeless.

How could that be when I was also standing here by the window? I looked down at the legs supporting me. Legs, body, arms—all mine. And yet, there I was in bed too.

Huh.

This wasn't my first out-of-body rodeo. I searched the rest of the room, expecting to find some divine figure running the show. I found only Jacoby sprawled at the foot of the bed, twitching in his sleep. Mason slept in the stuffed chair on the other side of the bed. Grim perched on my bureau, his gaze fixed on Mason.

I leaned over my still body to examine my face. An abrasion scarred my left cheek, probably from the fight with the vamps. I hadn't even registered it on the way home. My lips moved as if I was chewing a piece of gristle. Jeez. Is that what I looked like when I slept?

I turned away to focus on Mason.

He hadn't changed his clothes. They were covered in dirt and blood. His beard told me he'd been sitting there for at least a day. I laid my hand on his arm, but he didn't stir.

"He can't feel you."

The voice seemed to come from right beside my ear. I jumped and whirled.

A woman stood by the end of the bed.

Her hand rested on the head of a giant raptor with golden wings that dripped flames.

A mountain devil.

She scratched the leathery skin on its crown. The bird watched me with predatory determination.

With effort I pulled my gaze back to the woman. She was tall and regal with masses of brown hair that hung in waves past her hips. She wore a simple gray wool dress. It looked homespun. I'd never seen her before and yet, she was familiar. It was the eyes. They watched me with the same feral intensity as the mountain devil.

I'd seen those eyes before.

"You're her. The woman from the mountaintop. Terra."

I'd dreamed of her once, just as my cousin completed the rite that had infected me with the Maid Mother Crone disease. Something in Gunora's magic had sent me a vision of a primeval woman and thousands of her disciples.

This was the same woman. She might wear a different skin and different clothes, but this was Terra, heart of our world, god of every living creature on it.

She inclined her head. "You may call me Terra, though I have many names. One is as good as another."

The devil left her side. It didn't hop like a bird, but stalked like a prowling hyena. It approached the bed and my still form. Grim's head jerked up. His hackles rose as his gaze tracked the beast. Interesting. The night jaguar could see this vision too.

Terra sat on the edge of the bed and stared down at my sleeping body with an unreadable expression.

"Am I dying?" I felt much too calm to be asking that question.

Terra turned her gaze on me and smiled. Her face was ageless, her dark skin unlined by wrinkles, but her eyes were too wise to be young.

"No. I chose you. You have no time to die."

The room shifted. Suddenly, Terra was standing by the window and I was on the other side of the bed. Grim hissed and did his best Halloween cat impression. The mountain devil hissed right back and flexed its wings. Flames melted from his feathers, but I felt no heat.

Was this all an illusion? Was I dreaming? I swallowed down my feelings of disorientation. Whatever was happening here, it was important. I needed to focus on Terra. No matter how they came to me, I needed to heed her words.

"You chose me?"

"Yes."

Terra's lips never moved when she spoke. Her communication wasn't unlike the dragons' mindspeak. Only it felt…more. Her words didn't just come into my thoughts. They infiltrated my entire being, as if they sprang from my own DNA.

"Chose me for what?" I sounded breathless.

"To fight for me. For the forests and the inhabitants of this world."

"Inhabitants? You mean the people."

"I mean all the lives in my care."

The room tilted again and we switched places. The mountain devil now stood by the window. Terra stood next to Mason, frowning at his sleeping form. She held her hand over his head, palm down like a benediction. I had a sudden rush of protectiveness.

"Don't touch him!"

"He is lost in the darkness." She frowned, and even this didn't mark her face with lines.

"He'll be fine." I said it to assure myself as much as her.

Terra tipped her head to look at me.

"His darkness is not mine."

I was having a hard time following her logic. My thoughts felt sluggish. "What do you mean not yours?"

"Not of this world. It is alien. But then I have sheltered so many aliens since the breaking."

"The breaking? You mean the Flood Wars?" It was a good description of a time when the world broke open, letting in people and creatures from all different dimensions. It had been a terrible time for us humans, but I'd never stopped to wonder how much more terrible it would have been for the spirit of our world. Had Terra suffered each tearing of the veil like a knife wound? Did the alien creatures feel like fleas crawling over her body?

Terra let her hand drop. "He is not my concern. You are. I chose you."

"You said that, but I don't understand."

"When the doors opened, creatures from different realms came to me, predators and prey alike. I harbored them all. I could do nothing else."

Her expression turned stern. She spoke like she'd been forced into it, but what kind of power could force a god? Before I could articulate that thought into a question, the room shifted again. I stumbled against my dresser and Grim hissed in my ear.

"But there is one predator who must not be allowed to continue. One who disrupts the balance." Terra gazed out the window.

"Humans." I knew it. We'd pissed her off one too many times and now she was going to wipe us out like the parasites we were.

"Not humans. Not yet, anyway." Terra smiled. "I am still hopeful that your people can learn from past mistakes." "But the opji get no more pardons from me." Her eyes blazed and her expression grew terrible and awesome. "They kill for pleasure. Great swaths of my forest burn for their greed." Terra filled the room, floor to ceiling. Behind her, the mountain devil flamed, blasting me with heat. They towered over the bed, and I shrank back. Grim howled.

"And now they have a shar-lil!" Her voice boomed. "I will not let it be!"

I cringed, squeezed my eyes shut, and covered my ears with my hands. None of it helped. The voice echoed like thunder, and seemed to invade the very core of my being.

When I opened my eyes, Terra had shrunk to her previous form. She looked tired.

"I will not let it be," she repeated, quieter now.

I had no idea what had just happened, or what she wanted from me.

"The shar-lil, what is that?"

"They don't know how to use it, or even what they have. But they will learn. And they will destroy everything."

"But what *is* it." My frustration was showing.

Terra held her hand out, palm up. A ball of light appeared. It swirled and morphed, like a small sun spinning in her hand.

"You must find it before it's too late." Terra's face, lit by the thing in her hand, looked smooth and youthful and sad.

I clenched my fists, trying to keep my frustration in check. It was never a good idea to antagonize a god.

"But. What. Is. It?"

The mountain devil growled and jumped on the bed. It pawed at my unresisting body laying there. Flames burst from its wings and encircled me like a pyre.

On the other side of the room, Terra closed the gap between us and shoved the shar-lil at me. Her hand, holding the glowing orb, smashed right through my chest.

I choked and struggled for air. My eyes felt hot and ready to explode. I couldn't breathe. I couldn't move. Terra had her fist around my heart.

"The shar-lil is the end of everything. It will remake the world." Her eyes bore into mine. "Find it. Destroy it. Before your enemies slaughter us all." Her voice faded away and the grip on my heart loosened.

"Please…I don't…" I didn't get to finish. Grim pounced on the mountain devil. A bright light flashed and the room turned upside down again.

8

I gasped and sat up with a start, expecting to find a mountain devil on my chest. Instead, I dislodged Grim. His fur stood on end. He hissed and swiped at my hand, then seemed satisfied that I was awake, jumped off the bed and sashayed from the room.

I looked around. My eyes were gritty and clouded, but when I tried to lift my hand to rub them, it felt weighted with lead. Everything hurt, even my eyelids.

Light filtered through the crack in the curtains. I was in my bed. There was no mountain devil and no cryptic god hounding me from the corner.

The familiar smell of our sheets comforted me. I pulled myself upright with great effort. My muscles felt as dried as old leather, and my tongue was thick and rough in my mouth.

A quiet *zzz, zzz* told me Jacoby slept at the foot of the bed. I struggled to sit up, barely making it onto one elbow before the effort became too much.

Mason was asleep in the chair beside the bed.

I reached for the glass of water on the night stand and spilled most of it before cupping the glass in two trembling hands. I drank down the rest of it.

"Easy. Don't overdo it." Nori stood in the doorway. My heart sank when I saw her. They'd brought in the kitsune healer. That meant my wound was as severe as I'd thought. I rubbed at my bandaged wrist. It ached, but not any worse than a bad bruise. Somehow, Nori had drained the venom from my blood. I'd seen her brand of healing before. It took a lot out of her.

She came in and laid a cool hand on my forehead.

"What happened?" I rubbed my head. I was so groggy. "I remember the stampede and then…" Memories came back in patches. The most vivid of those memories was the visit from Terra, but I didn't want to tell Nori about that. I'd sound like a crazy woman.

Nori was a tiny kitsune shifter with glossy black hair that she wore in a tight pony tail. She usually had an air of elegance about her, like an early movie star. Today, her eyes were hooded with dark circles and her skin looked ready to crack. She had obviously spent the night healing me.

I rubbed a hand over my face and ordered my thoughts. The bandage pulled at my wrist.

"The peyochip. It stung me."

Nori nodded. "The venom was bad. I don't think it would have killed you, but the pain made you thrash about and lose consciousness. He didn't handle that well." She glanced at Mason, still asleep in my chair.

"Your cat did something to him. I'm not sure what. But he's been out ever since."

So Grim had gone all night jaguar on Mason's ass. That could only mean that he'd been close to losing himself to the darkness again.

"That's three patients in one night," Nori said. I should really be charging you folks more."

"Three patients?"

"Your rodent friend came back with a pregnant woman."

I stared at her as the words tried to make sense in my head. Then I remembered Soolea. Raol had made it home then. I didn't think he'd like being called a rodent, but I could forgive Nori a lot right now.

"Is Soolea all right?"

"A bit shook up, as can be expected. But she's due any day now. Angus gave her a room in the gatehouse. I think I'll stick around until the baby comes. No point in running back and forth from the city."

Tears wetted my eyes. I was amazed I had enough moisture to make them. Nori was a good friend. She hadn't always been. Because of her affection for Mason, she'd made some bad choices when we first met, but I couldn't fault her for her care to me and mine. She'd saved Jacoby once and now it seemed she'd saved me, if not from death then at least from days of excruciating pain.

"And Mason?"

"Let him sleep. That's the best thing for him. I'll check on you both later." She refilled my glass from a jug on the nightstand. I tried not to chug it down. Then I held the glass in my lap with shaky hands.

"I'll tell Dutch to bring you something to eat, but go easy. You might still feel some nausea. Let me see your ankle too."

I'd forgotten about the wojak bite. I folded back the blankets to reveal my bandage-wrapped foot. Nori peeled off the bandage. The wound was nearly healed. Only the pink skin of a fresh scar remained.

Nori nodded, satisfied with her healing and rose to leave.

"Nori?" I called. She paused at the door. "Thank you."

She shot a glance at Mason and smiled.

A few minutes later, I dropped the glass on the night stand with a clatter that woke Mason.

"Sorry. Go back to sleep. Or better yet, come to bed." I patted the mattress beside me.

"You're awake!"

He shot from the chair. His clothes were rumpled and muddy. He wore a two-day beard and his hair stuck up at all angles. And he was beautiful.

He reached for me and stopped, as if his touch might shatter me.

"Are you okay?"

"I've been better. Feels like a truck backed over me."

Then my big, strong man crumpled. He sank to his knees and pressed his face into the mattress. His shoulders convulsed with sobs that he tried to hold in. His voice was thick with unshed tears and muffled by the blankets.

"I thought I'd lost you. I couldn't get home fast enough. I couldn't…"

He raised his face, cheeks smeared with tears. And his eyes were black as coal.

"Mason?" I reached for him with my hand and with my keening. His magic was wild and burgeoning, like a summer storm. "It's okay," I soothed. "I'm okay. You did it. You got me help in time."

His lips quivered. He nodded and took a deep breath. The black bled from his eyes.

From the foot of the bed, Jacoby snorted and rolled, flinging out a hand and a leg to take up most of the bed.

I laughed, the sound as rough as gravel on stone. "You should move him."

"Let him sleep. He was awake all night too. Besides I don't need much room."

He shucked off his dirty shirt and pants, climbed into bed and wrapped his whole body around me, as if he could shield me from all the evils of the world.

THE WINGED DEVIL

March 16, 2084

Three blog posts in one week! You'd think I have nothing else to do. To be honest, I'm laid up at the moment, recovering from that peyochip sting. So I thought I'd catch up on some critter research.

Lately, I've been fascinated by the mountain devil, a creature that has often been confused with the phoenix. Both have wings of flame, but the significance of those flames differs. A phoenix usually symbolizes rebirth, while a mountain devil is known to pluck the eyes from the deceitful. Instead of a regal raptor head, the mountain devil looks more like a vulture on fire. Not pretty, but pretty intimidating.

I'm curious about other stories related to the mountain devil. There was a mention of it in Pylee's Homestead Reference that suggested it once prowled the hills of Pennsylvania. I might be going crazy, but I think I saw one not too far from Montreal Ward. Has anyone heard about other sightings?

COMMENTS (4)

Feel better, Valkyrie367!

Toots12 (March 16, 2084)

Mountain devils have been long associated with tutelary deities. They are watch dogs of gods that guard the land and sky.

Professor-T (March 16, 2084)

> Gods of land and sky? Like Terra?
>
> *Valkyrie367 (March 16, 2084)*
>
> > Terra is only one name for something mutable and unnameable, but yes. You could call Terra a tutelary god. The Terran priests call

the mountain devil a guard dog, though what it is supposed to be guarding is not clear.

Professor-T (March 16, 2084)

Two days later, Nori declared me fit enough to return to work. I dressed in jeans and my Valkyrie Pest Control work shirt. The dark green was flattering to my complexion and I looked a lot fresher than I felt.

Walking into the kitchen, I found Mason feeding Holly. She sat on his knee. Small pieces of muffin and fruit were mashed on the table in front of him.

My little angel saw me and immediately spat out a wad of chewed muffin.

"Mama!" she shrieked. Holly did everything at high volume—speaking, running, playing. Thankfully, she also slept like a pro or we'd never get any peace.

I sat at the table and Mason passed her to me.

"You should take another day off. Maybe two," he said.

Apparently, I didn't look as fresh as I thought.

I rolled my eyes and bounced Holly in my lap. If he had his way, I'd stay home for another week. The crease never left the spot between his eyebrows as he watched me pick at my breakfast.

"I'll be fine." Holly grabbed one of my braids and tried to stick it in her mouth. I gently extricated it from her sticky fingers and gave her my coffee spoon to play with. She squeezed the spoon tightly in her fist and let out a shriek, just because she felt like it. We can learn a lot about self expression from toddlers.

"Eat something and then maybe I'll let you go," Mason said.

I broke off a huge piece of Dutch's fabulous morning glory muffin and stuck the whole thing in my mouth, grinning as I chewed.

We both knew that Mason didn't "let me" do anything, but I gave him a pass. I might have been the injured one, but thanks to Nori, my wounds were healing faster than his. He still watched me with that haunted look, like I might spontaneously combust. I couldn't blame him. I'd almost lost him a couple of times. It never got easier.

I swallowed the muffin and felt a little queasy. I hid it by chugging down lukewarm coffee.

I had only one job that morning and saw no reason to cancel.

"I'm just going to Hedge to check on the new construction," I said. "A scouting mission only. Besides, you're the one who asked me to go. You said it was important."

"It is important, but not so much that you need to go today." He spoke while trying to clean Holly's hands. She'd gotten a hold of my muffin and was now rendering it to goo that oozed out between her fingers. She flailed and fussed in my lap while Dad tried to pry open her tight little fists.

"Gah!" she said, then let out a shriek that instantly wilted every potted plant in the room.

Oh, boy. We'd have to work on that. Holly's green magic was off the charts. I'd have to teach her to control it or we'd soon be living on a desert homestead.

I distracted her with a book about animal ABCs. It was made of some fancy new indestructible material, probably suited for space exploration but was perfect for toddlers who liked to tear things apart. I opened the book. Holly grabbed the page with a coy-bear on it and tried to stuff the whole thing in her mouth.

"Where were we?" I asked.

"We were discussing you staying home and not driving all the way out to the south shore today."

"Oh, right."

More than three years ago, Gerard Golovin envisioned a grand industrial complex to complement his railroad. Parliament approved it almost immediately, but construction had been stalled first because of the fae prince's attempted coup, then because of disruptions to the railroad by the godlings.

Terran fanatics had taken these setbacks as signs of displeasure from the god who abhorred anything that encroached on her forests. They set up camps outside the proposed site and tried everything from sabotaging construction vehicles to hunger strikes in order to stop the clear-cutting. In the end, Hub militia had arrested them all. It had been all very hush-hush, and no one heard from the Terran protesters again.

That happened before Mason became Prime Minister, and though he deplored Hub's high-handed tactics for stamping out the protests, he believed the expansion was important for bringing new prosperity to Montreal. I agreed.

The railroad to Manhattan brought opportunities for trade that hadn't been seen in the ward for over fifty years. There were already plans for a new rail line going west to Toronto. The world was becoming united once again.

In recent months, building at the complex had restarted. The plan had been to extend the city's ward through the site and join it up with the railroad's ward. And that's when they ran into a new snag.

Montreal was desperately short of Apex stones. The rare gems were feats of alchemical wonder. In the same way carbon could be crushed into a diamond, magic was harvested and pressurized to make Apex stones. It was a long and expensive process, but the stones were invaluable. They fueled everything from cars to electric lights to the protective ward itself, and Montreal was expanding too fast for the alchemists to keep up with demand.

But you can't keep a good alchemist down, and they came up with another way to stop the forest from reclaiming the newly cleared site. Everything had been progressing according to plan until they found a pest that could derail the entire project. That's when Mason had asked me to have a look.

"I'll just drive to Hedge, get a quick look at the problem, maybe take some pictures and come home to file a report. I'll be done by noon."

"Uh-huh." Mason didn't seem convinced. He knew as I did, that simple jobs were never simple. But I hoped this one really would be. I wanted time to visit the New Temple of Terra before coming home. I needed some answers about a certain creepy dream I'd had about a god and a mountain devil. At least I hoped it had been a dream.

I finished my breakfast and handed Holly to Mason. She squirmed until she found her footing on his lap and started to bounce again.

He looked at me over her blond curls. "But seriously. The job can wait. I don't want you taking on too much."

"Someone's got to pay the bills now that you're on a measly civil servant's salary." I grinned. Being Prime Minister of the Alchemist Party had its perks, and the enormous salary was only one of them. I didn't need to work, but I wanted to. Even when that meant doing the job on a day when I'd rather head back to bed.

"If it makes you feel better, I'll get Emil to come along for the ride."

"That would make me very happy." Mason didn't look happy. I decided we needed to change that.

I perched lightly on his knee, the one that wasn't already occupied by our daughter and twined my fingers in his hair.

"Why don't we go out Friday night. Just you and me. Somewhere private." I kissed the corner of his mouth where his lips met his unshaven cheek. I loved that spot. It was equal parts soft and bristly, just like Mason.

"You think we can find a babysitter?" He quirked an eyebrow, and I was glad to see some of the sternness leave his face.

"I'm sure a certain banshee won't mind. She's a sucker for a love story."

"A date it is, then." He kissed me long and deep.

"Gah!" Holly screamed.

I sighed and drew back enough to lean my forehead against his. Holly grabbed our ears and shrieked again.

Mason laughed. I kissed them both and left feeling lighter than I had in days. Some couples argued about kids or family or money or the dozens of other things that could break a marriage. Mason and I rarely argued. We understood that everything we held dear could be taken in an instant. It was the reality of the world we lived in. And when we'd taken our vows, we'd sworn never to take any of it for granted.

The only thing that could come between us was fear of losing each other. I was glad that Mason seemed to be over my brush with death. I had complete confidence that he would get control of his dark magic, and I would put it all behind us too.

I headed outside. My van was parked beside the gatehouse where the Guardians lived.

Angus had decided to hang out on the roof for the day. I gave him a wave, knowing that he could see me in his stone form, even if he couldn't respond.

I thought about knocking on the gatehouse door to check on Soolea, but it was only eight o'clock and I didn't want to wake her. I'd see her when I got back.

Jacoby arrived with his work belt slung over one shoulder like a bandoleer.

"You're supposed to be on vacation," I said.

"Vacation's borings." He watched as I sorted through my kit in the trunk, making sure I was well stocked.

Jacoby took his apprenticeship duties very seriously. So when I'd told him that all employees should get at least two weeks of paid leave a year, he'd accepted it. And since my schedule was reduced, I decided this would be a good time for Jacoby to relax.

It was day three of R&R, and he was already bored.

"You need a hobby." I backed him up so I could trigger the van's trunk door to close.

"Hobby?" He scratched the poodle fur behind his ear.

"Yes. A hobby. Something that's kind of like work, but you get paid in fun instead of money."

His nose scrunched up as he tried to understand.

"Like gardening. For me that's fun and relaxing. It's a good hobby."

"Gardening's dirtys."

"There are lots of other hobbies. Infinite possibilities."

"Like what?"

"Like woodworking, painting…some people even collect things, like," I struggled to think of something he could collect, "like antique bottles or sea glass."

Jacoby still struggled with the concept.

I crouched so I could look him in the eye and squeezed his thin shoulders. "The point of having spare time is to find something new about yourself and have fun doing it. Dekar is working on the barn for the new horses today. Why don't you help him? Maybe building things is your secret talent."

He puffed up his chest. "I coulds build things."

I watched him trot off to find Dekar. I felt bad for foisting him off on the goblins, but I truly did believe he needed some time away. And I didn't need him tagging along when I visited Terra's temple later in the day.

Twenty minutes later, I parked outside Valkyrie Pest Control. It still felt weird to come here only for business. It had been my home for so long. Emil now occupied the little apartment behind the office. I made right for the garage where we stored weapons, tools, first aid products, traps, and all the other paraphernalia needed for the job. The curtain in the window upstairs twitched, and I gave a friendly wave to Mr. Murray, our nosy upstairs lodger.

After refilling my kit, I headed for the office.

As it turned out, I didn't have to ask Emil to accompany me. He took one look at me and said, "I'm coming with you."

I nodded in resignation and tossed him the key fob. "You drive."

I really needed to get a better concealer.

10

The gray sky drained all color from the shanty town that lay outside the South Gate. Hedge was a lawless place. Its residents had no rights or protections from Hub, and the militia only stepped in to govern when the gate or the ward were threatened. Any other crime was just another Tuesday in Hedge.

A storm had blown through last night, leaving a blanket of fresh snow over the muddy March mess already on the ground. Most of that was trampled to slush from the day's foot traffic.

Emil drove slowly through the streets clogged with pedestrians, mule carts, and horses. The only alchemical vehicles besides ours belonged to Hub, and these were heavily armored trucks parked at most corners. Soldiers stood beside them in full body armor with blasters ready. The closed visors on their helmets gave them an alien, menacing air.

"Is it just me, or are there more people in Hedge than ever?" I said as I watched the street outside my window.

"Definitely more." Emil had turned off the auto-drive and gripped the steering wheel with grim determination. When a mule cart laden with furniture blocked the intersection, he leaned on the horn. An elderly man with fae ears and a wisp of white hair turned on the cart's bench and gave us the finger.

Emil sighed and put the van in park. While we waited for the traffic snarl to clear, I studied the crowds. Most were human, with a few class two fae in the mix. I saw families of goblins and wood trolls camped at the side of the road. Dirty human children wearing nothing but rags ran among the stalled carts, grabbing at anything that wasn't tied down. An ogre carried a massive wooden beam on one shoulder and the crowd gave way for him to pass. The town was over-crowded, noisy, and dirty. Even with the windows closed, I could smell its distinct scent—something like stagnant water plus rotting food.

Mason had saved Arriz and his family from this fate, but we couldn't save everyone. Still, I thought someone should do something about the conditions here. But who? Parliament? Many long-time residents of Hedge were staunchly anti-government. They were homesteaders at heart, and wanted nothing to do with Hub or Parliament. Hedge was the perfect compromise. They enjoyed the protection of Montreal, without having to adhere to any of its regulations. I wondered how they felt about the influx of refugees to their little ramshackle paradise.

Finally, the Hub soldiers pushed away from their truck and began sorting out the traffic. Why they'd waited so long, I didn't know. Tensions were running high and they broke up a fist fight that had erupted between two stranded cart drivers.

"Look at those fancy boys, finally doing their job," Emil said. "It's about time."

The soldiers demanded that the mule cart blocking the intersection turn down an alley. The old man argued with hands flying and hair whipping in the wind until a soldier leveled his blaster at him.

"A bit harsh," I said, but it worked. The cart pulled away and traffic continued.

As we headed through town, the sights went from dismal to appalling. We passed several burned out buildings full of squatters and the long wooden structure that passed for a hospital. My stomach ached when I saw it.

There were bodies, wrapped in dirty sheets piled up outside the hospital.

Bodies. Plural.

By the All-father, I knew the flu had hit hard down here, but this was epidemic-level hard.

A woman and a goblin carried another body and dumped it on the stack like cordwood.

"That can't be from the flu, is it?" My voice sounded small and hollow.

Emil glanced at the macabre site, then kept his eyes on the road ahead. "It's taken hold in both Barrows and Hedge," he said, meaning the other shanty town outside the North Gate. "There have been cases inside the ward too. The hospitals are on the brink of being over-run."

"I didn't know that." Where had I been? Oh, right. Recovering from my own near death experience.

"But Parliament can't know how bad it is here. They would have done something by now." If nothing else, Mason would have made a bigger fuss about me coming to Hedge this morning.

Emil shrugged. "It's Hedge. There's always something bad happening here. If not plague, it's fire. Or gang wars, or a drug feud. It's not really Parliament's problem, as long as the trouble stays outside the gate."

But it was Parliament's problem if the sickness spread to the ward. I'd be bringing this up to my representative as soon as possible. Having my rep as a captive audience at dinner would make that easy.

We drove on and left the traffic, sickness, dirt and poverty behind. Near the southern edge of town, the roads widened and the buildings, though not pretty, were more sturdy. We passed barracks for Hub soldiers and housing for the farmers who tended Montreal's greenhouses and fields. Here the militia presence was ubiquitous. There were no more children running loose. No more mule carts.

The new train station was the heart of this new town. Built from plain gray stone, the station was a huge structure flanked on one side by the rail yard and warehouses on the other. Looking at it, I couldn't help thinking it was a symbol for the progress of our new world. And as a symbol, it lacked all beauty and refinement.

We left the train station and barracks behind. Emil stopped the van at the top of a hill.

We gazed at a spiral of new roads in a vast clear-cut zone. Mason had shown me the map of the proposed industrial complex, but I hadn't understood the immensity of the place. When finished, the complex would be the size of a small city.

It would eventually be home to warehouses, office buildings and factories, all linked to the railroad by a private rail line. For now, it was eerily empty. The only activity was happening in the western portion of the giant clearing, where one completed warehouse stood.

Emil whistled long and low. "That's unbelievable."

In a time when commerce had been severely curtailed to fit the diminished population, building a new industrial complex was already amazing. And even more so because the builders thought they could keep the Inbetween from reclaiming the land.

The city and railroad were protected by wards to keep the Inbetween's magic at bay. There were no Apex towers within the new construction zone.

"How do they think they're going to manage this?" Emil looked at me with raised eyebrows.

"I guess we'll find out." I pointed vaguely toward the lone warehouse and he drove on.

The site's foreman, Adam Marat, met us beside the warehouse as we parked. The sound of backhoes, dump trucks, and chainsaws made it difficult to do more than smile and nod when he introduced himself.

The site was busy with workers excavating foundations, pouring concrete and building frames for more warehouses. Others were clearing trees to expand the already vast footprint of the complex.

Adam indicated that we should follow him.

Emil leaned in and whispered in my ear, "You go. I'll look around."

Adam didn't seem to care about Emil wandering off, so I followed him into the warehouse. The light and the noise dimmed. The building was empty except for piles of lumber waiting to be put to use. I studied Adam as we walked across the vast empty expanse, heading for a door on the back side of the building.

He was tall and sturdy, the kind of guy you went to when you couldn't get the lid off a pickle jar. His hair was hidden under a hard hat, but from his ruddy complexion, I guessed it to be blond or red.

He marched across the smooth concrete floor like a man on a mission, and I had to lengthen my stride to keep up.

"Have you had any trouble with the opji?" I stank at small talk, but I wanted to know if the south side of the island was also feeling the heat of the opji movements.

He shot me a frown. "The vamps? Nah. Not that I've heard. Why? Should I be worried?"

"Probably not," I assured him quickly. "But they've been spotted in the north. Homesteads have been attacked."

"We've got a bigger Hub presence down here. What with the trains and the farms. The opji would have to be pretty stupid to attack."

Stupid or desperate, I thought. But it was true that Hub spent more resources on the south shore where most of the farms and greenhouses that fed the city were located.

"My, uh, contact said you have a new way of curtailing the forest encroachment." Adam didn't need to know I was the wife of a prime minister. People tended to treat me with kid gloves when they knew. And I wanted to be sure he spoke openly with me.

Adam puffed up his chest. "This whole complex will be built ten years faster because of it. Really amazing stuff, but I'll let you see for yourself."

He opened another door on the opposite end from where we'd entered the warehouse, and we strode into sunlight again. The noise of the ongoing construction was muted here. This warehouse—the first of many, I assumed—was built up against the western edge of the cleared land. Two hundred paces away, the forest grew like a wall of brambles. In the summer when that wall was full of leaves, it would be nearly impenetrable.

"How long since you clearcut this?" I asked.

"Over a year." Adam rocked back on his heels, squinting in the bright light.

A year? Without wards around our homestead, the forest would grow back in days. But regular wards were unstable and had to be reinforced regularly. They weren't practical on a large scale like this. Not unless you had Apex stones to back them up.

I pretended to admire the bare land. In truth, it gave me a sinking feeling.

"Seems like you've got everything under control," I said. "So what's the problem?"

"Over here." Adam motioned for me to follow him. "With the shortage of Apex stones, the alchemists found a new way to block the wild encroachment. I guess you could call it a militarized plant."

As we walked toward the tree line, my eyes grew accustomed to the bright light again and I finally saw it.

A line of mushrooms grew at the edge of the forest. I'm a great fungus enthusiast. The abundance of mushrooms near our home never ceases to amaze me. They are beautiful and earthy. If I tap into my green magic, I can feel their magic burrowing through the dirt, connecting all life together in one great harmony.

These weren't those mushrooms.

These were bone white protrusions that pushed through the dirt like skeletal fingers, as if I stood beside a massive grave and all the corpses had decided to dig their way to freedom. And the fingers weren't still. They bent and stretched in a slow pulsing beat, like they were trying to squeeze invisible fruit.

Creepy, but also kind of cool.

I moved to kneel in the dirt to examine them, but Adam cautioned me.

"Don't get too close. Look." He pointed to the right where one of the fingers suddenly exploded in a yellowish puff of spores.

I closed my eyes. By the All-father. Were these people really that stupid? Why had no one warned me about the potential danger of an unknown exploding spore spreader?

I sighed. It was too late now. My hazmat gear was in the van. If the spores were poisonous, I was already contaminated.

"We call them knucklebones," Adam said. "I forget the official name, you know…the scientific one. I can ask, if you need it."

"Yes. I'll need everything you've got."

I took out my widget to snap a few pictures. The bony protrusions grew from a carpet of gray-green lichen. It was hard to tell if the fingerlings and the lichen were the same fungus or a parasite-host combination.

I knelt—keeping well away from any potential exploding fungi—and sank my magic into the earth.

I keened the mycelium of the knucklebones immediately. It was like a black smear of tar. I shuddered. Unlike the mycelium of regular mushrooms, this one connected nothing. In fact, when I pushed my magic further, I keened the reluctance of the rest of the forest to even touch it. It was an effective barrier against encroachment.

It also felt wrong. Unnatural. If I had to guess, I would say this fungus wasn't native to Terra. It had probably come through a tear in the veil. Or some over-eager alchemist had spliced a native mushroom with something alien.

I reeled in my magic and stood.

"Interesting." I couldn't say I approved, but it seemed like a good barrier against encroachment. "So what's the problem?"

Adam flicked a finger, motioning me to follow him. We walked along the ring of fungi. Several fingers released puffs of spores as we passed. I pulled a bandanna from my kit and tied it around my face in a futile attempt to keep the spores from my lungs.

We stopped at a small tool shed. The knucklebones grew right up to the back of the shed, and one entire side was covered in the lichen that grew around the knucklebones. The wood underneath was eaten away.

"We think the spores are causing this," Adam said. "It's got me worried that the fungus might spread to other buildings."

Great. Now I wanted a shower. In a decontamination tank. I could only hope that since Adam was still walking around breathing, the fungus didn't affect humans too.

"Who's the lead alchemist on this project?" I asked.

"Hubert Bauch."

"He must have a plan to contain the fungus if it gets out of hand?"

Adam twisted his lips and ran a hand along his jaw, a classic stalling gesture. He had something to say and he didn't want to say it.

"Bauch left us with a fungicide to use if it spread too far. But it stopped working about a month ago. It's almost like the fungus adapted to it. That's about the same time this stuff started growing on the shed."

Terrific.

"Bauch left if for you? Where did he go?"

"He died," Adam's voice was flat. "The flu took him six weeks ago."

"And that's all he left you? A fungicide?"

Adam's face turned red, from embarrassment or anger. I couldn't tell which.

"It was an ongoing project. We didn't expect to be without our lead alchemist. But that's why you're here, to take over the project."

No way. No sir. No how. They couldn't pay me enough to take over care of the knucklebones.

"I'm not an alchemist. I'm only here to assess the situation and make recommendations to the ministers."

"So what're your recommendations?" He crossed his arms and narrowed his eyes.

My recommendation was to raze this place to the ground, fungi, warehouse, shed and all of it. But I realized that wouldn't be a popular opinion around here. It also suddenly occurred to me that I was completely alone with this bear of a man, on the edge of the forest and not within earshot of anyone else on site.

I smiled and said, "My first recommendation is that everyone on site gets a physical. I don't think those spores are harmful, but best to be sure, right?"

He nodded reluctantly, and his shoulders relaxed.

"Then I'll do some digging and see what I come up with, okay? But I'm sure the minister will want to get a new alchemist out here asap."

He'd better. After the scolding I had planned, he'd better get a whole team out here.

I made my goodbyes to Adam and promised he'd get my full report in a few days.

Emil was waiting in the van.

I dropped my tired self into the passenger seat. Emil saw the frustration on my face.

"Was it that bad?"

"Just a sec." I typed a message to Oscar.

Where are you?

A few seconds later, he answered.

Agora

Perfect. He was working at his lab behind Abbott's Agora, the market right near my office.

"Can you drop me off at the Agora before you head back?" I asked.

"Sure thing. Is something wrong?"

"Let's hope not."

I texted Oscar again, detailing the problem.

A ripple of unease washed over me as I thought of those dancing knucklebones and the millions of potential knucklebones that could be nesting in the cracks of my skin at that moment.

ost alchemists had two or more labs. One within the city for official party business, one on Perrot Island where they could conduct more sensitive experiments, and one completely private lab on their own property.

I was lucky that Oscar was currently working at his lab behind Abbott's Agora, the sprawling market that took up most of the grounds of the old college. The Alchemists had purchased the study halls and dormitories and turned them into offices and labs.

Oscar met me at the door to the Penfield Building. We bypassed the nosy imp guarding the reception desk who tried to make me sign in with his digital scanner.

"Out of the bloody way, you oaf!" Oscar snarled. "This is important business!"

"But Mr. Lewis!" squealed the imp, "it's protocol!"

Oscar waved him away and pulled me down the hall to the last door.

"I hope he won't get in trouble for that," I said as we entered the lab. "Poor guy was just trying to do his job."

"Jona? Nah. I'll take care of it if he does." Oscar closed the door behind us and shut the blinds on the glass door, effectively cutting us off from prying eyes.

"I find I have less patience for meaningless protocols as I get older," he said. I didn't think that screening visitors coming into a lab full of tech secrets, bio-hazards, and dangerous artifacts could be called meaningless, but I let it go.

Oscar had his quirks, but he was the best alchemist in the city.

He stood a full foot shorter than me. His head was round and smooth as a cue ball with a fringe of white wispy hair around his ears. What he lacked in hair on his head, he made up for with his eyebrows. They were like bushy white caterpillars that writhed on his agile face when he changed expressions.

"So tell me what this big emergency is all about."

I held my specimen jar in both hands but hesitated to give it over. "You didn't call Mason, did you?"

The bushy caterpillars arched. "No. Should I have?"

"No." I let out a sigh. "He's been overly protective lately. That's all."

"And you think he has reason to be worried about that?" He pointed to the jar still clasped in my grip.

"I'm not exactly sure what this is but it's all over the new dig site in Hedge, and…" I paused, feeling a bit foolish. "I might have got some on me."

The caterpillars stretched to the top of his head. "Might have?"

"Okay, I did. I know I should have been more careful. It was stupid—"

"Where?" Oscar cut me off. He frowned and the caterpillars slammed down to his nose.

"On my face, probably. And my clothes."

To his credit, Oscar didn't swear or scold me. He took the specimen jar, then ushered me into a contamination shower conveniently located next to the door. From a cupboard, he selected a bundle of gray clothes and two white towels. He added a large nylon bag to the pile and handed it all to me.

"Take everything off. Bag all your clothes. Boots too. Use the soap provided in the stall. It won't be gentle on your skin and it smells like sulfur, but it'll kill anything."

"You really think this is necessary?"

"Better safe than dead. Go on, go on." He shoved me toward the tiny shower. "By the time you're done, I'll have a better idea what we're dealing with here." He left and shut the door, leaving me sealed in.

I did as he ordered and stripped down. The room was chilly until I turned on the water. There was only one temperature. Scalding. The soap did smell like sulfur, but I lathered up my hair with it anyway, then did the rest of me. I stayed under the hot, stinging spray until I felt like an al-dente noodle.

By the time I was done, my skin was bright pink and tender as a sunburn.

Thankfully, the towels were soft and fluffy. I gingerly dried off and opened the bundle of clothes. White t-shirt, socks, gray sweatpants and shirt. I even found a pair of terrycloth slippers tucked into the mix. It made me wonder how often Oscar had visitors in need of decontamination that he had bundles of clothes in various sizes at hand. Ah, the life of an alchemist. Always exciting.

I dressed and searched through the drawers until I found a comb. Oscar's hellfire soap hadn't done my hair any favors and it took several minutes to comb through the snarls and tangles before I could plait it into a braid down my back.

I left my contaminated clothes in the bag beside the shower and went to find Oscar.

He was sitting at a desk in the farthest corner of his lab. He'd pulled up Hubert Bauch's work on the Alchemist database. A vid screen was projected on the wall above his desk. Numbers, graphs and images scrolled up the screen. Oscar frowned and zoomed in on one image that showed the bony white protrusions sticking out of the ground, then he sighed and turned to me.

"What's the verdict?" I asked. "Am I already being eaten up inside by this fungus?"

"No. And it's not really a fungus at all. At least it's not fungi like we understand them."

"You think it's alien?"

Oscar nodded. "Possibly. Or something horribly mutated by magic, but that seems unlikely. In any case, it's completely inert in the human body. You're safe."

"I wish I'd known that before I scrubbed off my epidermis."

Oscar didn't seem concerned about my epidermis.

"It's a fascinating species whatever it is."

"The site crew are calling it knucklebones." I pointed at the screen.

"That's as good a name as any."

"If it isn't a fungus, what is it?"

Oscar rubbed his wispy hair, making it stand up.

"They're plants that digest other plants, but they aren't passive like fungus. They're hunters, in a way."

"You're kidding."

"Not at all. Scientists have known for years about bladderwort and the way it lays traps for algae."

"Like a Venus flytrap?"

"Like that, only not carnivorous. Or not *only* carnivorous. It seems Bauch found these knucklebones and cultivated them to eat any cellulose-based organism they come in contact with. It's pure hubris, really, to think that he could contain it." Oscar pounded the desk and an empty coffee mug bounced.

"Adam Marat said he had a pesticide to control it, but it hasn't been working lately."

"Of course not. If Bauch weren't dead, I'd have him strung up for this. Fool." Oscar shook his head. "According to his notes, the pesticide was only half the treatment. The knucklebones repel the forest. That's their purpose, if it works."

"It does. I keened it. It was like the trees and the bushes were cowering away from it."

Oscar nodded. He was one of the few people who knew the extent of my magic and I trusted him to keep my secrets.

"So without any plant matter, you have to ask, what were the knucklebones eating?"

I stared at him in confusion, and then the answer hit me. "Bauch was feeding them."

"Exactly." Oscar made guns out of his fingers and shot me for emphasis. "And when he died, the knucklebones went looking for something else to eat."

"The shed."

Oscar grinned and shot me with finger guns again.

"And that means it will keep spreading." By the All-father. It could take over the forest.

"As I said, hubris. An alchemist's untimely death can undo years of careful experimentation. Bauch thought of everything, except that he wouldn't be there to feed his monster."

"So we burn it down."

"Not so fast. The ward is in no imminent danger. And Bauch was onto a good thing. This isn't really my area of expertise, but I've got a really good crop of interns this year. I think we can find a solution that doesn't include a scorched earth policy."

"Interns? That's your solution?"

Oscar patted my hand.

"Don't worry. You did the right thing, bringing it to me, but we'll take care of it from here."

He turned back to his desk and lit up his widget, probably calling in his team of infant alchemists.

I trudged back to the bathroom and pulled my boots from the decontamination bag.

I was going home to lodge a complaint with my local parliamentary representative.

C H A P T E R

12

"That whole place should be shut down." I paced around our living room. I'd told Mason about my encounter with the knucklebones and Oscar's findings in Hubert Bauch's notes. The wine in my glass swirled, dangerously close to spilling. Mason sat on the couch by the fire, one ankle crossed over the other knee. He still wore what I called his PM's uniform, a dark blue custom suit that fitted him to perfection and showed off the strength of his shoulders. He'd pulled the tie loose and a bit of skin showed at the open collar. He watched me with an expression halfway between alarm and amusement.

I wasn't done pacing.

"What were you thinking when you approved such a scheme? An unknown fungus? Really? Not to mention the whole idea of an industrial complex to begin with. Do you realize how big it is? How much of Terra's forest they claimed? It goes against everything the founders of our ward stood for."

I paused for a breath and a big gulp of wine.

Mason uncrossed his legs and patted the over-stuffed ottoman in front of him.

"Sit."

I squinted at him, not sure I wanted to be soothed. I downed the rest of my wine before I sat, facing him. He took my empty glass and put it aside. Then he turned the ottoman with me on it until I faced away from him. His fingers dug into the rock-hard knots on my neck and shoulders.

I might have groaned.

"First of all, I didn't approve any scheme. This project has been in the works for years. It was proposed by our favorite *connard* Gerard Golovin. The land was already being cleared by the time he died."

He meant by the time I killed him. By the time my blade cut his throat and he bled out all over me. I shuddered. Golovin had used his influence as Prime Minister to push through his plans for the new rail system, until Polina had twisted his mind to suit her own motives.

Three years had passed since I fought Golovin on a train, surrounded by his evil golems. Mostly, I'd dealt with the things I'd done there, with the people I'd lost in the aftermath. But every once in a while, it hit me. Polina and Golovin had nearly torn down everything the founders of Montreal had worked to safeguard, and years later, we were still living with the effects of their scheming.

My shoulders inched up to my ears again. Mason gently pushed them down and continued with his ministrations.

"By the time I took over, the land was cleared and the foundations already laid for the first buildings. Hubert Bauch was a bit eccentric, but he was a brilliant alchemist. No one could deny that. And his plan to keep the forest at bay seemed to be working. So far, there's been no encroachment."

"Until now."

"Until now." Mason's hands stilled, but he rested them on my shoulders. They were warm and solid. I leaned into the touch. He pulled me backward onto his lap and wrapped his arms around me. His mouth tickled the soft spots under my ear and down my neck.

The house was quiet. After a long day of trying to keep up with Raven and the goblits, Holly was sleeping hard. Raven too, had fallen asleep with his widget in hand as he texted his friends. The rest of our charges were making themselves scarce. I closed my eyes and let myself be immersed in Mason, the feel of his chest pressed against my back, his warm, woodsy scent, and the dark presence of his magic. I wanted to put away the worries of the day and just be here. Be present.

But the memory of that scarred raw earth that would soon be a bustling hive of commerce, and those unnatural knucklebones…it shook something in me.

"It's wrong. I don't know how to explain it. I touched the magic of those knucklebones. It was unlike anything I've ever felt. Green magic should be, well…green." I was explaining this badly. "It should feel like sunshine on your face and the ocean lapping at your toes. Does that make sense?"

Mason grunted an assent. I felt it rumble through his chest.

"The knucklebones were black."

"Mmm."

"Like death."

"Like a demon."

I punched his shoulder softly. "You're not taking this seriously." I looked up at him. He was grinning.

"You live with a demon and you're worried about some mushrooms?"

I sighed and thumped my head against his chest again.

"It's more than that. The whole operation just stinks somehow."

"Some would argue it's progress."

He was right, but it felt odd to think of progress as a good thing. The Flood Wars had beaten that idea out of us. It felt dirty to want things, to strive for bigger and better. To wish for humankind and fae to grow and prosper.

"Terra won't like it," I said softly.

Mason's laugh shook me. "You've never been one to worry about hurting the gods' feelings."

"I know. I don't. It's just…" I saw her dark-pooled eyes again, staring right into my soul. "It's just that she can be quite persuasive."

Mason's hands had been roving gently down my arms and across my hips as if they might be considering a way inside my jeans. Now they stopped.

"She? As in Terra?"

"Uh-huh."

He picked me up and dumped me on the couch beside him. "I knew there was something you're not telling me."

His hair was messed and I reached up to smooth it down. He caught my hand in his. The crease between his brow told me I wasn't getting out of this one without spilling the beans.

"It's nothing really. At least I think it's nothing." I trailed off. We sat in silence for a long minute. Mason was a master negotiator. He wasn't going to let me off the hook. The silence dragged on to become uncomfortable, until I fairly squirmed in my seat.

"Okay, it's about when I was stung by the peyochip. I didn't want to say anything because you were so upset."

He still didn't speak, but one raised eyebrow encouraged me to continue.

"While I was unconscious, I sort of had…I guess you could call it an out-of-body experience. And I met Terra." I looked down at my hands twisted together in my lap. I realized how ridiculous this sounded. "It's not the first time either. When Gunora passed her curse onto me, I met Terra then too, though I wasn't sure it was her at the time."

"And now you're sure?"

I nodded.

"What did she want."

"She has a quest for me." I laughed. It was a harsh sound. All of this talk of Terra made me irrationally nervous, as if she might be lurking behind the curtains, listening to everything I said.

"She wants me to find something called the shar-lil. Find it and destroy it."

Mason's frown increased. "The shar-lil? Are you sure."

"That's what she said."

"Tell me everything. Start at the beginning."

So I did. I told him all about waking up and seeing him sleeping in the chair, then seeing my own unconscious body. I told him about the mountain devil and Terra's oblique words.

"You think this shar-lil has something to do with the industrial complex?" he asked.

"I don't know. I don't even know what the shar-lil is. Maybe it *is* the complex. Maybe I'm supposed to destroy that. Or maybe it's a person, or something that has nothing to do with any of it."

I ground my teeth in frustration. This is why I hated dealing with the gods. They loved to play games for reasons that us mere mortals couldn't understand.

Mason rose and poured more wine. He undid the knot in his tie and pulled it out of his shirt collar. "I don't like surprises, especially from a god."

I agreed.

"You should have told me." He was using his low voice. To those who didn't know him, it sounded fierce and angry. I knew he was hurt. I undid the buttons on his cuff and pulled up his shirtsleeve. The tattoos scrawled past his elbow now in black lines that looked like the text of some alien language if you squinted at them just the right way.

"This is why I didn't tell you."

He brushed off my concern by pulling his sleeve down.

"The alchemists on Perrot Island have a decent library," he said. "Some of the texts are ancient. I'll ask around. See if the name shar-lil comes up."

I nodded again, but reluctantly this time. Terra hadn't said this shar-lil was a big secret, but then she hadn't said much really. And if she expected me to do this all on my own, she was the one in for a surprise.

"Tomorrow, I'm going to visit the temple of The New Terran Church. Maybe they'll have some answers for me." What with the potential bio-hazard, I hadn't made it there today as planned. But learning more about Terra had become a priority.

Mason took my hand and pulled me up. "Good plan." He kissed me. "But we can't do anything about it tonight. So I have another plan."

"Does it involve a hot bath with a hot Guardian to scrub my back."

"Possibly." He tucked my loose hair over one shoulder and ran a thumb along my jaw. This never failed to cause my insides to puddle in my knees. What was so sexy about a thumb?

"But Angus is on patrol. Will this Guardian do?"

I ran my hand under his loose shirt, over his hard muscles, and was pleased to feel him tense.

"Oh, you'll do just fine."

I turned and beckoned him toward the bedroom.

"Bring the wine," I said over my shoulder.

Several hours later, Mason I thought slept beside me. He faced the door with his back to me and the window. I pulled the sheet away and the light from the moon fell on black lines that stretched over his shoulder and down his back. I traced one with my finger. It scrawled like writing, and I wanted so badly to decipher it.

"Promise me." His quiet words startled me. The shoulder under my tracing finger flexed, but he didn't turn.

"Promise you what?" I continued to trace the black lines. They were mesmerizing.

"Promise me that if the demon takes over, you'll kill it."

I let my hand drop. Kill the demon. Kill him. He knew what he was asking. And I knew what I was agreeing to when I whispered, "I promise."

"You really don't have to come with me again." I looked at the morning's job manifests. I had to clear a brownie nest from a church basement where they wanted to set up a thrift shop. "Brownies are easy."

"That's what you said about yesterday's job," Emil countered. And he was right. I still shuddered when I thought of those knucklebones. So I let him drive me around and tried to enjoy it.

It turned out the brownies *were* easy. I bribed them with chocolate and they agreed to leave the basement. This involved some coaxing while the brownies lobbed missiles made of anything they found on hand. I dodged coffee mugs, shoes, old hats, dishes and more. The church ladies weren't pleased with the mess, but I quoted them critter wrangler rule number eighteen: if critter wrangling isn't messy, you're doing it wrong. Okay, I just made that up on the spot, but it got them to sign off on the manifest with only a little grumbling. I billed them for the chocolate. That stuff's expensive.

I had one final stop before going home—a visit to the temple of The New Terran Church. It was a long shot, but maybe they'd have some insight into my out-of-body experience and Terra's odd demands. I debated dropping Emil off at the office first, but we were already downtown and the temple was only a few blocks away.

"Do you mind?" I asked. "I have a quick errand before we head back."

"Sure thing. Where to?"

I gave him the address. He gave me back a funny look, but said nothing as he started the engine.

The central heart of The New Terran Church was situated in an ancient basilica once devoted to St. Patrick. Levesque Boulevard ran in front of the church and had been a major artery through the city, but a flash bomb tore it up during the war. Insidious magic still lingered in the area, causing any man-made structure to be taken over by thick foliage—trees, shrubs, moss and all kinds of flowering plants—within weeks of building. Unable to siphon off the magic, alchemists for the city's zoning council had simply rerouted the boulevard, and the ancient basilica had been left to rot.

Covered in greenery, it was the perfect spot for a church devoted to Terra.

There were no usable roads leading to the churchyard, so we parked a few blocks away in front of a run-down tavern with a winking neon sign advertising "Danseuse Nues."

"You really going in there?" Emil pointed at the forest-shrouded church.

"Just wait here. Or go have a morning shot and peep show." I nodded toward the titty bar.

"I might do that." He grinned back at me, somehow looking boyish and wolfish at the same time.

I got out of the van and opened the trunk to change out of my work jacket. I couldn't do anything for the stained pants, but at least I could show some respect inside the temple by not wearing a dirty jacket. I pulled on a light and clean windbreaker. As a last thought, I pulled the knife from my belt and left my sword too. I wouldn't risk angering Terra by going into her house armed.

A fountain marked the entrance to the only path leading to the church. "Fountain" is perhaps too fancy a word for the tumble of fieldstone with a spout of water cascading over it. I assumed it was a man-made construct, but the magic in this area was unstable. For all I knew, Terra had blessed her own church by dragging a natural spring from the depths of the earth. She pulled bullas up all the time. Why not a fountain?

I paused at the shrine, unsure if I should bow or cross myself. I didn't really know the etiquette here. I dipped my fingers in the pool below the fountain and tasted the water. If Terra didn't like that, she could tell me herself.

Terra didn't pop up from behind a hedge with her pet mountain devil. Nor did any priests come running out to shoo me away.

I continued up the path.

The trail was clear and solid underfoot, but the trees and bushes alongside were so dense they choked off all sound from the city. Branches met overhead, and I walked through a tunnel of greenery. I emerged, blinking in the sudden light and looked up. Way up. Dozens of stone steps had been cut into a hillside and above those, looming like a Gothic castle, was the temple of The New Church of Terra.

The ancient blocks of gray stone were barely visible under clinging vines of ivy in full bloom of glossy green leaves, something that shouldn't happen in Montreal for another two months. The Terran priests no doubt took that abundance as a sign of their god's favor.

The building was shaped vaguely like an arrowhead with a main steeple flanked by two smaller steeples, a sloping roof and two more pointy structures, just in case the approaching supplicant didn't get the hint to look to the heavens. A round stained-glass window was set in the middle of the facade like the eye of a giant cyclops.

The temple of the New Church was old, far older than the Terran religion, which only came into its full glory during the Flood Wars. The temple was housed in what was once a Roman Catholic Church. Even before the wars, the Catholic Church had lost much of its congregation and been forced to sell off some of its properties. Churches were re-purposed into trendy bars or restaurants. Others became private homes.

Then the wars brought a renewed interest in religion, an understandable reaction when faced with annihilation by forces beyond one's control. But the Catholic Church, and most of the old-guard religions, didn't fare so well in post-war times. Perhaps people lost faith in them, since those gods had done little to save their families when the bombs started to fall. Or maybe it was the proliferation of new gods, which ironically were mostly ancient gods come again. Many of these new gods found homes in old churches.

Like Terra.

I couldn't help feeling small while gazing up at the mighty Gothic structure, which was exactly what the original architects wanted. We should all feel insignificant in the presence of the gods. But now that I was here, I also felt ridiculous. Who was I to think I could be chosen by Terra for anything? Surely, the whole "find the shar-lil and destroy it" had been a hallucination brought on by the peyochip venom coursing through my veins.

I wasn't sure what I expected to gain by this visit. Maybe I just wanted someone to tell me I wasn't going crazy. I almost turned back, but the sound of Terra's voice still echoed in my bones. She hadn't just been insistent. She'd been scared.

And that brought up the question: what could scare a god?

I strode up the last few stairs until I faced the sturdy double doors. They were as large as castle gates and bound by iron bracings.

Now what? Did I knock? I suspected the door was at least six inches thick. My knuckles would barely resonate on it, and I didn't see any kind of knocker or doorbell. Then I spied the brass knob of a smaller door off to one side and nearly hidden under the masses of foliage. I turned the knob and the door swung inward with a rustling of leaves.

"Hello?"

I stood in the doorway, not daring to intrude any further without an invitation. No one answered. I stepped into the gloom and waited for my eyes to adjust. Before me stretched a massive building. For a moment, I had one of those existential crises that comes when magic distorts reality. This hall couldn't possibly fit inside the building I'd seen from the outside. Then I remembered that the old church had taken up an entire city block. This building really was that big, and made to look even bigger because it had been gutted. No pews, no nave, no sacristy. Just one gigantic hall, dimly lit by stained-glass that peeked through the verdant foliage.

If I'd thought the outside was overgrown, that was nothing compared to the inside. Ivy covered the wall at my back and spread to every corner. Trees lined one long aisle and their canopies brushed the ceiling. In their shadows, an abundance of wildflowers grew in every color, though their hues were muted in the shade. Birds chirped in that lazy afternoon way. It was an oasis of natural beauty in the middle of the city.

It shouldn't be possible. My foot scuffed slabs of gray stone. How did the trees take root in that? How was there enough light, enough rain, enough soil to support such a thriving ecosystem?

Apparently, having Terra's favor had its perks.

"May I help you?"

The voice startled me. I turned to see a man standing only a few feet away. I hadn't heard him approach. He was slender with a full head of shaggy brown hair, delicate features, and overly-large eyes. He wore some kind of homespun, and it might have been a trick of the light, but for a moment, I thought the brown cloth was a pelt.

Shifter, I thought. Selkie maybe. The big brown eyes had that puppy-dog look.

"Um, I'm not sure." A bluebird swept down from the trees, catching my attention. When I finally pulled my gaze back to the man, I felt like I'd been standing there for hours. He watched me patiently.

"Beautiful, isn't it?" His voice was melodious, like he'd learned to speak by listening to the birds. "The abundance of our Mother. Makes one wonder why anyone would want to live out there," he nodded toward the still open door, "with all that noise, and clutter."

"You're a priest?"

He inclined his head. "I am. My name is Almarick. You are welcome here in Terra's house, Miss…?"

"Greene. Kyra Greene."

His hands were clasped behind his back, so I didn't extend mine in greeting.

"Of course, Ms. Greene. We've been expecting you."

"You have?"

"Walk with me."

The door swung shut behind us, cutting off my only escape. And yet, I felt no need to run. For the first time in weeks, I felt truly safe.

We walked up the path. I could no longer think of it as the aisle of a church. It was like walking in the perfect forest, the kind you only saw in paintings or dreams.

"Did Terra tell you I was coming? You can talk to her? Can *I* talk to her?" I peppered him with questions, but Almarick ignored them all.

"Do you see there? Look." He pointed to a tree that had grown with a crook halfway up its trunk. In the shadow of that crook, an owl perched. If its eyes hadn't tracked our movement, I would have missed it. The camouflage was that good.

"For every bend in the road, for every seeming misstep, there is meaning for another."

I rolled my eyes. This was going to be one of *those* conversations. Why couldn't the gods—and their acolytes—speak plainly?

We continued on with Almarick pointing out particular flowers or interesting fungi.

I like the forest as much as the next person, more so even, but I was getting impatient. I wanted answers, not a nature documentary.

"Ah, here we are." We'd walked the entire length of the temple. The priest stopped at a stone wall, easily two stories high. It was carved in a relief. A giant bird with wings spread wide and beak pointing to the sky. The feather tips seemed to fade away like flames.

It was the mountain devil from my dreams.

I stared at the carving for several long minutes. My emotions ran the gamut from irritation to wonder.

"She's real," I finally said.

"She is." To his credit, Almarick didn't smirk. But his eyes twinkled with humor.

"She speaks to you too?" I turned to face him, daring him to put me off again with some vague platitude.

"She does, when the need arises."

"And she told you I was coming?" He nodded. "Why?"

"Why did she tell me? I wouldn't presume to know. Why are you here? Only you can tell me that."

I let out a hard breath.

In my heart, I'd known it wasn't a dream, but I'd needed verification. Staring at the giant bird seemed like a good validation.

"Okay, if I'm not going crazy, then Terra asked me to do something…I'm not really sure what. But it seems dangerous. I'm not sure I can do it."

"The Mother never asks more than you can handle."

I side-eyed him. That was exactly the kind of religious mumbo-jumbo I didn't need. I turned away. A squirrel darted up a tree nearby, and stopped on a branch to scold us.

Almarick laid a hand on my sleeve.

"If she chose you, it's because she believes you can do it. Perhaps that *only* you can do it."

"Then maybe she should have given me more info. I have a family to think about. A job. I can't go running around on some wild goose chase."

"I understand."

I watched a beetle crawl along the edge of the stone wall, right over the talons of the mountain devil.

I decided to cut to the chase. "Do you know what a shar-lil is?"

"Where did you hear that?" Almarick's tone was so sharp, I turned to him in surprise. His gentle gaze now had an edge.

"Terra told me. That's what I'm suppose to find. Find it and destroy it."

His face went white. His magic blurred, and for an instant, I was staring at the face of an otter. Then he seemed to recover. He blurred back to a man and straightened.

"There is a shar-lil in Montreal?"

"Maybe. I'm not sure. I'm not even sure what I'm looking for exactly. Terra just said I need to find it. I don't even know where to start looking. And how do I destroy it? Is there some rite? Should I bring it here?"

"No!" Almarick burst out. "Not here! It's too dangerous. You must take it away…" His words faded. He stared at the mountain devil as if the carving had the answers. He hands twisted the homespun fabric of his robe.

"Tell me," I said gently. "What is it? What is the shar-lil?"

"It is a weapon. A terrible weapon that must be kept away from anyone who could use it for ill. You must not bring it into the city."

Okay. Shar-lil bad. I got that already.

"What do I do with it then? Assuming Terra is right about me and I manage to retrieve it. What then?"

"The Mother must have a plan. She will make that clear in good time. I will look for guidance, but you must go now. I can only say that you need not seek the shar-lil. It will come to you. The Mother has seen as much. Now go. Go!" He ushered me back along the forest path. At the door he stopped.

"I understand now why she gave you the gift. Use it in your quest with the Mother's blessing."

"Gift? What gift?" But the door had already shut behind me.

I didn't look back. Almarick would have no more answers. I just had to have faith that Terra would provide.

Unfortunately, faith in the gods was not something I had in abundance.

I descended the steps that led back to the city and found another priest in a homespun robe holding the reins of the most beautiful horse I'd ever seen.

He was easily seventeen hands tall, and opalescent white with silver dappling across his haunches.

"This is for you," the priest said. "With compliments of the mother."

I stared, open-mouthed, my heart racing at the sight of such pure equine beauty.

Then the horse reared, hooves pawed the sky and white wings snapped open from his back.

"His name is Gallivant." The priest held out reins that were attached to a halter, not a bridle. One didn't force a bit into the mouth of a pegasus. A small saddle, not much more than a leather pad, was strapped to his back.

Gallivant tossed his head and eyed me warily.

"He's a bit green." The priest patted the nose fondly. "Not sure of his own wings. You won't get him to fly yet, but he'll run you where you need to go faster than any horse and even most cars."

"I can't possibly accept him." My hand was already reaching out to pet the velvety neck. Gallivant held still, but he didn't lean in to my touch.

"You must. The Mother was quite insistent."

Pegasi were extremely rare. Even in Asgard, the Valkyries trained on normal horses. Only a select few got to ride the king's pair of winged steeds that were kept for ceremony. Of course, my aunt Dana never chose me—the half-blood mongrel—for such an honor, so I'd only ever admired a pegasus from afar.

The priest didn't give me another chance to protest. He simply handed me the reins, patted the horse and headed up the stairs toward the temple.

I stared at Gallivant. He stared back at me. I was thinking, "What am I going to do with you?" And I was pretty sure he was thinking the same.

I tugged on the reins and he stepped forward easily enough.

Maybe this won't be so bad.

That thought lasted less than a minute. We came across a branch lying in the path. His eyes rolled to white and he sang out a shrill whinny.

I tugged on the reins. Gallivant dug his hooves into the dirt and wouldn't budge.

"It's just a stick, you big goofball. Come on."

He backed up, pulling me with him. His tail shot to the sky like a great white plume.

"Big baby." I soothed him with long strokes on his neck.

But I didn't move the stick out of the path. That would be a colossal mistake. I had to show him who was boss right from the beginning. There was nothing worse than a bratty horse.

I gave him a moment to settle, talking to him in a soft voice. Then I stepped over the stick and back again.

"See? It's not going to hurt you."

Gallivant turned his head away. He wanted nothing to do with me and my evil stick. I jumped over it and back again. A few minutes of this and I felt like a kid playing hopscotch.

Finally, my mighty steed seemed calm. I gently tugged on the reins and he stepped forward, right to the edge of the killer stick's territory. The muscles on his haunches bunched and he leaped into the air like a champion hunter-jumper sailing over a six-foot fence to win gold. Well, maybe not that gracefully. His legs splayed out and his wings flapped, but he got impressive air out of it. He landed on the other side of the stick with ruffled feathers and a hard thump. Then he looked at me as if to say, "What are you waiting for?"

Horses. This is what you got from a thousand pound animal with prey mentality.

"Come on." I shook my head and we continued down the path.

The short walk took us fifteen minutes because Gallivant stopped for a swirling leaf and a particularly nasty shadow. He also didn't like the feel of wet leaves sticking to his hooves or the sound of the gravel under his feet when we reached the road.

By the time we made it to the car, I was out of patience and Gallivant was prancing with nerves.

"What in the hells is that?" Emil asked when he spied us.

"A gift from the Terran temple."

"A gift from Terra, you mean."

"I guess." I wasn't sure where Emil's belief system lay, and I hadn't confided in him about my visions.

"Wow." Emil circled behind the beast and Gallivant kicked out, missing Emil's front teeth by an inch. "Nice! He's got spunk."

"Yeah, he's ferocious as long as you aren't a stick, or a shadow, or a fluttering leaf."

"A bit spooky, is he? That's all right. That just means he's got brains. Some of my favorite horses started as spooky colts."

"I didn't know you rode."

"Are you kidding? Lady Lughwaite made sure I took part in all the fancy activities. Horses, dance, piano—anything that could put her pet vampire on display." Emil's adopted mother was a minor noble at the Winter Court.

"Huh. Dance?" I said. "Are we talking ballet or modern interpretive dance?"

Emil stuck his nose in the air. "Ballet of course." He lifted his arms in a graceful arc and did a pirouette, landing in a perfect third position pose. I'd had a couple of years of ballet too, before I'd convinced Mom that soccer was more my speed.

"Well, he doesn't fly yet," I said, "which is a good thing. I'm not ready for that. He's still pretty green."

"Can I give him a go?" Emil rubbed his hands together.

"He's got no bit. I don't know how you'll steer him."

"We'll do just fine. Won't we, fella?" He stroked Gallivant's gleaming coat. The horse responded with half-closed eyes and a relaxed stance.

"If you're sure."

"I am."

I handed him the reins, then cupped my hands to give Emil a leg up. He waved me away. With inhuman grace and strength, he leaped onto Gallivant's back and settled on the small saddle.

Vampires. Such show-offs.

I watched them walk off down the road. Horses, mules and carts were common on the post-war streets of Montreal, but Gallivant stood out even among those. He was a head taller than most horses, and the sun caught his sleek coat, bringing out a rainbow of highlights.

As soon as Emil found his seat, he pushed Gallivant into a trot. The horse seemed to glide through the traffic. At the intersection, Emil brought him to a stop. A car whizzed by them. My heart clenched when Gallivant's front hooves left the ground, sure he was going to pitch Emil to the concrete. Not that I worried for Emil's safety. It would take more than that to hurt the vamp, but I didn't want to have to tell the Terran priests that their gift had taken off at a run through the city.

Emil kept his seat and brought the spooked pegasus under control. When the light changed, he crossed the intersection and trotted back to me.

"I can't wait to get this fella into a full gallop! He's fierce." Emil's eyes shone with glee.

Fierce wasn't the word I'd choose, but he sure had strength and stamina. His sides weren't even heaving after that run.

"Want me to run him back to your place?"

That would be the most practical thing to do, but if I was going to accept this gift horse, I needed to learn to ride him.

"Just take him back to the office. There should be some hay in the garage." We kept all kinds of critter supplies on hand. "Set him up in the backyard. I'll be there in a couple of hours."

Emil saluted and swung Gallivant around. It was amazing to see. Without a bit, Emil had to be guiding him with only the pressure of his knees.

I watched the two of them trot lightly through the traffic on Levesque Boulevard. They looked good together. I was a little jealous and thought that I should have made Emil drive the van instead.

I sighed. I'd get my chance on the pegasus soon enough. For now, I turned my attention to my next appointment for the day and the mysterious reason why Gabe had requested a lunch date.

15

Because of the peyochip, I'd postponed my meeting with Gabe by a day. He'd sent me a text that morning asking if I was still up to meeting at The Gobbler. He knew it was my favorite restaurant in the tiny village of Pointe-Claire. It was also the priciest in the area. I wondered what he was up to. My birthday was weeks ago. Was it his birthday? I wracked my brain, but if I'd known Gabe's birthday, I'd forgotten it. The fancy location seemed suspicious if he just wanted to chat about some new side hustle, but I wasn't one to refuse a free meal, especially if that meal included The Gobbler's famous French onion soup.

The gravel parking lot on the south side of Pointe-Claire's Main Street bled into the rocky shore of Lake St. Louis. I remembered coming here as a child with my mother to eat ice cream and walk through the park to the beach. I'd wanted to go swimming so badly, but back then we called the lake "Pooey Louis" because it was so polluted. Now the water was steel gray, clean and ice-cold.

The Flood Wars had done more than clean up the lake. They'd flooded this entire area and eroded the shore. Once there had been a line of stores, restaurants and pubs where the beach now lay. I glanced around, thinking I'd parked right on the spot where my old favorite pizza joint had once stood. Luigi's had mastered the perfect cheese-to-sauce-to-crust ratio and had been a staple for my birthdays. Mom used Luigi's pizza as her secret weapon when dealing with a grumpy teenager in need of cheering up. My heart hitched a little thinking of it. She'd been gone from my life for over a decade but only since my trip to Asgard had that loss really hit home.

I turned away from the shore and the memories and headed inland. When the floods had receded, some fifty years ago, a few buildings still stood. Others had been built up around them, re-establishing the centuries-old village.

The Gobbler was one of the buildings that withstood the floods. In fact, the tiny fieldstone house had stood for over two hundred years. Along with floods, it had survived wars, famine and fires. Nope, they just didn't build them like they used to.

I turned the antique porcelain doorknob and shoved hard, knowing the door could stick, then ducked under the low lintel. The restaurant's interior boasted only one small room with half a dozen tables pushed against bare fieldstone walls. Stairs led to a more modern upper level, but these were cordoned off for the lunch crowd.

It wasn't hard to find Gabe in this setting. He sat in a corner, with the light from a window bathing him in a cold glow.

He wasn't alone. My foot faltered on the uneven floor when I saw who sat with him.

Dimitrios Dukas, leader of the Olympian Pantheon, godling of the almighty Zeus, and all-around douche-bag. The last time I'd seen Dimitrios in person Hub officers were escorting him from a hall in handcuffs, the night Mason had announced his run for Prime Minister. In an effort to garner attention for his cause, Dimitrios had staged a scene at Mason's press conference and several people had been hurt. Of course, I'd seen him since then on the news, particularly the time he blew up the new railroad, killing Hub soldiers in the process. Nice guy.

Now I understood the reason for the fancy restaurant. They were trying to woo me.

For years, the godlings had been petitioning for a fourth political party. They felt that none of the existing parties—fae, human and alchemist—fairly represented their needs. So far, they'd managed to make a lot of noise, destroy public property and kill a few people, but the one thing they couldn't do was agree on who should lead this new party.

The godlings weren't a homogeneous group. Gabe's family led the Saivites, the Hindu Pantheon. Dimitrios led the Olympians. There were dozens of smaller factions to represent pantheons from all over the old world, including the Pharaohs, Mayans, and Japanese Kami. They rarely agreed on the menu for lunch, let alone a leader.

A couple of months ago, Gabe asked if I would join their fledgling party. Apparently, as the only Aesir in the new world, I had the unique privilege of being a godling, but also standing apart from all the other factions—perfect leadership material.

I'd refused him. The idea of a fourth political party intrigued me, but I didn't like the methods the godlings chose to make their voices known, and I didn't believe that by adding my voice, I'd be able to change their fundamental ideals. Gabe had seemed to accept my decision, and he hadn't said anything about it since.

Now the leaders of the two most influential godling factions were sitting at a table, sipping wine and waiting for me.

I almost turned around and left. If it hadn't been for the smell of French onion soup wafting in from the kitchen, I would have. Instead, I pulled the chair back with my toe and sat with arms crossed over my chest, my eyes on Gabe.

"How can you eat with this scumbag," I asked. "Even The Gobbler's chef doesn't cook well enough to overpower the bad taste just looking at him leaves in my mouth."

"Ms. Greene, there's no need—"

I cut Dimitrios off. "I wasn't talking to you. I won't talk to you. In fact," I glared at Gabe and pushed my chair back, "this conversation is over. Thanks for the ambush."

Gabe grabbed my wrist a little too hard.

"Kyra wait."

I stared down at his hand with a frown. I'd left my sword in the truck, but I keened its anxious excitement as it sensed my anger. Anger usually meant it was about to get wet and it liked that.

"You don't think you can restrain me here, in a public place, do you?"

Gabe pulled his hand back. To his merit, he flushed and fussed with his napkin. Good. If he was entirely comfortable with this scenario, then the Gabe I knew—my trusted assistant and friend—was already a lost cause.

His big shoulders hitched and he sighed.

"We're not trying to ambush you. We just want to talk."

"I have nothing to say to a murderer." I still wouldn't look at Dimitrios, but from the corner of my eyes, I could see he was relaxed, leaning back in his chair. He was enjoying this.

"If it makes you feel better, I'm not a murderer by trade, only by accident." Dimitrios spoke with a Greek accent that was entirely put on. The guy was born and raised in Montreal.

"Right." I snorted. "'Honest, officer, he fell on the knife, twenty-seven times.' That kind of accident?"

Now I did glance at him. Dimitrios watched me with a grin on his face that was one shade away from a smirk.

"These things happen." He spread his hands in a what-can-you-do gesture. He was entirely too handsome for a shit-head. Dark-eyed with black hair swept back from his forehead, cheekbones that looked sculpted from marble.

The waiter arrived and poured me a glass of red wine that I didn't ask for. A second waiter followed with steaming bowls of onion soup topped with cheese-crusted bread. Someone had taken the liberty of ordering for me. I hated that. Maybe I'm over-sensitive, but unless you know me really well, don't presume to know what I want to eat.

Except that I would have totally ordered the French onion soup. I have naughty dreams about The Gobbler's French onion soup.

I grudgingly dipped my spoon into the bowl. It came out strangled by cheese and onion strings.

I shot Gabe an angry look. "No fair, Devi."

He shrugged and tucked into his soup. Conversation stilled as we all took a moment to savor the oniony goodness. The Gobbler should have been the official caterer for the Parliament. The ministers would get so much more done. No one could argue when there was Gobbler soup on the table. It left a warm, fuzzy feeling in my stomach, and calmed me enough that I no longer wanted to strangle Dimitrios.

When my bowl was empty, I pushed it away, crossed my arms over my chest and glared at Gabe.

He gave me his most charming grin. "You weren't kidding about that peyochip bite. You look like crap."

"Thanks. It was a sting, not a bite." I wasn't going to let our friendship lull me into cordiality.

"I think Ms. Greene looks stunning as usual." Dimitrios leered at me. "I certainly wouldn't kick her out of bed for eating crackers."

"Gee. That's sweet. You're a scumbag." I refused to let baby Zeus affect me. I focused on Gabe. "I haven't changed my mind, you know. I won't be a part of your godling revolution, and certainly not as a leader."

Dimitrios leaned in, forcing me to acknowledge him. His smile displayed perfect white teeth. "Ms. Greene, that's not what this is about. In fact, we don't need you. We have a new leader, one who has united our party."

I waited for the server to place elegant plates of spring greens topped with goat cheese and balsamic glaze on the table, then said, "I don't believe it." No one had been able to unify the godlings. I looked to Gabe for confirmation, but he was pretending to be engrossed with his salad.

I chewed over the idea while munching my greens. If there was a chance that the party finally came together, that could mean big changes for Montreal. Whether those changes were for good or evil would depend entirely on the tactics of this new leader.

"Do you understand the impetus behind our push for our own party?" Dimitrios asked.

"Let me guess, no taxation without representation?" It was an old idea that got twisted to meet new rationales.

"Not exactly. After all, we can vote with the humans or the fae, if we wish." He sat back, elbows on the armrest, and laced his fingers over his chest. "You know that godlings have always had power."

"You mean magic."

He made a piffling noise. "That's such a flighty word. Let's face it. We have power. You feel it too." His eyes raked me up and down. I felt dirty under that gaze. "We've always had it to some degree or another," he continued. "But when magic flooded our world, many of us woke to this new burgeoning for the first time. We're not willing to give up that power."

"And who is going to make you?"

"The humans. They fear us and so of course they want to silence our power." He leaned back in his chair. The t-shirt he wore barely stretched over his exaggerated pecs, but just to be sure I marveled at his greatness, he ran his hands over his chest. It was a creepy, over-the-top gesture, even for a Zeus-ling that had probably been raised on sex and wine.

I put down my fork and wiped my mouth with my napkin. "Thank you for the mansplanation, but that's bullshit."

A small minority of humans lobbied for a magic-free Montreal. But there was also a group who wanted to elect a camel as Prime Minister. That didn't mean it would ever happen. The godlings were using the no-magic sentiment as fuel for their violence. *They* weren't the aggressors. No! They were only protecting themselves from those who would banish their kind. It was a ridiculous argument. Montreal was built from magic. Its wards were the most sophisticated spell the world had ever known. The fae, the alchemists and the majority of humans enjoyed a world with magic. And even if they didn't, there was no putting the genie back in the bottle now.

Gabe touched my hand, gently this time. "Look, Kyra, we don't want anything other than for you to meet her."

"Her?"

"Nici, our new leader. Just listen to what she has to say."

"Why?"

"Because we think she'll change your mind about us," Dimitrios said.

My gaze swiveled to him. I was starting to feel penned in. "And why should that matter?"

Dimitrios shrugged and Gabe said, "Because you have influence with the alchemists and the fae."

I started to protest, but Gabe spoke over me. "Don't deny it. Even before Mason was elected, you've always had an audience with the fae whenever you wanted it."

It was true, but those had been in the days of Queen Leighna's reign. We'd had a connection through my father. My connection with Merrow Farsigh, the new Fae Prime Minister, was based on the fact that I was the only one who knew she'd betrayed her queen. That didn't make me a welcome guest at the Winter Court.

The moment of silence lingered as I worked my way through this twisted confrontation. Gabe and Dimitrios watched me. Finally I said, "Say I meet with this…"

"Nici," Gabe supplied.

"Say I meet with Nici, and say I like what she has to say. What's your end game. What is it you expect me to do?"

"All we want is a seat at the table," Gabe said. "A chance to put past wrongs to right and plead for our cause in a civilized manner."

Dimitrios was grinning as if he thought the idea was hilarious, but he didn't contradict Gabe. They really were working together. If for no other reason, that made me curious to meet this Nici.

"Fine. I'll go. But don't expect much. Not my support. Not my approval. I don't guarantee anything more than a handshake, and maybe not even that."

"I think you'll be pleasantly surprised," Gabe said. "We meet tomorrow in Barrows. I'll text you the address."

The server whisked away the salad plates just as I rose to leave. The second server followed with the main course—homemade pumpkin ravioli in rosé sauce. The aroma hit me right in the saliva glands. But I couldn't sit another minute with the Zeus-wannabe eyeing me up as his next conquest.

I turned to the server. "Can I have this to go?"

C H A P T E R

16

Someone was standing by the small, fenced-in yard behind Valkyrie Pest Control when I arrived. The squat figure saw my van pull into the parking lot and scurried away. Was that…could it be?

Yes, it was. Mr. Murray bolted up the metal staircase to his apartment and slammed the door. It seemed that even my reclusive neighbor wasn't immune to the charms of a pegasus.

Emil met me outside. We watched Gallivant snuffle the ground, looking for shoots of spring grass.

"He settled in all right," Emil said. "The hay in the garage went bad, but I gave him a couple carrots and an apple. He's a bit of an attention hog too, aren't you?" He held out a hand and Gallivant lumbered toward it, blowing out his nostrils.

"I see that. Mr. Murray even came out to see him." I couldn't remember the last time I saw Mr. Murray set foot outside his apartment.

Emil nodded. "He's quite the draw. People keep stopping to gape at him. Had the kids from across the road over here too, wanting to know if they could ride him."

I looked at him aghast. "You didn't let them, did you?"

"'Course not. But you should get him home soon." As he said this, a car slowed down to take a look at the massive, winged horse. Even in a world full of fae creatures and magic, a pegasus stood out.

The car sped up after a good gawk. I had no reason to think they had anything devious in mind, but Emil was right. It was time to get Gallivant home.

Emil showed me where he'd stored Gallivant's tack beside the shed.

"Hey, did you know Gabe's working with Dimitrios?" I asked as he passed me the saddle and reins.

"Dimitrios? The Olympian?"

"That one."

"Huh. Gabe said something about trying to sway the Olympians who still advocated for violence, but I thought his father was spearheading those talks."

"Apparently they are. I just met with both of them. Gabe's all excited about some new leader in the group."

Emil rolled his eyes. "That would be Nici. She's all he could talk about last night."

"So she's legit, then."

"Seems to be. Gabe said his father had high hopes for Nici to unite the clans."

That made me feel better. If Nici could stop the bloodshed and make the Olympians work within the system, then she was worth meeting.

Gallivant stood nice and still while I saddled him. And he lifted his foot when I asked to pick out his hooves. The priests had trained him well.

Emil gave me a leg up and I perched in the saddle. Wow. The ground seemed very far away. Gallivant shuffled sideways.

"Give him lots of rein," Emil said. "He gets nervous when you hold on too tight."

I loosened my grip, and dug in my heels. Emil opened the gate and we shot through into the street.

"And text me when you get home," Emil called after us. "So I know you aren't lying in a ditch!"

I waved to him and focused on keeping my seat.

Gallivant wore no shoes and his clip-clops were muted. I steered him down the road. A car whizzed by and Gallivant shied. I led him to the shoulder where the ground was softer than the concrete. He pranced and I fought to bring him under control

He'd have to get used to cars. Luckily, when we merged onto the highway, there was a line of stopped vehicles waiting to leave through the gate. I nudged him to walk alongside the cars. He balked.

"It's okay." I patted his neck. "They won't hurt you."

Someone honked and Gallivant's wings spread wide. We lifted off the ground, only an inch or two, then he slammed down and pawed the earth, nearly unseating me.

That was about enough of that.

"Gallivant, *hael!*" I shot magic into the word. Of course, a horse wouldn't understand the command, but he felt it. *I* felt it. As soon as the word left my mouth, I keened his magic latch onto mine. He calmed and we were soon trotting up to the gate.

The Hub soldier on duty whistled when he saw us approach. "That's quite a beast. Does he fly?"

"No, but he does a good hop," I said.

The guard waved us through.

The only traffic out the South Gate was for the Perrot Island where the alchemists managed the Apex towers and maintained their more dangerous labs. These cars turned off the highway right after the bridge. Gallivant and I kept going.

Without the traffic, I gave him his lead and he took off. His wings might have been immature but, wow! His feet could move. I sure felt like we were flying as he ate up the miles to Dorion park.

I understood now, why pegasi needed no bits. Our magics had mingled. It felt like we were one beast, one muscle that needed no direction. I keened his pure joy at the race too.

We sped along. I barely felt the road beneath us. Then his muscles bunched and he leapt.

We were flying. Actually flying!

The trees fell away. Gallivant's magic cocooned me. I had only to think "left" and he banked slowly, circling over the canopy. It seemed the priest's predictions were wrong. He was ready to soar.

In its sheath across the back of the saddle, my sword hummed with joy. I pounded the sky with my fist and whooped. For the first time in my life, I truly felt like a Valkyrie.

Suck it, Aunt Dana!

C H A P T E R

17

The roads through the Inbetween were chancy. They could be closed to vehicles at any time. Random storms, pools of magic, and rogue monsters all made travel dangerous. Normally, to meet Gabe at the rather obscure coordinates he'd given me, I'd have to go through the city, take the Crystal Bridge and drive through Barrows to the western outskirts of town.

But I had a pegasus.

So instead of the three-hour drive, I chose the shorter flight by pegasus that took us around the island of Montreal to meet Gabe and his mysterious Nici.

It was no easy feat getting him tacked up though. He hadn't been left alone since I brought him home. The younger goblits insisted on stuffing him full of carrots. Jacoby and Raven took turns brushing his coat until it shone. Even Gita couldn't resist the lure of a pegasus and had come out of her nest to weep over him.

Gallivant took it all in stride, like the attention was nothing less than his due.

"No more carrots," I admonished when I saw Tums and Tad heading for the paddock again.

"Aww!" Tums whined. "But he likes them."

"And soon he'll be so fat, he won't be able to get off the ground."

The twins pouted.

"Go on now. You can feed him when I get home." I shooed them away and turned my attention to Gallivant. "You ready to fly?" He whickered and pranced in place. The fine line of his neck bulged with muscle. He was so ready.

I didn't push him into flight right out of the gate. The priest was right. Gallivant was still green. Even if we'd had a good test yesterday, I didn't know how long he could sustain flight. I'd save flying for when it was needed.

We got off to a rocky start when Gallivant balked at loading onto the ferry to Oka. The ferry driver was used to ornery mounts though, and she quickly scolded mine into line.

"Nice beast," she said, eyeing him a little too covetously for my liking. I'd have to come up with a glamor to mask those wings.

The trip across the Ottaway River took less than fifteen minutes. On the water, the pall of smoke in the west was more visible and the fishy air had a bitter underlying scent of smoke. The forest was still burning somewhere in the Ottawa Valley. I was glad our journey would take us east.

Leaving the ferry landing, a squonk ran across our path and Gallivant squealed like a frightened mouse. The boar-like creature wasn't fazed by flailing hooves or flapping wings. It snorted and shuffled off on its own unhurried schedule. It took a lot of smooth talking on my part to calm Gallivant after that, but he seemed to find his courage the deeper we went into the forest. A true child of Terra.

Eventually, I tapped into that strange magic that let me direct him with a thought and we rode on without further distractions.

The road heading north-east was the only obvious path through the thick forest. Gallivant trotted as fluidly as a gaited horse and we ate up the miles.

The animals of the forest were still restless. Could the fire be the cause? It seemed unlikely. It was too far away to cause panic here. But I had no other explanation for the constant flow of restless energy I keened nearby.

Once, Gallivant reared and nearly unseated me when a flight of deer darted across the road right under his nose. I spied wood trolls running through the trees too. They were usually too stealthy to be seen, but maybe the disquiet of the creatures had them disturbed. And once, I thought I spied the flaming wings of a mountain devil, but I could have been wrong. Or maybe Terra was keeping tabs on her chosen one.

Eventually, we passed a few homesteads and I knew we were nearing Barrows.

The town got its name because in the first battle of the Flood Wars, fortifications had been built to protect the valuable bridge onto the island.

Then bombs dropped on those fortifications, turning them into tombs. Terra reclaimed the land, covering the massive ruins in soft grasses and flowers until they resembled ancient burial mounds. In a quirk of fate, the mounds protected the land, creating a tiny temperate micro-climate that attracted settlers.

The first urban planners for Montreal tried to dissuade these squatters. They cleared the town by force, even burning the ramshackle buildings on numerous occasions. But the settlers always came back, and by the time Hub was installed as the military force in Montreal, Barrows was an established town.

I suspected that, like Hedge, Barrows was full to the brim with refugees. Luckily, I wouldn't have to witness any of that extreme suffering today. The address Gabe had provided was on the west side, well away from any prying Hub eyes. We wouldn't have to go into the town at all.

We did cross over one of the barrows the town was named for. The hillside was a mess of brambles, with no clear road over it.

"Now's your time to shine." I patted the pegasus's neck. I barely had to think the word "fly" and we were airborne. Even though the sun shone, the air was cooler up here. Wind pulled tears from my eyes and whipped them away. Gallivant pumped his wings until we reached the summit of the barrow. Then Gallivant soared.

Over the barrow, I quickly spotted the target Gabe had set as our meeting ground. Several cars were parked in the muddy yard around an abandoned cottage. That had to be the place. I urged Gallivant to close in on the cottage.

From on high, I could also see larger animals moving through the forest. They seemed to be converging on Barrows. It was truly a great migration, but to what end?

Gallivant landed in the muddy yard. His hooves touched down with barely a sound. I trotted him in circles trying to calm him. Flying was new to him too, I realized. He pranced and whinnied, seeming more unsettled than necessary.

It had to be the animals in the forest. I keened critters watching us from within the trees. That would be reason enough to unnerve a horse.

I dismounted and walked Gallivant toward the cottage and tied the reins loosely to a tree right by the front door. He was still stamping and twitching. I soothed him with long strokes on his neck and withers, pushing just a bit of magic into my voice.

"You're going to stay here, right?" Maybe it was our unusual connection, but I felt like he understood me, and he finally calmed. I figured if Terra really wanted me to have him, she'd make sure he stayed put.

I didn't ride with my sword across my back, so I unslung it from the saddle bag and shrugged on the harness. No way would I go into this meeting unarmed.

I turned to examine the cottage. The windows, long since broken by storms and squatters, were boarded over with fresh wood. Someone had made an attempt to tidy the yard and the entrance, but it still looked like a cottage that Hansel and Gretel might chance upon.

Gallivant snorted and shied again. I almost scolded him for being flighty, when someone grabbed my waist and spun me around. Before instinct made me reach for my sword, Gabe planted a kiss on my cheek.

"You shouldn't sneak up on people," I snapped.

"You look lovely this fine afternoon. And that's one hell of a horse." He tried to pet Gallivant, but the pegasus shied away.

"He was a gift."

"A gift fit for a Valkyrie." He grinned.

"You're unusually chipper." His cheeks had a rosy flush to them and his eyes were bright.

"Life is good when you don't sweat the small stuff. I'm glad you could come."

"Me too, I guess. I had to see for myself the woman who could finally unite the godlings." I paused. Gabe was beaming like a kid with a birthday cake. "You're really sure your father is okay with all this?" Gabe's dad didn't sound like the kind of guy who would easily give up authority.

"Definitely." Gabe rubbed his hands together. "Dad is crazy about Nici."

"She must be pretty amazing."

"She is. You'll see. You'll meet Dad too, come on. I told him all about you."

I made a noncommittal noise. I wasn't sure how I felt about meeting the patriarch of the Devi clan. He hadn't made life easy for Gabe. But I reminded myself that family dynamics always looked different when you were standing outside looking in.

"And Emil? Things are good there too? Or is he just more of the small stuff."

Gabe raised an eyebrow and grinned. "Definitely not the small stuff."

I punched his arm. "Don't be a perv."

He laughed. It was a sweet, easy laugh that I hadn't heard in a long time. Maybe things were truly settled in his life. I was glad. He deserved some happiness. Still, I couldn't help poking the sleeping bear.

"What about Uma? Did you settle things with her?" His sister-in-law had threatened to take their son and return to her parents' clan. Gabe's father urged him to marry her to keep the heir close. Gabe had refused.

"Uma's good. We worked things out. Nici convinced her to stay with us."

"Oh." That good news deserved more enthusiasm than I could give it. This Nici character seemed to have a long reach.

Despite its decrepit state, the cottage was marginally warmer inside. It had that damp, earthy smell of a boarded-up building left to rot. We entered a large, empty room with a closed door on a side wall. I assumed it led to a kitchen area. Instead of more expensive gleams, fat candles burned on tables around the outer walls. They did little to dispel the shadows and only made the lighting macabre. The leaves, dirt and garbage that you'd expect to find in an abandoned house had been swept away. Folding chairs had been set out in rows on the warped floors, and these were filled with people. Every head turned as we walked in.

Gabe and I took seats in the last row. Deciding our arrival wasn't newsworthy, the heads swiveled back toward the front of the room where a table was set up like an altar. Two unlit pillar candles flanked a strange gold sculpture that resembled a bird's nest made of thorn branches. One thick branch stuck up straight with a nasty spike on top. It had also been gold once, but was now mottled with black stains.

That wasn't ominous. Not at all.

Gabe smiled at me. Everyone seemed to be waiting for the show to begin.

Someone up front coughed and a chair creaked. The room had a hushed pall over it. A feeling of unease crept over my flesh. I let out my keening—gently, so I didn't alert any strong magic users in the room—and found the emotions that usually colored a large crowd— apprehension, excitement, a drop of irritation. Everyone sat straight-backed and forward-facing. No one seemed bothered by the cold and the dark.

I let my keening run over Gabe. His shoulders twitched as if he could feel my magic probe, but he only shot me another grin.

I had the sudden urge to be anywhere but there. Even as my feet pushed into the floor to lift me, the side door opened, and Dimitrios stepped through. He stared into the waiting crowd and smiled beatifically, like an old-time priest waiting to give a benediction. A second man followed him through the door. He looked like an older, slightly shrunken version of Gabe. This had to be Arjun, Gabe's father. Like Dimitrios, he took in the crowd with a sweeping glance, but his brow was furrowed low over his eyes and his full mouth pursed in disapproval.

All the heads swiveled again, this time to take in the new arrivals. My legs were still tensed to run, but I was frozen to my seat.

Dimitrios reached the altar, carrying a black sack that shimmered like crushed velvet. He reverently placed the bag on the table and opened the drawstrings that held it closed.

The tranquility in the room vanished, and I felt more than saw people lean in and hold their breath.

The sack fell away to reveal a...coconut.

What in the hells?

A murmur rippled through the crowd. A woman in the second row stood up and ran for the altar, but Dimitrios waved her off. "Not yet. Not yet. Patience Deanne."

The woman—Deanne—grumbled something unintelligible and returned to her seat. Her shaking hands gripped the chair in front of her, and the desperation on her face was that of an addict waiting for a fix.

I became aware of a low-grade hum, not quite a sound, more like a shiver running over my nerves. The keening wasn't always adept at deciphering magic, but I could tell, the source of this hum was the artifact on the altar.

Arjun and Dimitrios worked quietly to set up the rest of the display. Arjun placed a large jug with a cork stopper next to a simple stoneware cup. Dimitrios lit the candles.

During this process, Dimitrios's hand kept straying to touch the coconut. And once, Gabe's father leaned in as if to smell it.

This was just too weird.

Then the side door opened again and weird became terrifying.

Nici had arrived.

CHAPTER

18

She was tall and pale with long silvery-blond hair. Ice-blue eyes filled her narrow face, and she moved with the signature grace of a vampire.

I recognized her immediately. She was the opji at the faux court in Underhill that Queen Leighna's usurper brother had formed. She'd led the opji when they came through the door from Underhill to attack Montreal.

She'd killed Alvar, the fae prince.

My thoughts were in a jumble. What the hell was an opji doing here, so near the ward? And why were the godlings meeting with her? Not just meeting, they were *anticipating* her.

Gabe felt me rise and his hand clamped over my wrist.

"She's opji!" I hissed. A man in the next row turned and frowned at me. Like I was being rude. Like we weren't all about to be slaughtered by a vampire.

"Relax." Gabe gave my wrist a squeeze. "It's okay. Just listen."

He lost his smile, but his face showed none of the anger I expected. This wasn't right. My keening hummed with the wrongness of it. My sword picked up on my agitation and joined in the song.

Gabe had been part of that battle with the opji. He'd witnessed dozens of Hub officers killed by the vamps. He knew that the only reason we were all standing here today was because Gita had shattered the night with her banshee scream and given us all a chance to fight back.

His grip on my wrist tightened enough to hurt.

"Thank you all for coming." Nici's smile was cold. Blond bangs hung in a straight line, hiding her brows. The rest of her hair fell in long, thin wisps

114

to her waist. She was dressed all in black except for a blood red blouse that peeked over the edge of her buttoned jacket.

"My name is Nici. Some of you already know me." Someone in the crowd whined like a hungry dog. Nici acknowledged the sound with a faint nod. "Some of you are here for the first time, brought by trusted brothers and sisters. I'm sure you're wondering what's going on. All will be made clear to you very soon." She clasped her hands in front of her like a mockery of a prayer. "Now, we have a lot to discuss. Plans that need to be finalized, so let's get this party started!"

Everyone rose. Like automatons, they filed down the aisle to wait by the altar with varying degrees of impatience.

"Come on." Gabe, his hand still on mine, pulled me along with the others. There were too many bodies ahead of us for me to see what was going on, but I heard gasps and groans, some crying, and one woman who shouted "Yes!" so many times, I thought she might be having an orgasm.

I knew I should leave, should run as fast as I could to the nearest Hub station and raise a fuss until they came to shut this thing down. But morbid curiosity kept me in line. I couldn't leave until I knew exactly what this "thing" was.

The line in front of us shortened. People took their seats, some with obvious joy plastered on their faces. Others with vacant gazes.

The space in front of the altar cleared enough that I could finally see what was going on. A young couple stepped forward. The man confidently rammed his hand down on the spike and grinned as it tore through his flesh. His blood dripped onto the coconut.

Except it wasn't a coconut, I saw that now. It was too big, for one thing, and the brown shaggy husk didn't look quite right. Dark brown veins segmented it into diamond-shaped parts, and it had a golden quality to it that had nothing to do with the candlelight. The glow seemed to come from within.

With each drop of blood splashed onto it, the song of the coconut that wasn't a coconut rang out. The waves of magic were strong enough to make my sword wail. The blade's bloodthirstiness added to the confusing mix of emotions in the room. My keening had been buzzing in alarm for some time, and I'd already locked down my personal wards. I tightened them even more to block out the alluring call of the coconut.

The young man pulled his hand off the spike and held it toward Nici with a grin. She licked the wound.

Eww.

It was disgusting, but it also made sense. Vampire saliva had healing properties. In the days before the wars, that's how they fed undetected in large cities. Of course, nowadays, they didn't bother with niceties like healing their victims.

The woman with the young man was more hesitant, a newbie to this bizarro spectacle like me. She pressed her index finger to the spike, but not hard enough to bleed. Nici encouraged her with a grim smile and the woman pressed harder. A sharp cry escaped her lips as the spike spilled her blood. The man grabbed her hand and pressed the bloody finger to the artifact—for an artifact it was. The thing pulsed with magic.

The woman blubbered and tried to pull away as he mixed her blood into the macabre tapestry. Nici pressed the stone cup to her lips. In mid-sob, the girl tried to protest. Then the wine—or whatever was in that cup—touched her lips and she calmed.

The man took a big gulp too, then led his shaking friend back to the chairs.

After one more couple—older men who looked like brothers—we were next in line.

Gabe strode up to the artifact, drew the side of his palm along the spike with practiced ease and gave the coconut a bloody fist bump. After he sipped from Nici's cup he turned to me with expectation in his eyes.

"No way. Not gonna happen." I turned to run up the aisle. I had no idea what this was about, but I knew I didn't want to take part. Gabe caught me by the arm and spun me. I was too stunned by this betrayal to react, and in seconds, he'd dragged me back to the altar.

"Hold her," Gabe said to Dimitrios. The words dropped like icy rain down my back.

Dimitrios twisted my right hand against the small of my back. He gripped my shoulder while Gabe yanked my left hand. He was going to do it. Gabe—my Gabe!—was going to blood me in this unholy ritual.

I squirmed. I stomped on Dimitrios's foot. He cursed and jerked my right arm upward. Pain lanced through my shoulder, but my fingers brushed against my sword. Even sheathed, I could draw strength from it. I gripped the blade's tip, and it willingly pumped magic into me.

Gabe jammed my hand down on the spike even as I ramped up my wards with all the energy I could muster.

He smiled. His face looking oddly skeletal in the dim light.

Adrenaline kept the pain from me until Gabe yanked my hand from the spike. My flesh and my heart tore at the same time. I screamed. Gabe pressed my palm to the rough husk.

Magic burst from the artifact. It washed over me, buffeting my wards like an explosion from a blast furnace. Without the boost from my sword, it would have left me in a seizing, drooling puddle on the floor. Even so, I was gasping.

Nici picked up my bleeding hand and licked the wound. I closed my eyes, wanting this horror to end.

"Drink now." She pressed the cup to my lips. My stomach lurched as I smelled blood, not wine. I jerked my head away. The hot blood spilled down my neck.

"That's okay." Nici's voice soothed. "We'll do it the old fashioned way." Her sharp incisors cut a chunk of skin from her wrist and she jammed it to my lips, pinching my nose with her other hand. I jumped back, only to come up against Dimitrios's chest. Nici smeared the blood against my lips, forcing them open.

I couldn't breathe. The room spun. My knees gave out and I slumped against Dimitrios.

Instinct took over. I gasped for air, tasted blood on my tongue, and gagged.

Nici smiled. "Blood for blood. The ancient ways are always best. There now. Don't you feel better?"

I felt violated. Revolted. I burned with rage. And I used that fire to purge the vampire magic.

Dimitrios let me go. I could see they all expected me to step in line. I glance back at the young woman who'd gone before me. She'd stopped shaking and watched with a pleasant, if concerned, smile on her face.

If I let them know, if they understood that their little magic trap hadn't worked, I'd never leave the cottage alive.

I wiped my eyes with my unbloodied hand. Tears blurred my vision, but I put on a smile.

"Yes…" My voice hitched and I tried again with more confidence. "Yes, I feel better. Thank you."

Nici smiled like a benevolent savior. Gabe took my hand again, this time gently. The wound from the spike had already healed, but my palm was sticky with blood. He started to lead me back to our seats.

I pulled away and turned back to the bloody artifact, trying to imitate the same reverence I saw on all the other faces.

"May I ask, what is it?"

"It is something that will change the world," Nici said. "And you are helping it. Your blood," she paused and looked over the crowd of eager faces, "our blood will make it come alive and when that happens civilization as we know it will cease to exist. We will replace it with a society that answers our needs. All our needs."

Happy murmurs flowed through the room. As I headed for my seat, no one seemed concerned that I might run.

"Blood for blood," Nici had said. She needed an addicted herd of cattle to prime her artifact. And that's all these people were to her—cows. That's all humans ever were to opji.

Back in our seats, I slipped my hand around my back and sucked more power from my blade. It continued to burn away the vampire blood, but I felt queasy and jumpy. Already, I wanted to taste the blood again.

My eyes latched onto the coconut, and a new thought struck me.

The shar-lil.

Could it be? Of course it was. Terra had said the opji had it. And what had Nici said? It was something that will change the world. Those were eerily close to Terra's words, only she'd called it a weapon.

Now I couldn't leave, not without that artifact.

"If everyone is settled, let's talk business." Nici spoke from the altar. "Dimitrios, what news do you have since our last meeting?"

The Olympian turned to the waiting crowd. The sense of waiting had returned, but it was now accompanied by energy sizzling away below the surface. Whatever else Nici's blood had done to these people, they were eager to do her bidding. I would even say they were enthralled.

"We have four agents working inside Hub. Thank you Patrick." He nodded to the young man who had gone before me in the blood rite. Patrick nodded and smiled.

"We continue to struggle with infiltrating Parliament, but we're hopeful about a new lead in that direction." Dimitrios's gaze landed on me. I forced down a shudder and kept a stupid smile on my face.

I keened the blood in my stomach, sour like curdled milk and hot like burning embers. Behind my back, my fingers ached from gripping my sword. The blade continued to feed me magic, to fight against the opji blood, but I didn't know how long I could hold it off. My head ached and the room seemed to swell and throb around me.

I had to get the shar-lil and leave. Now.

Nici droned on about their plans. I tried to pay attention, but pain blossomed in my gut. The room felt hot and airless. She said something about breaking the ward and about needing more blood for the artifact.

"Pledge with me!" Her voice boomed. "I pledge to give my blood freely to the seed of life!"

Every voice in the room rose in unison to repeat the words. Gabe nudged me with his elbow and I mumbled along with them.

"I pledge to return in one week's time…"

The crowd chanted the words back at her.

"…to renew my bond with the seed of life…"

The crowd repeated.

"…to renew my pledge to the cause of freedom…"

Their voices echoed her, louder now.

"…and bring an end to tyranny!"

The crowd's chant ended in a crescendo of whoops and cheers.

Nici waited for their cheers to quiet. She had one more admonishment.

Her eyes blazed. "You will tell no one of this meeting. You will bring one new recruit with you next time." She bit out a last word that sounded like *cest-gash*. I didn't understand it, but I recognized a power word, no matter the language. She'd ordered us the way I did to Princess when regular commands didn't work.

The enthralled crowd murmured their assent as one. I added my noncommittal voice and squeezed my sword.

Finally, the meeting broke up. I gazed longingly at the door, but I couldn't leave without the shar-lil.

"Come on." The cheerful monster that had taken over my Gabe, pulled me toward the altar where Dimitrios was packing up the strange artifact.

Nici reached for Gabe and kissed him. She was tall enough that she didn't need to stretch. Their lips met in a kiss that was decidedly more than friendly.

Oh, Gabe. How long had this been going on?

"Thank you, my love." Nici stroked his cheek with one sharp nail. "You did well."

Gabe grinned like a kid on his first date.

Nici turned to me. "I have a special project for you, Valkyrie."

I wasn't surprised that she knew me. I got the feeling nothing happened at these meetings without Nici's orchestration.

"Of…course." I stumbled over the words, and she frowned. I pushed back against the burning ember in my gut and put on a confident—if docile—face. "Anything you need." My eyes were trained on the shar-lil as Dimitrios packed up the altar, but Nici would expect that. Others filed past the artifact, brushing it with last desperate touches. One woman leaned down to kiss it.

"Good." Nici dragged my attention back to her. The candlelight flattered her pale complexion, but up close, she wasn't as glamorous as she seemed. Fine lines were etched around her eyes and mouth. The opji weren't immortal, but they were very long-lived. How old did she have to be to show signs of aging?

My resolve to steal the shar-lil wavered. I wasn't facing one of the post-war vampires. She'd been around for centuries. That would make her harder to kill. Harder, but not impossible.

She tucked a long-nailed finger under my chin and tipped it up so I was forced to look her in the eye. "You will bring your husband to me. Here. Tomorrow morning. Before the sun rises." Nici smiled and patted my hand. I fought the urge to shrink away. "Do you understand?"

"Yes. I will do it."

"Of course you will. That is all."

And we were dismissed.

This was my last chance to snatch the shar-lil.

Dimitrios packed it reverently back into its bag, and the side door opened.

My heart sank. Four more opji came in to escort Dimitrios and the artifact away.

I had no chance against five opji. I watched them leave, thankful that Nici had already given me another shot at the shar-lil. Tomorrow morning, I'd meet her again.

Gabe and I left the cottage. My legs felt like hollow sticks. I could still keen the animals lurking in the trees, but that problem seemed inconsequential now.

I had to get away. I had to get somewhere safe before the power of my sword drained and my wards cracked under the pressure.

Gabe walked me over to Gallivant. The pegasus was agitated by the activity in the yard and the cars leaving the lot, but he hadn't bolted. I rewarded him with apple chips from my pocket. I worked out some of my agitation by rubbing his neck.

"Aren't you glad you came now?" Gabe asked, with a grin. I wanted to slap that stupid smile off his face. I wanted to punch his teeth down his throat. I was beyond angry at him for involving me in this.

I couldn't look at him without showing my rage, and decided to cut it short before he realized something was amiss. I made polite words of goodbye. Gabe got into his silver sports car and left.

I mounted Gallivant and pushed him into a cold canter, then into flight, wanting to get far away from Nici and her little cottage of horrors, and fast.

Twenty minutes into the ride, my rage against Gabe died.

Nici's blood had him under a thrall. And her magic had been amplified somehow by the shar-lil. How long would it last? Probably just long enough for her to boost it with more blood at the next meeting.

Someone had recruited him too. Probably his own father. And they would go on recruiting and enslaving people to the magic of the shar-lil until there was no one left to fight for Montreal. Was that why Terra called it a weapon? Could it truly enslave an entire ward?

I still felt like I was missing something, some piece to the puzzle that cryptic gods and overbearing opji hadn't seen fit to show me yet.

But one thing was certain. Nici would get her wish. I'd bring Mason to meet her.

C H A P T E R

—————

19

ason had warned me that the PM's communications were never private. He wasn't sure if the fae spied on him or the humans, or even someone in his own party, but he'd warned me never to tell him sensitive information until he was sure he had a secure line.

I called him anyway, as soon as I had a signal. He picked up on the first ring.

"Where are you?" I tried to keep the panic from my voice, but he wasn't fooled.

"What's the matter? Is everything all right?"

"Just tell me where you are."

Even though the call was audio only, I imagined him running his hand through his hair.

"I'm still at the office."

"Good. I'm almost home. I'll be there in two hours, tops. It's date night, remember?"

"I remember." His tone told me I wasn't fooling him. He knew something was up. I hung up before he could question me further. He'd stress about the call until I got there, but that couldn't be helped.

Gallivant and I arrived home at a full gallop. Dekar came running at the sound of hooves. I dismounted and tossed him the reins.

"Can you untack him? I've got an emergency in the city."

Dekar nodded. "No problem."

I'd been trained to always take care of my own mount. It didn't sit well with me to give Gallivant over to Dekar. But I had no choice now.

Inside, I found Gita snoozing in the chair by the big window. The house was quiet. That meant Holly was down for her afternoon nap. Damn. I'd wanted five minutes with her before I took off again.

I shook Gita gently. She snorted and clacked her teeth together before taking in my worried face.

"Someone is dead?" she asked.

"Not yet."

"That's good." She settled back in her chair.

"I have an emergency in town. I have to leave now."

Mason and I had planned a date night in the city and Gita had already agreed to babysit, but I was leaving hours early.

"S'okay." Her eyes were already closing. I bit my lip. Was I asking too much from the old banshee?

Dutch came in from the kitchen.

"I'll be home tonight too."

That made me feel better. I didn't know how superheroes saved the world everyday without a full crew at home.

I ran to my room and packed a bag. There would be no time for fancy dresses and cocktails tonight. I packed warm clothes for traveling the Inbetween at night and weapons.

A quick goodbye to Raven and I was out the door, only to stumble over Jacoby.

He didn't look happy.

"Vacation's no funs."

I walked right past him and he followed me to the van, watching while I tossed my bag in the back.

"I thought you were helping Arriz, you know, trying out woodworking as a new hobby."

"Hobby's no funs either," he grouched.

I ground my teeth. I didn't have time for this.

"There are lots of other hobbies." I tried to sound cheerful. "Ask Suzt if she can teach you to bake." If I believed in such things, I'd be going to hell for foisting off the dervish. Thankfully, I didn't believe, but I'd need to repay some favors to Arriz, Suzt and Gita when all this was done.

Jacoby watched me with big eyes. Puppies had nothing on those eyes.

They were round, and dark, wet with burgeoning tears and fringed in drooping gray fur.

I crouched on the gravel and gave him a hug.

"I'm sorry I haven't been around," I said. He sniffled. "I promise that this weekend, we'll find you the perfect hobby. But right now, I need to go into the city."

"You needs 'prentice?" The fringe of fur around his eyes perked up.

"Not tonight. I'm meeting Mason. It's date night."

His shoulders slumped. I patted him on the back. "I think Dutch just made cookies inside." That cheered him up again. Yep. I was truly going to hell.

I didn't wait for Jacoby to make it inside. I jumped into the van, backed up and turned in the driveway.

Soolea was standing on the steps of the gatehouse, one hand resting on her round stomach. I waved to her and fought off another wave of guilt. The young homesteader was another one of my responsibilities that I was failing at.

This weekend, I vowed. I'd make time for them all this weekend, if I could just get through the next twenty-four hours.

Ten minutes later, a Hub soldier was waving me through the West Gate and I rolled onto the bridge.

I normally didn't like to drive on autopilot over the bridges. It was probably perfectly safe, and I was probably being superstitious. Probably. But the light was fading and my guts roiled with sour vamp blood. My hands shook like I'd drunk three pots of coffee. I felt safer with them off the wheel.

I rested my head back and forced my eyes to stay open and on the road. I thought about what I'd seen that day, about Terra's dream-warning, about all of it. But mostly, I thought about Gabe. Tears welled in my eyes and fell freely down my cheeks. I wiped them away with my sleeve.

When I pulled into the parking lot underneath Mason's building, I cut the engine and sat in the dark feeling drained and jittery all at once.

Suddenly it felt like a very bad idea to bring Mason into this mess.

Nici wanted a thrall in Parliament. My Valkyrie magic had resisted her, but just barely. I wasn't even sure I was in the clear. I could still feel her blood fighting for dominance inside me. How could Mason face her?

I restarted the van. I'd tell Mason that I changed my mind, that I'd been coming by for our date night, but decided I was too tired or that Holly needed me.

A hand knocked on my window. I jumped in my seat.

The crease between his brows told me Mason had been waiting and worrying since I called.

I killed the engine again and got out of the van.

"What's going on. Tell me now."

"Not here." I glanced pointedly at the surveillance camera on the wall. "Kiss me and pretend everything's normal."

His arms circled me, and I pressed against him, taking comfort from his heat, his scent and the aura of his magic, all so familiar.

"You're shaking." His voice was rough and low and right beside my ear.

"I'm okay, I think. Let's go somewhere private."

He held my hand during the elevator ride to the ninth floor where his Alchemy Party offices were. The reception area was lit only with a few floor lights, but some people lingered in the glassed-in offices. Mason waved at a woman sitting at a security desk and a man watching the nightly news feed in the break room. He pulled me past offices of ministers and their aides, right to the end of the hall. He opened a nondescript door, ushered me inside and flicked on the light as the door shut behind us.

I blinked in the bright light. We stood in a tiny office supply cupboard. Metal shelves lined three walls. They were stocked with coffee, dry goods, electronics and cables and all the other knickknacks a busy office required.

"Why aren't we in your office?" I whispered.

"You said privacy. This is probably the only room on the floor that isn't bugged."

Wow. Sometimes I didn't appreciate how stressful his job was.

"Tell me what's going on and I'll decide if my office is safe."

I took a deep breath and began by telling him about the lunch meeting with Gabe and Dimitrios. By the time I got to my arrival at the cottage, I could see a muscle bulging at his jawline. He didn't like that I'd gone alone.

"I was meeting Gabe," I said. "I thought it'd be okay, you know?"

He nodded and I continued. My hands gripped both of his fiercely as I told him about Nici, the shar-lil, and the brainwashed godlings.

"Gabe too," I finished with a choked-back sob. "He's under the opji's thrall. I don't know what to do."

A bag of coffee flew off the shelf. A second bag followed, and a third. They hit the opposite wall like missiles and exploded in a clatter of beans.

Mason had let my hands drop and was breathing heavily as he tried to rein in his rage.

"Did…did you do that?" I asked. "How?"

"It seems that manipulating the dead means more than just flesh. Anything once alive is fair game."

"Anything?"

He shrugged "I haven't tested it much."

By the All-father! Was that how telekinesis really worked? Maybe it was just a manipulation of the dim life-force surrounding an object. I'd have to bring this up with Errol. My bodach magic teacher might have some insight into this game-changer.

I waited for Mason to get himself under control. I wouldn't reprimand him for losing it. We'd had that conversation, and I knew he was working really hard to temper the dark magic.

"I'm okay," he said finally. "What about you? You said the vamp forced you to drink her blood."

My stomach was still tied in knots just thinking of it. "I'm not sure. I feel okay. Disgusted and kind of shaky, but okay. I don't think I'm under her thrall."

"How would you know?"

"Because she told me to bring you to her tomorrow and I'm absolutely not doing that."

"Yes you are."

"No. I'm. Not." I crossed my arms over my chest and glared. He ran a hand over his already-messy curls and rubbed the back of his neck.

"We'll discuss it later. First we neutralize that vamp blood." He laid one hand on my belly and the other along my cheek. His eyes reflected concern. "This is going to hurt. I'm sorry."

His hand slipped behind to cradle my head while the other one pressed firmly into my stomach.

Fire burned through me. I bit back a scream. My muscles seized while flames tore through my veins. The pain vanished in an instant. I crumpled and Mason caught me.

"I'm sorry. It's done now. It's over." He gathered me close and whispered into my ear, over and over, until I caught my breath and was able to stand again.

"What did you do?"

He smoothed a tear away from my cheek and tucked a braid behind my shoulder. "I told the undead blood to go away. Forcefully."

"You could have warned me." I shoved his shoulder, but it was a pale, half-hearted gesture. Already, I felt free of the vampire's bond. My hands relaxed and the jitters left me.

"I thought it better to get it over with. You okay now?"

I nodded, still feeling a bit numb. "Sounds like you've been practicing."

"Oscar has me on what he likes to call his demon regimen."

Oscar was one of the only friends who knew about Mason's dark blessing. They'd been working together so that Mason could master his magic.

I looked around. The floor was covered in coffee beans. The rich java scent filled the small room. Such a waste. But at least my stomach didn't recoil at the smell. I felt stronger and the queasiness was gone.

Finally, when the awkward silence had stretched long enough, I said, "I'm not taking you to meet Nici. That's exactly what she wants—a high ranking official under her thrall. They even said as much at the meeting."

"I'm not saying that I'll swap blood with her. But she thinks you're under her thrall, right? She won't see it coming."

I kicked coffee beans as I thought about it.

"And what happens when you refuse to take part in her unholy ritual. Then what? She'll realize that I'm faking it and kill us both."

He cocked an eyebrow. "You think I can't take on one little vampire?"

"She won't come alone! For all we know she could have an entire wojak army waiting."

"Then we won't go alone either. But we're going." He held my face in both hands. I stared into his beautiful silver eyes—beautiful and full of worry.

"Kyra, you know we have to. This is serious. Up until now, the godlings have been a minor irritation. Now they they've hooked up with the opji. This is no longer a protest. It's war."

I turned my face into his palm and kissed it. He was right. I'd known it since I first saw Nici in that cottage. There was no way this was going to end without bloodshed.

I nodded. "Okay. But I need food and rest before we start planning our attack." What I really wanted was one night at home, a hot bath, a snuggle with my daughter and a good night's rest in my own bed before the world as we knew it ended.

He kissed me and went to look for a broom to clean up the coffee beans.

The Alchemy Party's base was housed in the iconic Sun Life building in one of the busiest sections of downtown Montreal. It served as the headquarters for the ministers, but it also had private labs and living quarters. On nights when Mason worked too late, he stayed here. On gala evenings I sometimes joined him.

At twenty-four stories high, the Sun Life building was the tallest post-war building, but only the first ten floors were inhabited. The rest extended outside the ward.

Mason's private apartment was on the tenth floor.

"Come on." He took my hand and wrapped my arm around his waist. "I thought you'd be too tired to go out anyway, so I brought date night in. Supper's all ready upstairs."

I nodded, wondering if I'd even make it that far before exhaustion took over.

We left the elevator for a small hall with only two doors—one for Mason's apartment and one for his deputy, Ramona Becker.

Mason opened the door on the right and we went inside.

"I'm calling in reinforcements." He opened a drawer in a small table by the front door and chose one of a dozen identical widgets. They were throwaways. He wasn't kidding about the trackers.

He wandered into the living room and paced by the fireplace. I followed him and flopped onto the couch.

Captain Glenda Lowe picked up his call after several rings. He put her on speaker so I could listen in. I heard a baby crying in the background. It was strange to think that the terse captain had a life away from Hub. I couldn't imagine her in anything but the black and gray uniform.

She sounded tired when she said, "Prime Minister, what can I do for you?"

"I need a militia team ready to leave in," he paused to look at a clock on the mantle, "in six hours."

Give them an hour's travel time and that would mean Hub would arrive at 3 a.m. Hours before Nici's sunrise deadline.

"I see. And do I get to know why? Or is that above my pay grade?"

I could hear the weary smile in her voice. Nothing was above Lowe's pay grade.

Mason filled her in on the details of the latest godling caper. I lay back on the couch. I wouldn't get much rest tonight.

I texted Dutch to check in. He sent back a quick note.

Gita has Holly in the bath. R sulking in his room. All's quiet. See you in the morning.

I put down my widget. I had a tight feeling in my chest that had nothing to do with being poisoned (again) by an opji.

Mason ended his call.

"How do you know Lowe's phone isn't tapped?" I asked.

"I don't. But if the news of an imminent opji attack is leaked, at least we've narrowed down the suspects."

I was glad I didn't have to live in his rat's nest of politics and intrigue. Give me a leech infestation any day.

I gazed around the living room. It was a beautiful space, decorated in grays and blacks with a hint of blue on a throw pillow or a splash of color on the abstract art that covered the walls. It was all very chic and generic and not my style or Mason's—less a home-away-from-home and more of a private hotel.

"Why don't you have this place redecorated?" I asked.

He sat on the couch and pulled me onto his lap. I felt the heat of his breath as he nuzzled my neck.

"Because I never want to be too comfortable here. It's not home. Just a rest stop."

I leaned into him and reached up to tangle my fingers in his hair. It was too long again, just the way I liked it.

"We have a couple of hours before we leave. We should really get some rest." His voice was muffled against my skin as he continued his barrage of kisses. I keened the passion in his magic—passion and something else. A dark urgency.

"You know it makes me crazy when you go off to fight the bad guys on your own."

"I know."

His hand found the hem of my shirt and slipped inside to grip my waist and then, more gently, my breast.

"I was terrified when you called. I knew something was wrong…"

"I know."

I was kicking off my shoes even as he worked on the clasp of my bra. He picked me up and carried me toward the bedroom, not bothering to turn on lights as we went.

"You make me crazy," he repeated, but this time with less anger and more fervor.

"I know."

And then I didn't know anything else but the heat of Mason's passion. For at least an hour.

I lay in bed listening to Mason putter in the kitchen. His love-making had been rough and desperate. I touched a finger to my lips that were swollen from his five o'clock shadow. I felt a little raw inside too, like someone had just pulled me from the ocean's undertow and scrubbed the sand off me.

He returned to the bedroom wearing only boxers and carrying one plate piled high with delicate hors d'oeuvres, canapés, fruit and cheese. In his other hand, he carried a bottle of sparkling water and two glasses.

"I thought this would be better than a heavy meal."

"It's perfect." I stuffed a tiny shrimp confection into my mouth and grabbed another, only now realizing how hungry I was.

Mason ate sparingly, then called Angus. He gave him the coordinates for the cottage in Barrows.

"Get there as soon as you can. Scout the area, but don't be seen. Then watch for any incoming activity. We'll be there before three." He disconnected the call and picked up a grape, but didn't eat it. I could sense his mind racing through scenarios.

"You should tell Lowe that the Guardians will be in the area," I said. All we needed was one nervous soldier to shoot a gargoyle.

Mason shook his head. "I don't want them to know just yet."

"You don't trust Captain Lowe?"

"I don't trust that every soldier in her militia hasn't come in contact with Nici."

Good point. If she'd gotten to Gabe, anyone could be under her thrall. Suddenly, the savory shrimp canapé turned to ash in my mouth.

THE MILITIA TEAM WAITED for us at Hub station in Barrows. They drove two armored vans that carried six soldiers each, besides the driver. The soldiers wore body armor over their uniforms.

"Sergeant Cloutier, sir!" A soldier stepped forward to greet us. "A message from Captain Lowe, sir. On a secure line." He held out a widget. Mason leaned in to read the screen, then grunted his approval.

Cloutier tucked the widget into one of his many pockets. "We're ready to leave when you are, sir. There's room in each van for one of you."

"We ride together," Mason said.

The sergeant didn't argue. After some reshuffling, we left the Hub encampment with Mason and me riding in the second van.

"What did Captain Lowe say?" I spoke in a low voice, though everyone in the van could hear me.

"We have orders to kill the opji on sight. But she wants the godlings brought in for questioning."

A bit of tension eased from me. I was worried about Gabe. It was unlikely that he'd be with Nici at this time of night—unlikely, but not impossible. She might be using the godlings as shields. She could make him do anything, even attack the soldiers to ease her escape.

"Good. We should remind everyone that these people are under a thrall. It's not their fault."

"With all due respect, ma'am, the godlings got themselves into this mess," Cloutier said from the front seat.

"Maybe so, but not all of them were involved in the railroad bombing. I know that for a fact."

"If you say so." The sergeant didn't sound convinced. I glanced at the soldier sitting beside me, but his eyes were locked on the road ahead.

I sighed. No doubt some of these men and women had fought against the godlings in the railroad attack. Some had probably lost comrades or even been wounded. I hoped they would obey Lowe's command and not give in to vengeful prejudices.

It was past two in the morning. More than four hours until sunrise. The early arrival would allow us to scout the area, hopefully before the opji arrived.

"Oh!" The thought burst from me. Several heads turned my way. "I'm sorry, but I forgot to tell you one important thing."

Mason squeezed my hand. "Go on."

"The animals. They're still on the move. A lot. We may face stampedes again."

"What does that mean?" Cloutier asked. I could tell he didn't like being left out of the loop. "What kind of animals?"

"Every kind, I guess." I rubbed a hand over my forehead. It was hot in the van, and my eyes felt gritty. "I didn't see them very well."

"Then how do you know they were there?" Cloutier swiveled around in his seat to look at me. He seemed older in the dim light, older and more stern.

"It's hard to explain."

Mason interrupted me, "Kyra can sense animals. If she says they were there, they were there."

"What does this mean for us? Do we need more backup?" Cloutier asked.

"I don't know. I don't think so." I sounded wishy-washy. He was probably thinking, "Why do I always get stuck with these stupid civilians?"

"Look," I said. "We're almost there. I think we should check it out. If the animals are a threat, I'll let you know and we'll back off."

Cloutier stared at me for a long moment, then nodded. He spoke into a radio, giving instructions to the soldiers in the lead van.

A kilometer down the road from the old cottage, we drove the vans into the forest and parked. Two soldiers efficiently swept away the tracks that showed where we'd pulled off the road. I didn't think this would fool an opji, but it was probably protocol. The others kitted up with weapons and body armor.

Cloutier insisted that I wear an armored vest over my jacket.

"Why? The opji aren't going to shoot us," I grumbled.

"You want to join the party?" Cloutier said, over his shoulder. "You wear the armor. You too Prime Minister."

Mason didn't complain. He slipped off his jacket and donned the armor. I fussed with my sword's harness. It didn't fit over the vest. Finally, I opted to carry the sheathed blade. No way would I leave it behind.

We walked the short distance to the cottage, careful to keep off the road. Anyone really looking would spot our tracks, but not if they were only passing in a vehicle.

"Anything?" Cloutier asked me.

I had my keening stretched as wide as I thought safe, while still keeping my wards locked down tight. I sensed no animals nearby, at least nothing more than the usual night crawlers that could be found in any forest.

"Nothing." After a moment of quiet with the crunch of our footsteps the only sound, I added. "They were here this afternoon, though. I swear."

Mason turned to give me a quick smile. Cloutier didn't respond.

When we reached the edge of the clearing that marked the cottage lands, the soldiers fanned out. Within seconds, I lost sight of them as they found cover to sit and watch, leaving us standing with Cloutier and one other soldier.

"We're going to clear the inside," Cloutier said. "Wait here." The two soldiers crept to the cottage door and slipped inside.

Standing in the cold and the dark, I felt lost at sea. The sudden recollection of falling overboard and the cold, suffocating St. Lawrence River came back to me. That was the time Polina had kidnapped me and sent me downriver on a cargo ship to mess with Mason. I shuddered and gulped the damp air. I was overtired and my imagination was picking a fight with me.

"I won't let anything happen to you." Mason rubbed my back. I barely felt it through the layers of jacket and armored vest, but his confidence was soothing, even though we both knew his words were empty comfort. Not that Mason wouldn't do everything in his power to keep me safe. He would lay down his life to save mine, if it came to that. But my recent poisoning by a simple peyochip had underlined how fleeting life was and how arbitrary death could be.

Still, fake it 'til you make it and all that. So I put on a shaky smile to reassure him.

The moon had risen late. It was only half-full, but it lit the chimney of the cottage in a silver glow and painted darkness under the dormer windows. Nothing moved in the yard. No lights came from inside. Then a shadow on the roof broke away from the other shadows. A gargoyle was watching.

Cloutier chose that moment to return. He heard the sound from the roof and turned with his blaster raised. I keened the faint whine, telling me it was primed and read to kill.

"Stand down," Mason said. "He's one of ours."

"Would have been good to know," Cloutier said and lowered his gun. He was a man used to being in charge and didn't like having the responsibility of keeping a Prime Minister safe while still deferring to him.

Angus stretched his stumpy wings and did a floating hop down from the roof. Sort of. It was more of a planned fall. He landed with a heavy thump on the frozen ground.

Angus stretched his neck as if sitting on the roof had given him a kink.

"Anything to report?" Mason asked.

"Only that it's a beautiful night for a wee stroll, even if it's cold as a yeti's teat."

"What does that mean?" Cloutier said. He still held his blaster with both hands and his eyes didn't stop scanning the shadows around the cottage.

"It means I've been freezing my arse off for over an hour on that roof and no one has come or gone." Angus rubbed his chest as if it pained him. He did that a lot lately. A couple of years ago, a ghost named Naomi had possessed him. He finally found a way to separate from her, but he rubbed that place in his chest as if it seemed hollow. He didn't talk about Naomi and I didn't ask. If he wanted to tell me, he would.

"Good," Mason said. "Get back up there and keep watch. We're going inside."

Angus coughed, hiked up his pants and spat on the dirt. "I'll watch the road. Young Bartholomew is up there." He wandered off, still grumbling about the cold. I glanced at the roof, but couldn't spot Bart. Gargoyles were good at becoming one with the shadows.

"The house is clear," Cloutier said. "No one inside. We're going to walk the perimeter." The soldiers each headed in a different direction and we quickly lost sight of them in the shadows.

Mason and I waited for Nici inside. The cottage was cold and dark. I fished a small gleam from my belt, activated it with a shake, and tossed it in the air. It hovered above our heads, giving just enough light to make the shadows threatening.

We stood in the open doorway. My breath came out in shallow puffs of frozen air. Just being back here set my nerves on edge.

The room was empty with chairs stacked in a corner and candles snuffed.

Mason motioned for me to stay and went through the door to the kitchen. I waited by the strange altar. The candles had burned down to nubs, and drops of blood marred the tabletop.

I rubbed my hands together, trying to warm them.

Mason returned and shook his head. We were alone.

He pulled out two chairs and set them up, sitting heavily on one. I stayed standing where I was. My keening was on high alert so I could sense anyone coming, and the traces of blood on the altar shone in my mind like flecks of burning lava.

"It makes no sense," I said.

Mason tilted his head, questioning.

"The blood rite. I get why Nici forced the others to drink her blood."

"Makes the thrall stronger."

"Exactly. But why blood that artifact. It didn't do anything but sing."

I thought of the weird coconut thing. If Nici had been expecting the blood to activate it in some way, she must have been disappointed.

"Maybe it needs more blood," Mason suggested. "Like it's being primed."

"Maybe." I would have to ask Avie about that. Avalon Moodie was my best friend and a strong witch. She wasn't into blood magic, but she might know enough to explain the odd rite.

I looked around at the empty room and then at my widget. It was past three in the morning. Nici wanted Mason before sunrise. That was in less that three hours.

"Now what?" I asked.

Mason extended his legs and crossed his arm, hunkering down in the chair. "Now we wait."

ici didn't show. Just before sunrise, Angus returned to say he'd wait out the day with Bart on the roof. I paced to keep warm. Mason and I watched from the front porch of the cottage as the sky went from bruised plum to tangerine. Still no opji.

An hour later, Cloutier drove us back to our van in Barrows.

"I'll file a report with Captain Lowe," he said in a neutral tone. He didn't seem put out by the waste of time, but I couldn't help feeling like the girl who cried vampire.

Mason and I drove home in silence. On the bridge, heading into the city, the river lit up like a carpet of crystals. I vaguely wondered if that's where Crystal Bridge got its name, but my brain was too mushy to hold onto that thought.

Traffic was light at this time of morning, but we'd have to cross the city and another bridge before we reached home. When we hit Highway 20, Mason put the van on auto drive and leaned back in the seat. He only did that when he was really tired. I decided I'd better stay awake, just in case.

I called Gabe. It went right to voice mail. I left a curt message asking him to call me.

"What do you plan to say to him?" Mason asked.

"I don't know. To stay away from Nici, I guess."

"Do you think he'll listen?"

"No." I was gripping my widget so hard, my fingers ached. In fact, I ached all over. Lack of sleep and constant tension were finally getting to me.

"You won't like it, but it might be best if we restrain him until this is over," Mason said.

"Like kidnap him?"

"Yes."

"I'll think about it."

I knew he was right, but trying to work out the logistics of kidnapping the heir to the Saivite clan was too much in that moment. My eyes felt like glue and my thoughts were sluggish. I leaned back in my seat and the next thing I knew, Mason was gently shaking me awake.

"You should rest. I'll see to Holly."

I took him up on the offer and crawled into bed without even getting undressed.

I WOKE TO A cooing sound. Holly was in bed with me. She'd kicked off the blanket and was examining her toes. On her other side, Mason snored softly.

I want to wake up like this every day, I thought.

Then the memory of the previous day came back—the blood rite, the opji…and Gabe.

I reached for my widget and tried his number. Again it went right to voice mail.

I turned back to my baby girl and pulled her into my arms. She squealed with delight, and I decided we'd better get up before we woke up Daddy.

We had a late breakfast and Suzt arrived just after eleven to take over babysitting duties. Holly squealed again and held out her arms until Suzt picked her up. I tried not to be jealous. Suzt was a godsend. Holly loved her, but that didn't mean she loved me any less. My head told me that Holly was a lucky girl to have so many people who cared for her. My heart would catch up to that idea one day.

I left Suzt to clean up the applesauce in Holly's hair and went to get ready for work, only to trip over Jacoby in the hallway.

He was sprawled on the floor with several lengths of long rope tangled around his legs and arms. His widget was open and he concentrated on the screen with his tongue poking out the corner of his mouth.

"Watcha doing?" I asked.

"Mr. Dutch says knots tying is goods hobby."

"Did he." I suspected Mr. Dutch just wanted a few moments of peace without a certain dervish hanging around.

"So you're enjoying your vacation then?"

Jacoby made a distracted grunting sound and I left him to his knots.

Before I hopped in the shower, I tried Gabe's number again. Still no answer. I thought of calling Emil, but I didn't want to alarm him. I'd wait until I got to the office to break the bad news.

I PULLED INTO THE parking lot of Valkyrie Pest Control. The curtains on the second floor trembled. Mr. Murray checking out the new arrival. No need for a high tech surveillance system when your tenant was a nosy-pants.

I found Emil in the office. He was just finishing up a call with a client.

"That was Mrs. Henderson. She says the raccoons are nesting in her chimney again."

"Right." The last time I'd visited Mrs. Henderson, the "raccoons" in question had been a dervish. "She wouldn't know a raccoon from a jackalope."

Emil grinned. "I told her you'd be there this morning."

"Wonderful." I slumped in the chair behind my desk. The desk was really superfluous now, since I spent very little time at the office.

"You okay?" Emil asked. "You looked a little ragged around the edges."

"Have you heard from Gabe today?"

"No. Why?" Emil crossed his arms and sat straighter in the chair. His posture reminded me of Nici—straight-backed, but not rigid, like a willow tree able to bend with the wind. Maybe it was an opji thing, that casual grace.

"I have to tell you something and you're not going to like it." I fiddled with the keyboard on my desk.

"Okay." Emil fixed me with his big, amber eyes. I saw worry in those eyes. This wasn't going to go well. Aw, hells. There was no helping it. I bit the bullet, ripped off the bandaid and leaped into the breach.

Once again I told the whole story, starting with my lunch date with Gabe and Dimitrios. His expression darkened as I told him about meeting Nici, the blood rite, and her growing army of thralls.

"It can't be true!" He stood up. Spots of red blazed on his pale cheeks.

"Gabe wouldn't deal with the opji."

"He's not himself. Nici has him under a thrall."

"That's ridiculous. I would have noticed."

"I didn't. Not until I saw the blood rite."

Emil picked up the coffee cup from his desk and threw it against the wall. It shattered on impact, leaving a brown smear.

"Not fair! Things were good, and now you tell me that he's under a vamp spell? I thought it was because he'd reconciled with his family…and because he'd finally realized his feelings. For me." A breath hitched in his chest. He ran both hands through his hair, tugging on the long curls as if he wanted to pull them out.

"One thing doesn't necessarily negate the other," I said. "Gabe's feelings for you are obvious. I'm sure Nici has nothing to do with that."

Emil snorted. "Right. Because Gabe just happened to fall into my bed the same week that a vamp put him under a spell. It's a fabulous coincidence."

"Maybe not a coincidence, but maybe the thrall has freed Gabe from his responsibilities. That was the only thing really standing between you."

Emil grumbled something that could have been assent.

"Whatever the case, we have to find him. I've been calling all morning but he won't answer. Keep trying."

Emil nodded. He hunched over his widget, but paused before calling. "What do I say if I get a hold of him?"

"I don't know. Make up some excuse, but get him over here and don't let him leave." I didn't mention that we were going to restrain Gabe. Emil wasn't ready for that tidbit yet.

"I'm off to Mrs. Henderson's. Call me if you hear from him."

MRS. HENDERSON OPENED THE door and said, "What do you want?" She wore faded khaki pants and a beige t-shirt with the word "Hugs" surrounded by pink hearts. A reddish brown stain bisected one of the hearts like blood, but it was probably just spaghetti sauce. I sometimes forgot that the average citizen didn't deal in blood on a daily basis.

"Kyra Greene from Valkyrie Pest Control." I flashed her my official looking badge, which was really just a printout from my computer. "You called about something nesting in your chimney?"

"Coons. I told 'em it was coons." Her voice rasped like a smoker's, but looking at her rundown neighborhood, I didn't think Mrs. Henderson could afford cigarettes. They were a luxury in a world where farmland was micromanaged by Hub.

"I'd be glad to take care of your raccoon problem." No point in arguing with her. I'd gone through that before. Mrs. Henderson believed what she believed and nothing I said would change it.

"That's what you said last time." She was a good foot shorter than me, but she pushed into my personal space.

I didn't step back.

"And I did take care of them, as you might recall. I can't control the entire animal kingdom though. If they came back, it's because you didn't put a cap on the chimney like I told you to."

She squinted even though the sky was overcast. Her mouth twisted into a snarl, and I thought she'd yell at me to get off her lawn. Still, I wasn't in the mood to back down.

Finally, she turned and headed inside, leaving the door open.

All right then.

I followed her into the living room. It had the same musty smell with an underlying odor of cat urine that I remembered.

"So tell me why you think it's raccoons," I said as I laid my tool bag on the hearth.

"It *is* coons. I'm telling you, I hear them all night long."

"Hear what exactly."

"Rattling and banging. Like they've got a whole mariachi band up there."

"Doesn't sound like something a raccoon would do." I was pushing her, but I couldn't help it.

"Whatever. Just fix it."

I crouched on the hearth and shone a flashlight into the flue. Immediately, a rattling sound came from above. Definitely not raccoons. I was pretty sure Mrs. Henderson had rattlers. And not the snake kind.

I swept the light over a patch of bulbs bobbing on long stalks. The bulbs reacted to the light by shying away. That made the rattles on their stalks jangle, and a gray veil slammed shut over the bulbous end like an eyelid.

Yep, Mrs. Henderson had a good case of rattling peepers.

I tipped the light up the chimney. The bulbs nearest to me fell into shadow and they extended toward me again. The ones further up the chimney retracted in my light. More rattling. I lowered the light and after a moment all movement stopped. Then the rattling began again. They were singing the song of their people.

I pulled my head out of the chimney. "The good news is you don't have raccoons. You have rattling peepers. They're perfectly harmless. It's a lichen—a plant—that grows in dark places."

"A plant? No plant sounds like that."

"This one does. The bad news is I need a special tool to remove it."

"Special tool?" Mrs. Henderson seemed set on repeating everything I said. "Why can't you just poison them. Or burn them out?"

"Do you think if fire worked, they'd be growing in your chimney? And poison isn't effective. It's bound to leave some alive and they'll just grow back."

I was already packing my tools away.

"What are you doing? You have to get rid of 'em. I don't want no dirty lichen in my house!"

I looked pointedly at the filthy carpet and wombat-sized dust bunny in the corner. The peepers were probably the cleanest thing in this house.

"I told you I need a special tool. I'll have to reschedule." In fact, what I needed was a dervish who was small enough to climb into the chimney and scrape off the fungi. I took out my widget and scrolled through my calendar. "How about next Tuesday?"

Mrs. Henderson cursed me. It wasn't a very imaginative curse. I'd been threatened by badder asses than that.

I packed my flashlight back in the bag and hoisted it over my shoulder. Mrs. Henderson followed me to the door, calling down fire and brimstone on my entire family going back seven generations.

"See you next Tuesday," I said as strode down her front path. She might call another pest controller before then, but somehow, I didn't feel bad about losing that gig.

Dimitrios was leaning against my van, waiting for me. He pushed himself forward and brushed off the back of his coat.

"You really should take better care of your vehicles, Kyra. It's filthy."

"What do you want?" I walked right past him and opened the hatchback to put away my tools.

"I want you to know that Nici is displeased with you."

"So she sent her lapdog? Why can't she threaten me herself? Oh, that's right. She'll burn up in a fiery red mist if she tries to cross Montreal's ward."

Opji attacks were the reason for the ward's foundation, and no vamp had ever been able to break it. When Prince Alvar had committed his little coup, he'd bypassed the ward altogether by opening a door to Underhill.

"Is that what Nici wants?" I asked. "She's looking for a way into Montreal, isn't she? And she thinks her little thrall of wannabe gods will help her get it."

Dimitrios pounded on the side of my van. Blue light crackled over his fist. The energy spread along the metal van and zapped my hand where it rested on the raised trunk.

"Ow!" I yanked my hand away.

Dimitrios grinned. His shoulders swelled and he grew about a foot. He glowed with an inner light that suffused his face, making his eyes darker and complexion swarthier. Galvanic magic sizzled in his raised hand, and he shaped it into a spear.

Or a lightning bolt. Dimitrios was a descendant of Zeus, after all.

"Not all the godlings are wannabes, Valkyrie."

The air smelled of ozone, like the summer sun on hot tar. Every nerve in my body told me to run. Now that they knew I wasn't under Nici's thrall, they had no use for me. Dimitrios held his electric spear under my chin. It sparked and thrummed making the hair prickle on my scalp.

Then he wilted. The light behind his eyes faded. His shoulders sagged and the blue magic winked out.

"The might of Zeus has limits." It was my turn to smirk.

He leaned in, eyes blazing. "You shouldn't have betrayed us. We were watching. You brought Hub soldiers to meet with Nici. The next time you see her, she will tear your throat out."

"Huh. I wonder if the all powerful Zeus would have let himself become a slave to a vampire."

He slammed me against the van. One hand gripped my shoulders, fingers painfully digging into the muscle. His face filled my entire vision. A bit of froth flecked the edges of his lips.

"You are lucky that I don't hit women." His breath stank like alcohol.

"Yeah? Well, I hit men." I wound my free arm up and slugged him in the side of the head. It hurt. A lot. But he staggered sideways. I grabbed the first weapon I found in my trunk, a tire iron, and swung it like a baseball bat. It met his elbow with a satisfying crack.

He screamed and jumped back.

"You bitch! This isn't over. We'll—"

I swung the iron again, missing by several inches, but I hadn't meant to hit him. I only wanted to make it clear that I wouldn't back away from a fight.

"Yeah, yeah. You're going to get me," I said with a surprisingly calm voice. "Whatever. Save it for someone who cares."

I slammed the trunk, got into the van and drove off. In the rear view mirror, I saw Dimitrios standing in the road, cradling his arm and talking on his widget.

I turned the corner, put the van on auto-drive and leaned back in my seat. That's when I started to shake.

I drove in no particular direction for ten minutes, then pulled the van to the side of the road before getting on the ramp for the highway. Cars whizzed by me. It started to snow in fat, wet flakes that melted as soon as they hit my windshield.

I called Emil. He answered before the first ring ended.

"Did you talk to Gabe?" I asked.

"No. Dammit!"

Emil's voice was distant and overwhelmed by a hissing sound. Wind, I thought. He was outside. I heard traffic in the background. Someone shouted "Back off!" and there was a muffling sound as if Emil covered the mic. The call went dead. Two seconds later my widget rang again. It was Emil.

"Where are you?" I demanded.

"On Chemin Street. Standing outside Gabe's neighborhood."

Mount Royal dominated the city center, and Gabe lived in a gated community just west of it. It wasn't really a mountain, more like a lopped off hillock, but it had always been the heart of Montreal.

"I got tired of calling, so I came over to bang on his door instead, but the damn security guard won't let me past the gates. Says I'm not on the approved list of visitors." Again the muffling sound, and "Screw you!" Emil came back on the line.

"Kyra? You still there?"

"I'm here."

"I don't know what else to do." He was out of breath now.

"Just slow down."

"I can't. The guard is chasing me. Oh, wait, the fat fuck slipped in the slush. Isn't that too bad."

"Emil, stop fooling around and listen to me." I waited a breath to make sure he was paying attention.

"Okay, I'm listening."

"Do not, I repeat, do not do anything stupid."

"I just need to see him." Emotion clouded his voice.

"I know. But wait for me. I'll be there as soon as I can."

"What about the security?"

"I'll take care of it."

"Thanks, Kyra." He ended the call.

Emil probably thought I'd use my connections to have Hub override the community security guard. But after last night's failure in producing the opji, I didn't want Captain Lowe to think I was getting hysterical. Instead, I went home to arm myself with a hell hound and a bodach.

"THIS IS HOW IT'S going to work." I pointed a finger at the security guard. He was a short, chunky guy with a greasy little mustache and overly-prominent brows under more greasy blond hair. His expression was currently one of terror, but I couldn't take credit for that. Princess sat at his feet. The sun was peeking through the clouds and it lit the bone-white plating on her face. Drool hung from her muzzle. She curled a lip, showing off finger-long fangs, and a low, deep growl rumbled from her chest.

"Princess is going to wait here with you. We're going inside to talk to a friend. When we come out, you'll still be standing here and if you're alive it means you won't have done anything stupid. Got it?"

The guard nodded once.

"Princess, guard."

The hell hound didn't move. Her eyes were fixed on her captive's face.

"Won't he just report us as soon as we leave?" Emil said.

I turned back to the guard. "He won't do that because he'll see Princess's beautiful face in his dreams for months." I flicked his name badge. "Remy Proulx. Shouldn't be too hard to find out where you live."

His eyes flicked to me then back to the hound. He licked his thin lips.

I walked toward the gate, confident that my threat would hold for at least few days. After that?

"Can't you just put him in a thrall or something," I said to Emil. "You're a vamp. Use it."

"Can't. I never had the zycha."

"Right." I'd forgotten the zycha produced the power to enthrall. It was a blood rite that slowed an opji's heart to barely one beat per minute, extending their lives to hundreds of years. After the zycha, opji could only exist on human blood. Every opji underwent the rite at puberty—every opji except Emil who had been kidnapped and raised by fae since he was a baby.

"What are we going to do about the gate?" he asked. The home owners in the community could open it with a remote. The guard probably had one too, but I had a better plan that didn't involve patting down the already abused guard.

"Errol, you got this?" The bodach rode on my shoulder. He was no more than three inches tall. In one hand he grasped a tiny walking stick. The other hand hung onto one of my braids so he wouldn't fall off. Only his red, bulbous nose peeked out from behind his white beard and bushy eyebrows.

"Htpgtl," he said aloud. *Got it.* The affirmation appeared in my head. He pointed his stick at the gate. I heard a buzzing sound as Errol fried the electrical system.

"Try it now," I said.

Emil looked skeptical, but he grabbed the black iron gate and slid it sideways.

We were in.

I EXPECTED GABE TO turn us away at the door, but he smiled when he saw us standing on the stoop, then stepped back so we could enter. He looked like he'd slept in his clothes. Ice clinked in the glass in his hand as he motioned for us to follow him into a sitting room.

The curtains were closed against the daylight and several standing lamps with stained-glass shades lit the room. The walls, painted deep bronze, were cluttered with religious iconography. My knowledge of Hindu lore was rough, but I recognized Vishnu with his four arms and elephant-headed Ganesha. Images of Shiva, the patron god of the Saivites, dominated the room. A beautifully detailed statue of the god with his blue skin and third eye sat in the place of honor on the mantle.

Gabe put the glass on a marble sideboard and poured himself another shot of bourbon. He held up the half-empty bottle to ask if we wanted any.

"It's barely afternoon," I said. Gabe capped the bottle and shrugged. He sprawled on a plush couch and gave us that dopey smile again.

"So what's up?"

"You're kidding right?" The words exploded from Emil. I keened anger, fear and frustration churning inside him like a maelstrom. I touched his elbow and stepped forward to let him know that I would handle this.

"I went back to the cottage with Mason."

"Yeah, I heard." His sunny expression faded as his dark brows came together in a frown. "You shouldn't have brought Hub. Nici was pissed." And the grin was back.

"Is this just a game to you?" Emil snapped.

"Can I have a word with you?" I dragged Emil into the hallway. "You know he's under a thrall," I whispered. "Why are you provoking him?"

Emil ran a hand through his curls. "I just don't buy it. Gabe is stronger than that. He should be able to break out of any opji thrall."

"Not if it's been boosted by the shar-lil."

"We don't even know what that thing does." He hissed out a sigh of frustration.

"Exactly. So let's find out. Now just relax and let me talk to him."

Emil looked over my shoulder at Gabe who was leaning back on the couch, swirling the bourbon in his glass as if he didn't have a care in the world. The muscles at Emil's jaw bunched. "Fine."

We returned to the sitting room.

"You know that Nici is using you, right? You and the other godlings. She wants something, probably access to Montreal. Once she gets it, she'll discard you all, maybe even kill you like she did Alvar."

"I'm not worried." Gabe dipped his head side to side as if he was dancing to music only he could hear.

"You should be." I sat on the edge of the couch and let my magic mingle with his. There it was—the song that I'd felt more than heard when the artifact was blooded. That was the music Gabe was attuned to, hours after any thrall should have worn off. I probed the magic, looking for a way inside it—a way to reach Gabe—but it was a solid shield.

Gabe must have known I was checking him out on some deeper level, but he submitted to the probe with that same agreeable expression.

A thunk from upstairs told me we weren't alone. Gabe lived with his two sisters, sister-in-law, nephew and father. I couldn't discount the possibility that his whole family was under her sway.

I lowered my voice. "You have to listen to me. Nici has some kind of magical hold on you. You need to stay away from her until we can break it. Do you trust me?"

"Sure!" He nodded happily.

"Good. We're going to take you some place safe."

"No can do. Gotta stay here."

"Why?"

His faced scrunched up for a moment. "I don't know. I just do."

Great. Nici had him in a holding pattern. She'd probably told them all to go home and wait for her instructions. I couldn't let that happen.

Emil knelt beside us. "What about me, Gabe. You know I'd never hurt you right?"

Gabe swiveled his head toward Emil.

"Why don't you come with me. We'll wait together. Just not here."

"I…I can't."

"But remember, we promised to be together, no matter what."

Gabe's expression softened again and he ran a finger down Emil's jawline.

I hadn't realized their relationship had come this far. Tears crept down Emil's cheek and Gabe rubbed them with his thumb. Then he leaned back and let his hand drop.

"No."

Emil let out a ragged breath. "Then we're going to have to do this the hard way." He gripped Gabe by the shoulders. Emil was slimmer, but his opji blood gave him unnatural strength. He lifted Gabe off the couch.

A shriek came from behind us, and a woman jumped on Emil's back. Her nails scored his cheek and neck. Her voice rose in a ululation that rivaled my banshee's best scream. Under her weight, Emil fell onto Gabe and the three of them sprawled on the floor in a heap of flailing limbs.

I grabbed for the woman but got only her long black hair. She grappled with me. From his perch on my shoulder, Errol whacked her with his walking Twig. Uma punched me, a solid jab on the chin. I hooked her arm with my elbow and spun us both, taking her out of the fight.

"Bitch!" She spat. A small gob of saliva hit my chest. I gripped her shoulders and shoved, but not before she bit my arm.

I'd had just about enough of that.

My blade sang as I unsheathed it. I pressed the tip to her chest and backed her into the wall. She hissed and pressed forward until the blade pressed into her. One flick of my wrist and I'd skewer her. I couldn't risk it. A simple cut by my blade would be the end of Uma. And when Gabe finally beat the thrall, he wouldn't forgive me.

I backed off just as Gabe said, "Uma! Enough!" He untangled himself from Emil and rose to knock my blade aside. He stood between me and the manic woman.

"I'm sorry, Kyra, my fiancé is a very jealous woman."

"Your fiancé?" That came from Emil, who was now standing behind Gabe with a hand to his throat where Uma's nails had drawn blood.

Gabe didn't look at him. "Yes, my fiancé."

"What made you change your mind?" I had a sneaking suspicion that Nici was involved.

Gabe shrugged. "Father made me see it's the right thing to do."

"So you're all in then. You'll be taking over as head of the Saivites too?"

"In time."

"Is she in with Nici too?" I asked.

"Uma is under my protection," Gabe said, "and we're not going anywhere."

Uma was glaring at me with pure hatred as she clung to Gabe's arm. There was so much excess emotion in the room, my keening couldn't sort it all out.

"Nici will use you and throw you away. It's what she does."

Gabe's smile turned feral. "And you should know that my father has initiated me into all the secrets our clan keeps from the rest of the world." He glanced at a statue of Shiva on the mantle. "Shiva is often depicted as the benevolent one, the balancer, the mediator. But he is also known as the destroyer, and anyone who gets in our way should remember that."

His eyes sparkled and he seemed to expand. Maybe I was thinking about Dimitrios and how easily he had channeled Zeus's power, but I swore Gabe grew a foot and his skin was turning blue. I didn't want to wait around to find out what aspect of the god he could muster.

Errol spat out curses on Gabe's ancestry. I grabbed Emil by the arm. "Come on." I tugged him out of the house.

Snow was falling, covering the March slush in a fine white blanket. We walked slowly back to the car. At one point, I realized that I'd left Emil behind. I turned to find him standing in the middle of the road, looking lost. Snowflakes landed on his nose and cheeks and didn't melt.

"I've lost him." His voice was filled with emptiness.

"No—"

"I have! He's gone. One way or another. He's gone."

I crossed the space between us and gripped his hand. Errol jumped to his shoulder and patted Emil on the chin, mumbling about cursed gods.

Emil watched me with such trust in his eyes. I couldn't fill him with false hope.

"Then there's only one thing left to do," I said. "We break the thrall. We find Nici. We cut off her head and smash her damned shar-lil. We let the opji know that they have lost. Again." It was what Terra wanted me to do and I could no longer deny her.

Emil licked snow from his lips. "And how do we do that?"

I bit down on the bitterness roiling in my stomach. "We ask for help, but first I need you to tell me everything you know about the opji."

THE OPJI INCURSION. WHAT WE KNOW. WHAT WE NEED TO KNOW.

March 20, 2084

Hold onto your lug nuts, folks. This is a long post. Long but important, and I value any feedback you might have in the comments.

It's a well known fact that the original Triumvirate of Montreal created the Apex stones and the ward to safeguard the city against constant opji attacks in the last days of the Flood Wars.

For fifty years, the ward stood solid against the vampires. Until Prince Alvar of the Winter Court broke that peace in a childish fit of pique. He joined with opji forces in an attempt to overthrow the Triumvirate and his sister's reign at the fae court.

He was unsuccessful.

For Montrealers, this isn't news. What is less known is that, since that aborted coup, the opji have not given up their attempts to invade Montreal.

Barrows and Hedge are overflowing with refugees. And in the close quarters of those shanty towns, disease is running rampant. This is another offense we can lay at the opji's door.

The refugees are mostly homesteaders, pushed from their homes by the opji who have been steadily moving west from their home base of Vioska in the Ottawa Valley.

Why? What do the opji hope to gain by displacing homesteaders? That question has bothered me for some time. Logic would dictate they are trying to set up a base closer to Montreal—perhaps a military base from which to launch a new offensive.

But other stories from fleeing refugees make me uneasy. The few homesteaders who've escaped say that the opji are taking captives. Old, young, male, female, fit or ill, they don't care. Others tell of forest fires in the northwest filling the skies with smoke and ash. I can confirm this is true, as I have seen the pall of smoke on the horizon.

I don't doubt the opji are planning to attack Montreal. But what if there is more to their schemes?

What if the opji are attacking homesteads because of some threat to Vioska? I think this is the most likely scenario. Either the forest fires have decimated their land or, as some refugees have suggested to me, the flu epidemic that has hit the towns outside Montreal's gates has also infiltrated the opji's human breeding pens.

How much worse would the disease be to undernourished slaves kept in close quarters? It would also explain the desperate opji incursions, and perhaps why they have once again set their sights on Montreal.

So let's talk about vampires. What do we know about them?

It's hard to get any definitive knowledge about a normally reclusive race, but I'm lucky enough to have a close friend who has made a study of the opji for personal reasons. From him and the bits I have gathered by talking to refugees, here's what I know with some degree of certainty.

Opji are vampires in that they drink human blood. Other than that, they don't adhere to most of the old vampire myths. They are long-lived, but not immortal. Sunlight doesn't kill them, but they do seem sensitive to it and prefer to travel at night.

I don't want to get into a discussion about how to defeat an opji because I know the comments will blow up with trigger happy vampire hunters. But suffice it to say that holy water and garlic do not offend them.

The opji are proud of their ancient heritage. They are genetic vampires, meaning they are born that way. Or more correctly, they are born with the potential to be a vampire.

At an opji birth, the placenta is taken away to be dried with special herbs. The opji child grows much like any human, except for their rapid healing powers. At puberty (the exact age isn't known), the child goes through the *zycha* rite, where they eat the dried placenta, signifying their death and rebirth as an opji. There is, of course, more to it than chowing down on placenta jerky. There must be some other magic involved, but the secret of the rite is tightly guarded.

One thing I know, is that the zycha helps the opji contain their bloodlust. It slows their hearts, so the need for daily fresh blood diminishes. Without the zycha, an adult opji would have to fight the urge to drink the blood of every human they encounter for the rest of their life. On the down side, the rite also brings on their sensitivity to light. Talk about sympathetic magic. A dark rite that induces a love for the dark. Seems poetic.

With no more large cities to hide in and hunt in, the opji have become creative about fulfilling their blood needs. That's where the *krowa* come in. Krowa is the opji term for cow. And these poor souls are kept in pens just like livestock. The lifespan of a krowa isn't long. The constant blood-lettings siphon off good health along with the will to live. To combat this problem, the opji keep another group of humans as breeders, to replenish their stock. I shudder to think of those souls kept in squalor with death as their only hope of escape.

The opji aren't the only vampires in Vioska. They also breed an army of undead soldiers known as wojaks. These mindless soldiers are humans turned into undead drones through an unknown rite. They are considered less than dogs by the opji who use them as cannon fodder in their battles.

I've seen wojaks in action. They are monsters of wasted human proportions, terrifying precisely because they are so close to being human, and yet not. Their bodies have atrophied to leathery skeletons, leaving their faces fleshless and mad-eyed. They seem impervious to cold, fear or exhaustion.

What's not clear to me, is how the opji control the wojaks. Mindless as they are, the wojaks could run amok and decimate Vioska. And yet, the opji always seem to have them under control.

This brings me to the last opji subject for the day. Their magic. As I mentioned, they are born with heightened healing. The zycha rite seems to give them longevity. They have the ability to control minds, and their saliva has some healing properties. These skills were perhaps developed for ease of feeding in a past world that wasn't aware of magical creatures roaming the night. For it is likely, with all the stories of vampires through the ages, that the opji have been around since long before the Flood Wars.

I'd like to start an unofficial group to track the opji movements. I'm certain that Hub has committees dedicated to this problem, but the power of the people on the ground shouldn't be discounted. If you have spotted opji in your area, please let me know where. I will attempt to track their movements.

If you have any other information about opji that is relevant to the fight, I want to know that too. Let's pool our resources. Secret information helps no one but the opji!

COMMENTS (71)

So a steak through the heart, yea or nay?
MonsterHunter22 (March 20, 2084)

> Is that steak medium rare, dumbass?
> *Clued-Out (March 20, 2084)*

———•———

I bet decapitation works most things can't walk around without a head

BigGameGuy (March 20, 2084)

> Wow. Decapitation. Big words for a big guy. Did you have to look that one up?
>
> *Clued-Out (March 20, 2084)*

———•———

Fire cures all ills

SaintBecky (March 21, 2084)

———•———

I find if you cutting off nough parts a beast is bound to fall ventually.

Hercules-son (March 23, 2084)

———•———

Silver bullets? Put one between their eyes and I bet they won't get up.

Ilovewolves (March 23, 2084)

———•———

You guys make me sick. All people deserve to live. Opji are a noble and severely misunderstood race. We should welcome them with open arms.

DaisyGrace (March 23, 2084)

> You do that, sweetheart.
>
> *Clued-Out (March 23, 2084)*

———•———

I saw the opji outside of Barrows. They were watching the town. No one believes me.

Percy999 (March 23, 2084)

> I believe you.
>
> *Valkyrie367 (March 23, 2084)*

———•———

We see opji almost every day. So far they leave us alone, but I don't know

how long we can hold out.
North49 (March 25, 2084)

    Be safe.
    Valkyrie367 (March 25, 2084)

Vamps north of Barrows daily.
Homer-instead (March 26, 2084)

We've got 'em like a plague.
Annequin-Lodge (March 27, 2084)

The sky is on fire. The vamps can't be far
OnTheRange (March 27, 2084)

...+55 MORE COMMENTS

Since our visit to the cottage had turned into a wild goose chase, we couldn't rely on Hub for backup. I didn't need it. I went home and called in the troops. Our dining room once again became a war room.

Mason was sprawled in the chair beside me, looking tired and rumpled but still formidable. His magic simmered around him like a dark cloak, only adding to his air of menace. He looked like a man who could take care of business, whether that business was in a boardroom or a back alley. Thousands of years ago, that kind of man would have won the survival of the fittest contest. Other men would want him to lead. Women would want to him to mate. His confidence and brute strength would make them all feel safe.

My lizard brain wasn't immune to those charms. Even though I knew him intimately enough to see under that strength to the vulnerability at its core, there was still no place I'd rather be than by his side—in life and on the eve of battle.

He saw me watching him, gave me a small smile and squeezed my hand. He felt it too. Whatever was coming, it was bad.

I looked around the table at the rest of my crew. Everyone had come when I called. Oscar, our inventor extraordinaire, sat next to Avie, our magic specialist. Errol perched on the table by her coffee mug. Every once in a while, he'd dip his wool hat into Avie's coffee and suck the juice off the end of it. Avie didn't seem to mind. She had a pile of silver and copper charms in front of her and was busy stringing them onto leather cords.

I hadn't trusted Emil to drive after our confrontation with Gabe, and he'd come home in my van. He still looked shell-shocked by Gabe's betrayal. Angus sat next to him, with Dutch on Emil's other side. Berto and the remaining Guardians were patrolling the perimeter of our homestead, but would check in periodically.

Raol had come back from his latest tour of the Inbetween. He perched on the dining chair to report his findings. His fluffy tail curled up behind him like a puff of smoke.

"The creatures of the forest are restless, though I saw no more stampedes." For a little guy, he had confidence to spare, and he met every eye at the table. "They have some place to go, but don't seem to know where that is. I think we have to assume the disturbance has something to do with the opji."

The unease of the forest leached into the trees that tossed in the wind outside our windows.

Raol continued with descriptions of the opji movements and recent homestead attacks.

Grim perched on the end of the table, his body turned away so he could stare out the bay window, his ears twitching as he took in our conversation. Princess snored softly at my feet. Jacoby had nested himself into the fur on her belly, and Willow, my gray cat, curled up against her back.

Even Cricket, our hidebehind, lurked by the patio door, too shy to come closer. The goblins were snug in their cottage and Gita was reading to Holly before putting her to bed.

Raven appeared in the doorway, and listened to Raol give his report. I patted the empty chair beside me and he came to sit, looking awkward but pleased to be included with the grown ups.

Mason nodded and gave him a small smile. That was all Raven needed. He sat up straight and paid attention to Raol.

A wave of gratitude swept over me. Not long ago, I would have been sitting alone in my tiny apartment, feeding my critters after a long day at work, solitary and not even knowing what I was missing. We might be on the verge of war, but I wouldn't be fighting alone.

Only Nori was absent and that was because Soolea's contractions had started an hour ago. They labored in the gatehouse to bring a new life into this world. I just hoped that when we were done, there would be a world left to welcome them.

When Raol finished, I gave everyone the rundown of the past few days. When I got to the part about our meeting with Gabe that afternoon, Emil stood up, knocking his chair backward. He stormed into the kitchen. A few seconds later, I heard a glass shatter. Emil liked to throw things.

Dutch excused himself and followed Emil into the kitchen. I heard his low voice talking Emil down from the cliff.

I summed up my bad news.

"So it seems that the opji are trying to break into the ward. They're using the godlings to do it. I'm just not sure how. That shar-lil plays a big part. It might be some kind of weapon."

I let that sink in, giving them a moment to recalibrate and come to the inevitable conclusion.

The opji were preparing for war.

Silence stretched around the table. Avie's face was unnaturally pale in the dim light. Her hands stilled at her charm work. Oscar swore and pushed his chair away from the table so he could pace.

"Fifty years!" He punctuated his outburst with a raised fist. "Fifty years we lived without an opji incursion. Why now?"

Raol cleared his throat. "I think I can answer that. Traders are all talking about the flu. Entire homesteads have gone dark. Rumor says they're full of infectious corpses."

"The flu?" Avie said. "The opji don't get sick."

"But their krowa do." Raol's tail twitched.

"But surely a simple flu couldn't do that much damage." Avie looked at me for confirmation. I shook my head.

"You're used to the comforts of the city," I said. "Clean water, good food, medical care. It's not like that outside the ward." I remembered the camps in Hedge, the desperate eyes watching me from inside uninsulated tents. The bodies piled up outside the make-shift hospital. "And how much worse will it be inside the opji camps? A simple flu could decimate them."

Raol rubbed his hands together in a squirrel-like gesture of agitation. "That's exactly right. The traders all say the same thing. The opji are desperate for new blood."

"Desperate enough to attack Montreal." Angus shook his head. "Hellfire and damnation that's a rough piece of luck."

"So what do we do?" Avie asked.

All eyes turned to me. Why did everyone think I had the answers? I glanced at Mason, but he just gave me the same nod he'd given Raven, the one that said, "You can do this."

I took a deep breath and ordered my thoughts.

"We tackle this systematically. The way I see it, we've got a few separate problems. One, the vamps are using the godlings to do their dirty work. We have to find Nici and destroy this shar-lil. Avie I want you to research what kind of artifact it could be. It might not be easy to destroy."

"On it." She'd pushed aside her bits of copper and wire and was already typing furiously on her widget.

"Raol, I need information on the opji movements. Nici will have a base nearby. Where are they and how many?"

Raol nodded and flicked his tail.

I turned to Cricket who was lurking by the back door.

"Do you feel up to scouting?"

The hidebehind's eyes were huge and dark. His branch-like arms were tucked behind him and he nodded solemnly.

"Good. I need to understand the movement of the forest creatures. Where are they going and why."

"You think Nici is controlling them too?" Oscar asked.

"I don't know, but it has to be linked somehow." I didn't believe in coincidences.

I turned to Mason and laid a hand on his arm to bring him back from whatever far-away place he'd gone. "You have the hardest job. You and Oscar. Find out how far Nici's thralls have penetrated Hub."

Mason nodded. "I was thinking the same thing." The thralls were inside the ward. And each one of them was expected to bring someone in front of the shar-lil. How long before one of those new recruits was a Hub official or even a minister?

"Keep it discreet for now," I said. "We don't know how far this opji… infection has spread."

"Oscar, I want you to stay in touch with Avie too. If she figures out what the shar-lil is, we'll need a way to destroy it."

Oscar nodded. He was scrolling through his widget, already distracted by the problem at hand.

"I'd like to know more about that forest fire," Oscar said.

"Me too." I rubbed the back of my neck. We were spreading ourselves too thin. This was a monumental job and we were too few.

"I'll see what I can find out," Mason said. "Hub has to have some idea of how far it has spread."

"What about us?" Angus asked. He was captain of the Guardians now, but he still took orders from Mason.

"Stay close to home. We don't know where the opji are, but they're close."

That reminded me. "Errol, can you redo the wards around the house?"

"Ghhtbm." *Yes.*

I turned to Raven. "Go with him. Take Princess but keep her close, okay? Whatever is stirring up the animals might affect her too."

Raven nodded solemnly. He seemed pleased to have his own job. And All-father help me, I might be a bad parent, but we needed all hands right now.

Again, silence dropped over the room like a wet blanket.

I wasn't sure how I ended up in charge. I certainly didn't want the job, but my family, my friends, they all watched me now, waiting for our next move.

The door opened and Berto came in. His wings were outstretched, like he'd just landed on the doorstep. His duck-billed face was stern as he marched to the table.

"So what's next?" Angus asked.

"Nothing. At least not until we find out where the opji are hiding," I said, eyeing the new arrival.

"I can help with that." Berto ruffled his feathers into place. "We found an opji camp."

C H A P T E R

24

vie handed out charms to everyone. "These'll keep the opji from enthralling you. I think."

"You think?" Angus said. He held a charm in front of his nose. It dangled from a leather cord.

"Well, I've never made them especially for opji, but they work against mind-magic."

"Good enough." Angus tucked the charm into the brambles of his beard. Everyone was leaving. Oscar to start poking into parliament officials, looking for Nici thralls, Cricket to track the animals, and Avie to search her databases and contacts for anything related to the shar-lil.

She handed me a charm. It was silver, tooth-shaped, and wrapped in some kind of copper vine.

"I made this one special for you." She smiled and tucked the charm into one of my braids.

"Thanks. Hey, would you drive Emil home?"

"Sure," she said at the same time as Emil blurted, "No way. I'm coming with you.

"You're not," I said.

"I can fight the opji as well as anyone! Better even." His eyes were glassy and his voice had a maniacal edge.

"Your skills aren't in question. And you know it."

I laid a hand on his arm, but he yanked it away. I sighed.

"You're not going, and that's final."

A muscle twitched in Emil's cheek, but other than that, he seemed unimpressed by my mom voice.

"You can't keep me out of this fight forever."

"No, but I can keep you out of it until your head is on straight. Go home and cool off." It would take time to get over losing Gabe. Until he got his emotions under control, he was a liability. I didn't need Emil charging into the opji camp in a fury and giving our position away.

Emil was unmoving, until Avie tugged on his sleeve. "Come on. You can help me research that artifact. And if you don't mind chicken nuggets and fries, I'll even feed you."

I smiled, thinking of Emil surrounded by Avie's horde of screaming children. That should take his mind off things.

I walked them to the door. Avie pulled me aside and whispered, "You'll be careful?"

I made an X over my chest with my finger. "Cross my heart. This is a scouting expedition only. Hub will take care of the opji. We just have to point them in the right direction."

She nodded and pulled me into a brief hug. "Be safe." She turned away, but not before I saw the tears in her eyes.

It was just worry, I thought. Avie had some prescience, but her predictions usually came in the form of bizarre visions, spoken through her lips but in another voice. She rarely remembered having these visions, and surely, if she had some concrete knowledge of the future, she'd tell me. Surely.

I stood on the front porch to watch my team drive off, feeling a chill in my blood that had nothing to do with the March wind. I glanced at the sky. It was overcast, but no snow thankfully. The air smelled damp, with just the faint whiff of smoke.

I went inside to kit up.

I didn't relish the idea of trekking through the Inbetween at night, but waiting until morning wasn't an option. The opji would likely be on the move in the dark. We had to track them and let Hub know where to find them. By morning, the opji could be long gone.

I dressed in layers for warmth and buckled on weapons. I snuck into Holly's room to say goodnight, but she was already asleep, sprawled across Gita's chest, while the old banshee rocked her in their favorite chair. I kissed the sweet-smelling blond curls without waking her. Gita's sharp eyes took in my travel clothes and sword harness. She nodded once. I knew my baby would be safe until I returned. That didn't make leaving her any easier. It never did.

I met the others outside. Angus was talking to Jake, the younger Guardian who'd recently joined the team. When he saw me, he shooed Jake away.

"The boy's going to walk the perimeter of the ward all night." Angus spoke around a wooden stick that he was chewing. "To be honest, he's not the sharpest bulb in the drawer, so I'd better stay and supervise."

I nodded. "Good idea." We didn't need him to track the opji.

Angus spat out the stick and rubbed a hand over that hollow place in his chest.

"We'll hold down the hatches. Don't you worry, lass." Angus saw Mason coming and turned his back on him. "You just keep an eye on the bossman, got it?" Those last words were pitched for my ears alone. I nodded and felt a tightness in my chest. I wasn't the only one worried about Mason.

"Are you ready?" Mason asked. His eyes were lost in shadow, but I could read the tension in his shoulders.

"I'm ready. Are we driving?"

"Only part way. We'll have to walk the rest, so they don't hear us coming. Berto's already taken Raol to the rendezvous point."

Mason had a few last instructions for Angus. I waited for him in the van. Finally, he got in the driver side and flashed me a sharp grin.

"Just like old times, eh? The two of us on the road, fighting *les méchants*."

I tried to give him a smile. He grabbed my hand and squeezed. "It'll be okay. We always win, don't we. You and me. Together."

I nodded, furious at myself for the heat in my eyes. He wiped a tear that leaked down my cheek. "Hey, none of that. You're not pregnant again, are you?"

I punched him on the arm. "Not funny. And no, I'm not pregnant. I just can't help feeling like this is the big one, you know?"

"The big one?"

"Yeah, the fight we've been gearing up for. Like the opji have been planning this for years. We've been blind to their scheming, and now it may be too late."

"It's never too late. The ward still stands, just as it has for fifty years. That won't change. We'll make sure it doesn't change."

I took a deep breath, swallowing down my unease. We could do this. We could hunt vampires in the dark of night, get the information to Hub and be home in time for breakfast.

"Easy peasy." I nodded firmly.

The rest of the drive went by in silence. We parked at the ramp to the old north highway. Hub didn't maintain this route. It wasn't of strategic importance since most of the ward's farming industry fell far south of here. And westward travelers either went by riverboat along the St. Lawrence or they used the better maintained southern highway. Only a few isolated homesteads lay along the north road. Past those it ran into the Ottawa Valley and Vioska, the opji ward.

Mason pulled the van to a stop on the crumbling shoulder. I stared at the western horizon for a moment. It was lit up like the last dregs of a sunset. But that couldn't be right. The sun had set hours ago.

Fire. The forest was burning somewhere to the west. It was like staring into the first rays of the apocalypse.

I reached for the door handle. A dark figure leaped from the back seat. I let out an "oof!" as Grim landed in my lap, all twelve kilos of him.

"What the hell are you doing here?" I gasped.

His tail swished under my chin.

"Waiting for you to open the door."

His feet were digging into my thighs as he pranced around, trying to get his balance. I yanked the door handle and he leapt into the night. There was no use telling him to stay in the car. The grimalkin didn't take orders from me.

"What's furball doing here?" Mason growled.

"I don't know, but I suspect we'll find out."

"I don't like it. He's been acting odd."

"How so?"

"Just odd. Every time I turn around he's there. Watching me."

I chewed my lip considering this. Should I tell Mason that we—all his family—were worried about him? No. That would only make him more edgy. In truth, I was glad for Grim's backup.

"It's a cat thing," I said. "You can never know what they're thinking."

Berto and Raol waited for us, half hidden in the trees beside the road. Rain began to fall in a light mist. It did nothing to wash away the stench of smoke in the air.

The opji have incredible hearing and would hear the engine coming, so we left the van and walked about three kilometers along the cracked and overgrown road. After only a few minutes, the damp settled over us. I pulled the brim of my hat low and my collar up.

Nearly an hour later, Berto ushered us off the road and our pace slowed. We walked through the dense trees with no flashlights or gleams. The ground was mush. The trees were still bare of leaves, but without a moon or stars to guide us, the route was dark enough that I tripped on roots and stumbled into Mason's back more than once.

Berto, with his gargoyle night vision, led the way. Raol followed behind me. He was here only in case we lost the opji trail, and I meant to keep him away from any fighting. Grim slunk through shadows on a path of his own choosing.

Our passing was near silent on the wet, winter leaf litter. Most of the snow had melted, and we avoided the few mounds of ice that still dotted the path. We came to a clearing that seemed like any of the others we'd passed through, but Berto stopped. He used hand signals to communicate with Mason, telling us to split up and circle. Mason and I went one way, Berto and Raol, the other. Grim had disappeared.

The smell of smoke was stronger here. Mason knelt and scooped away mud that someone had used to smother a fire ring. He touched the blackened logs. "Still warm."

Someone had camped here recently. We continued around the perimeter and found more evidence. Trees had been cut down. For what purpose, I couldn't tell. To make a shelter? It seemed plausible, but the wood was chopped up as if someone had taken out their anger with a machete. Chunks of wood pulp littered the ground. Dozens of trees had been felled and discarded.

And then we found the carcasses. A pile of bodies lay at the far end of the camp—deer, rabbits, squirrels, coy-bears and a couple of wood trolls. The clouds chose that moment to part, and the full rising moon lit up the scene of an unimaginable slaughter.

So far from their feeding pens, the opji had turned to the forest creatures to feed their bloodlust. And like the trees, the sheer amount of death seemed wanton. Bodies were torn to pieces with much of the blood wasted. I understood that the opji needed blood to live, but this went well beyond survival. This was killing for the joy of it.

The stench of death was overpowering. I backed away and held my bandanna over my nose. It did little to block the smell.

"I'm no expert," I said, "but I'd guess that was enough to feed a whole lot of opji."

Berto joined us. He seemed unaffected by the gruesome scene. "We found another pile over there." He pointed to the other end of camp. "Probably for their wojaks."

Mason nodded grimly. "They don't seem too worried about hiding their tracks."

"Or they left in a hurry," I said.

"They've been gone about an hour," Raol said. "I picked up their trail. It shouldn't be too hard to follow."

A flicker of light caught the corner of my eye and I whirled to see the mountain devil burst into flames. It stood on two gangly legs like a stork, flapping its fiery wings.

Terra was watching. Not surprisingly, I found no comfort in that.

"I'm doing your bidding, already!" I hissed under my breath. "I'll get the damned shar-lil. Now leave me alone."

The devil launched into the air with one last raucous cry and flew over the trees, its flaming tail like a comet.

"What was that?" Mason asked.

"Mountain devil." I hunched deeper into my damp jacket. "It's a whole thing with Terra. The devil watches me, she watches the devil."

"I don't know how I feel about all this bonding you have going on with gods. It's not healthy."

"I'll tell Terra next time I see her."

Of course, the god would care little for my feelings. I was just a tool to her, a pointy stick to jab her enemies with.

Raol was already leading the others across the clearing to pick up the opji's trail. I motioned for us to follow, but Mason jerked backward.

"Stop." His voice rang out like a stone hitting concrete. His face twisted in an expression of pain meeting anger. Raol and Berto paused at the edge of the clearing, looking wary.

Then I keened it too. A miasma of death, strong enough to overpower the piles of corpses left in the camp.

The opji were here.

ojaks rushed into the clearing. The once-human creatures loped across the frozen ground with an ape-like gait. In seconds, we were overcome. A wojak bounded over the backs of its brothers and flew at me. Moonlight glistened on fangs as I fumbled for my hunting knife. No time to unharness the sword on my back.

Bony, near skinless fingers dug into my shoulders. The desiccated face loomed over me, all eyes and teeth. I plunged my blade into its gut and wrenched upward until I hit bone. Animated by undead magic, the wojak didn't even flinch. Its grip tightened, fingers clawing at my neck. I thrust one hand between us, pressing on its wasted chest. My shaking hand was the only thing keeping fangs from my throat, and it was losing the battle.

I couldn't shove the vamp away. And I couldn't let go.

With my free hand, I yanked the blade from its wasted guts and swung my arm in a wide arc, stabbing downward this time.

The blade glanced off skull bone. I stabbed again and found the leathery flesh of its neck. The wojak shrieked. I answered with a gurgling cry of rage. My blade dug deep. I sawed at sinew and bone until its head snapped sideways. The wojak crumpled to the ground with my knife stuck deep in its spine.

I fell backward, gasping for air as adrenaline spiked. Another wojak climbed over the body of its fallen brother and snarled, legs tensed to leap. I scrambled backward, ripped the harness off my shoulder and released my sword. The blade let out a high, enthusiastic note.

I beheaded the snarling wojak with one swift blow. My sword didn't get hung up on little things like bone. I sliced at the next wojak. A third leaped on my back. I grabbed its arm and locked it, then flipped us both. The wojak thudded to the frozen ground. I rose on one knee and stabbed through its dead heart, then turned and swiped the legs out from under another.

In minutes, I cleared a small space around me. Wojaks lay lifeless at my feet, nothing more than piles of skin and bone. Later, I would remember they had once been people. Now, I sucked in breath with ragged heaves, leaned heavily on my sword, and surveyed the ongoing fight.

Berto was surrounded. With his outstretched wings, the Guardian protected Raol against three wojaks. An opji stood nearby, patiently waiting for the inevitable outcome.

The gargoyle wielded a blade better than anyone I knew. His duck-billed face might look comical to some, but I saw only strength and ferocity as he cut and slashed, keeping the slavering wojaks at bay. They were pushing him back though, step by step, toward the tree line.

Then a second opji leaped from a tree and landed on Raol. The ratatosk let out a shriek.

"No!" The word burst from me. The opji turned, saw me standing alone and grinned. He prowled forward.

I stepped back, nearly tripping over a dead wojak. Where were the others? I couldn't see Grim. I hoped he'd done the smart thing and fled. Mason was fighting a core of wojaks at the other end of the clearing. The thunk of his stone arm echoed as he took down one undead after another.

It wouldn't be enough. He couldn't kill them fast enough to stop the opji master. I knew what was coming and I dreaded it more than an opji bite. Mason would give in. He'd break his promise to me and use his demon magic.

The opji was only a few feet away now. Tall, lean, black-haired with gaunt features, he looked like he'd be more at home in a Gothic castle than in the wilds.

The pile of bodies suggested a crew of opji. Where were the others? I glanced around, but saw only more wojaks. Was this opji a guard, left behind to secure their camp?

"Drop your sword, woman." His voice was low, but it rang in my head. He was trying to enthrall me.

Memories of my last lone encounter with an opji shuddered through me.

The pain of the bite. The overwhelming feeling of helplessness. And later, the confusion as his venom took hold.

I wouldn't let that happen again. I pulled on the magic of my sword and boosted my wards.

The opji grinned. He could probably feel my efforts to withstand his thrall. He didn't seem concerned. He glanced up. I followed his gaze and found only open sky. When I looked back he was standing right in front of me.

"Made you look." The stench of his breath wafted over me. He grabbed my sword arm. His fingers dug into the flesh above my elbow and my hand went numb. The blade fell to the ground. The opji wrenched my head sideways.

"Such a pretty neck." He licked the small scar from my first vamp encounter. "Too bad it's not a virgin. Someone has tasted you."

His eyes were vast pools of shadow, drawing me in to drown in their depths. My thoughts buzzed in darkness. I keened a small burst of magic from Avie's charm, then it fell silent. It hadn't stood up to the opji magic and neither could I.

I couldn't move. Couldn't breathe. And I wanted the bite. Wanted it so badly, I arched my back, offering my throat to his fangs.

Distantly, I heard something roar. A lion or a bear. A dragon?

The opji's head exploded. One moment I was waiting for the sting of his fangs. The next I was gaping at the stump of his neck and licking blood off my lips.

Mason loomed up behind the opji as his body toppled to the ground.

Only it wasn't Mason.

Fury had claimed him. He opened his mouth and let out a primal roar. His stone fist pounded at the night sky. He turned and focused his rage on the wojaks still battling with Berto. The Guardian was down on one knee, nearly overcome. I couldn't see Raol.

More heads exploded. Wojaks fell. Their bodies collapsed like tattered and bloody rags.

No one moved.

And still Mason raged. His voice filled the night sky. He screamed as if all the demons of hell were singing through him. The sound battered at my personal wards. It raked along my nerves like it wanted to tear me inside out.

"Mason stop!" My cry was a pathetic gasp against his, but he heard me. As the echo of his scream died out, he turned. His chest heaved. His eyes had gone black. Spittle foamed on his lips and a growl rumbled from his throat. His magic keened with pure hatred.

Mason had left the building.

A whimper escaped my lips before I could shut it down.

"Stop now." My voice cracked like brittle glass. "It's over. You stopped them."

The demon that had been my husband, my lover and my friend lowered his head and watched me the way a panther watches its prey.

"Mason, don't…it's me…you have to stop now. You kept us safe, and now it's time to let go."

I was babbling. My words were broken up by hiccuping sobs. Slowly, Mason advanced.

"Let it go, baby. Just let it go." I pleaded. Tears blurred the sight of my husband looming over me, close enough that I could feel the heat coming off him, his once handsome face now corrupted by demon magic into a mask of rage.

"Don't…"

His hands strangled off my protest. They closed around my throat and squeezed. The world shrank to his hate-filled eyes. The sound of my own desperate heart clouded my ears. The edges of my vision dimmed as if I looked through a vignetted lens.

Pain muddled with fear and my only thoughts were for Holly. How could Gita protect her from her own father?

I clawed against his grip on my throat, but my fingers were cold and clumsy. Useless.

My world went black.

And then I hit the ground. The impact slapped air back into my lungs. I gulped and gasped through my bruised throat, flopping around like a dying fish until feeling returned to my limbs.

I sat up. My chest heaved. My throat was raw. But my eyes were working just fine, and I saw the night jaguar sitting on Mason's chest. Mason thrashed, but the big cat easily held him down. The night jaguar leaned in and sucked the breath from Mason's lungs. Mason's eyes went wide. The jaguar continued to pull his breath as if he siphoned Mason's soul.

I thought of the old wives' tales about cats taking the breath from babes in their cribs. It couldn't be more horrifying.

Mason's eyes rolled back in his head, and he went limp. The night jaguar sat back and released his breath into the sky.

I keened a rush of magic, as swift and sure as a gust of hurricane wind. The night dimmed for a moment and then I was staring at the full crystal moon.

When I turned back to Mason, the night jaguar was gone. Grim sat on Mason's chest, licking a paw.

C H A P T E R

26

My brain was frozen. I couldn't feel my limbs. I took a step and stumbled over the opji corpse. I fell to one knee, and my fingers sank into still-warm flesh. My stomach lurched. I scrambled backward on my butt, soaking my jeans in muddy slush.

"Wh…what did you do?" My tongue felt thick in my mouth.

Grim hopped off Mason's chest. "I did what was necessary. Demons breed on fear. And the only thing he truly fears," he flicked his ears toward Mason, "is losing you."

I stood on shaking legs and went to Mason. He was breathing. His face was as pale as snow, but his magic had calmed. The demon was still there, simmering below the surface, but it had been caged once more.

I turned to Grim who was still meticulously washing his feet. "So you think this is my fault?"

"There is no fault here. But twice he has nearly been lost to the darkness because he feared for your life. This time I was able to subdue him, but the demon is getting stronger. I may not be able to dominate it again."

I dug my fingers into my temples and rubbed hard. The clearing was littered with corpses. The forest was eerily still, as if every creature of the night had stopped to watch the drama unfold. Then I spotted movement.

Berto lumbered to his feet. He shook himself and bent to pick up Raol.

"You okay?" I called out.

"He's bitten," Berto said. Raol lay in his arms, all bloody tufts of fur and torn riding leathers.

"Can you fly him home?" Nori would be able to deal with the effects of the vamp venom.

Berto shook his head and shrugged one shoulder. "Can't. Wing's been damaged."

I fished my widget out of my pocket. No signal. We were too far from the ward.

Dear All-father, couldn't you cut me some slack, just this once?

My head was starting to pound as adrenaline faded. There was no helping it. I'd have to leave Mason and Raol, hike back for the van, and hope for a signal. No way we could carry them out without help.

"Stay here," I said to Berto. "I'll be back as soon as I can."

The Guardian nodded and hunkered down beside Mason with Raol still in his arms.

I ignored the various aches of small wounds, and I ran.

CATS AREN'T KNOWN FOR their long distance stamina. They are more the sprint-and-kill type, but Grim kept pace with me as I jogged. When we reached the old highway, my widget got a spotty signal. I managed to put a call into Angus and relay our coordinates before the signal dropped. By the time we reached the van, two Guardians were waiting for us.

Angus whistled when he saw me. "Well don't you look like a bag of ass the cat dragged in." He grinned at Grim. "No offense, of course." Grim ignored him. He didn't even seem winded. I opened the van. He hopped into the passenger seat and dug into his toes to clean out stones and dirt he'd picked up from our run.

I sent Angus and Jake back to the clearing for the others and drove down the highway until I spotted them coming out of the woods.

Jake had been sculpted with the traditional grotesque features of the gargoyles that adorned the Gothic churches of old Paris. But he was bigger than any gargoyle I'd ever seen. Taller than Berto and broader across the shoulders than Angus. Raol looked like a child's toy cradled in his massive arms. Angus carried Mason over his shoulder like a sack of potatoes, and Berto limped along behind them.

It was nearly dawn when we loaded the wounded into the back of the van. There wasn't room for everyone, and Berto opted to spend the day in the forest. Once he turned to stone, his injuries would heal. Jake stayed with him to guard against any predators dumb or desperate enough to take on a wounded gargoyle. Angus jumped into the back seat with Mason and Raol.

I drove home with white knuckles and gritted teeth.

We snuck inside, hoping not to wake the kids, and laid the wounded on the couches in the living room.

There was no sneaking in on Dutch though. He was already coming down the stairs dressed in flannel sleep pants and nothing else.

Raol thrashed, incoherent with pain. The hallucinations brought on by opji venom had already started. He'd also lost a lot of blood and his right arm was clearly broken.

"Put him in the spare room," I said to Dutch, "and keep him there. He'll try to get up. Hold him down if you have to."

Dutch scooped up Raol and carried him from the room.

Angus glanced at the window. The sky was already turning gray with morning. "I'll wake the wee fox, eh? Before I head off to bed?"

"Yes, please."

I hoped Nori could come. Last I'd heard, Soolea was in labor. They could still be at it.

I smoothed Mason's damp hair from his forehead. If I didn't know better, I'd say he'd gone gargoyle again. His face was as pale as alabaster but warm to the touch—too warm.

Just as the sun lit the windows, Nori burst through the door.

"How's Soolea?" I asked.

"False contractions."

Nori was already focused on Mason. She ripped open his shirt and laid her hands on his bare chest. With eyes closed, her lips trembled like she was chanting something too low for me to hear.

She raised her head. Her eyes were inscrutable. "There's nothing I can do for him." My heart stuttered in my chest. She saw my stricken look and said, "I mean that he only needs rest. There's nothing for me to heal. He'll wake up when he's ready."

"Is this like…like with Jacoby. Is he gone somewhere?"

Nori smiled and took my hand. It was such a warm gesture from the normally aloof kitsune that my worry-o-meter immediately went into overdrive.

"No, he's not gone. He just burned himself out and needs time to replenish his magic."

"But he'll wake up, right?"

Nori bit her lip. "He will. He always comes back to you, doesn't he?"

I nodded. I wanted to believe her, but he looked so pale…so dead. I had to stare at his chest to reassure myself that it rose and fell in a slow but steady rhythm.

"I'll do some research to see if there is anything else I can do, but I think we just have to be patient."

I nodded numbly, and Nori left to take care of Raol.

I sat watching Mason. His breathing was so shallow, I laid my hand on his chest to feel the slow beat of his heart.

A few minutes later, Dutch returned and we moved Mason to our room.

I stripped off his filthy, torn and bloody clothes and washed him with a warm cloth. Then I undressed and scooted under the covers. His skin was hot but without the clamminess of fever. I thought I would lie there listening to his heart until he woke, but exhaustion tossed me into sleep as soon as I closed my eyes.

And I dreamed of a mountain devil chasing me through the forest.

CHAPTER

27

Mason slept for a week. Seven days during which I would slip away from my chores, my work, and from fronting a brave face for my family to sit by our bed and watch the slow rise and fall of his chest.

At night, I lay in bed beside him with my head on his chest, flicking through the news channels for any story about the opji invasion. Nothing.

I'd reported our encounter to Captain Lowe and she assured me she would handle it. I had to trust in the system, not something I excelled at.

Most nights, I would pace my room and stop at the window to stare at the dense forest, wondering how close the opji were and if they'd attack our homestead like they had the Hewitt's.

I prayed to the All-father, even though he'd never listened to my requests before. I didn't pray to Terra. Her watchdog chased me through my dreams whenever I managed a few minutes of sleep. That didn't leave me with any warm and fuzzy feelings for the god.

I canceled all pest control jobs for the foreseeable future. Holly was happy to have me home, Raven, not so much. Without Mason or I going into the city, he missed school. Other than the bullies, Raven normally enjoyed school. Now he chafed at the restrictions I put on him. No school, no friends and without Mason to supervise, no alchemy experiments in our basement lab. He sulked and spent long hours locked in his room.

Raol healed quickly. Two days after our encounter with the opji, he was back to scouting the forest, looking for more evidence of the opji. I wanted him to rest longer. He refused but promised to check in every day.

The only saving grace about these long days of waiting was that my battle wounds healed. I didn't want Mason to wake and see the print of his hands on my neck. It would undo him. I had forgiven him immediately. In fact, there was nothing to forgive. He was not responsible for the demon's actions. But he would never believe that.

On the afternoon of day seven, I sat in the kitchen with Soolea while she nursed one-week-old John Jeremy Mahingan.

Holly was playing on the floor with a pile of blocks and her dragon scale, given to her by our friend Ollie. Her toddler fingers weren't nimble enough to make a tower, but she tried her darnedest by piling the blocks in a heap and dropping the blue scale on top like a glittering cherry. It looked a bit like an Apex tower, and I wondered where Holly had seen one of those.

A spring snow squall had blown in overnight. I watched the white-washed landscape through the windows. Winter was hanging around this year. The snow was no longer picturesque. It was muddy and damp, and everyone cooped up in the house was ready for warmer days and green grass.

We drank tea and ate Dutch's latest breakfast confections. Soolea had eyes only for her son. He was a handsome baby, with Soolea's dark hair and his father's pale complexion. His fists kneaded his mother's breast.

"He's strong, just like his father." A small smile tugged at Soolea's mouth as she watched her son. She'd named him John Jeremy for his grandfather and father.

"Can I ask, what does the name Mahingan mean? Is it a family name?"

"It means wolf. He was born under the full moon. It is a good omen."

I hoped she was right. Without a home and a father, the kid was going to need all the luck he could get.

"Have you thought about my suggestion, to stay on at the gatehouse?" I asked. The Guardians could use a care-taker, someone who was awake during the day to see to the running of the house. They were pretty low maintenance and it would be an easy job for a single mother.

Soolea shook her head. "I thank you for the offer, but I think I must return to my parents soon. I won't be a burden to you much longer."

I waved away that comment.

"You can stay as long as you need. You know that. Are your parents around here?"

"North. In the mountains. They were originally in the Ottawa Valley, but the opji pushed them east."

That seemed to be a common problem these days.

"When did they move?"

"Three years ago."

I nodded. Three years ago, Nici led the coup of the fae court, using the naive Prince Alvar as her spearhead. Montreal had come together to beat them back—humans, fae and alchemists all working together. A lot could change in three years. I wondered if those factions would still be allies today if Nici managed to finally prime her weapon and break through the ward.

I also wondered what her end game was. Did she want to dismantle the ward so her wojaks could raid the living blood-bags inside? Had the pickings in the Inbetween become so slim that they needed to resort to such measures? Or did they have other plans for the population of Montreal? The smoke on the western horizon suggested that more was going on. I wished we could get scouts into the Ottawa Valley to find out what the opji were doing. Hub had tried, but the soldiers they sent never returned.

I brought my thoughts back to the present.

"I bet your parents will be happy to have you home."

Soolea nodded but her eyes looked troubled.

"You don't think they will welcome you?"

"Oh, yes. They will. I'm just worried. I haven't heard from them in months. Jeremy and I were planning to visit after the baby was born, to introduce them to their grandson and check on them, but…" Her eyes filled with tears and she didn't finish that sentence. I got it. Every once in a while, thoughts about Mason struck me hard, and I remembered that he lay in a coma, and there was nothing I could do about it. Soolea probably relived the horror of that last day on the homestead a hundred times an hour.

Holly grew bored of the blocks. She let out a shriek and smashed her tower, then got up and toddled over to the long table in front of the bay window that looked over the patio. I'd removed most of Mason's priceless artifacts that were within a toddler's reach. The table now held only a fern and

Willow, my utterly normal gray cat, who sat staring out the window, pining for spring.

Holly grabbed at the tail that swished in front of her nose.

"Don't pull the kitty's tail," I admonished. "She doesn't like that. Gentle with the kitty."

Holly tried to pat the kitty with a fat, sticky fist. Willow wasn't impressed and jumped down to find a more secluded resting place.

"She listens at least," Soolea said with a smile. Holly now turned her attention to the fern. I keened the focus of her magic. Her face screwed up into a little pug expression. The fronds of the fern shot upward, then danced side to side.

"Gentle with the green things too, baby." I walked over to pick her up and let her get a closer look at the fern. "See it's a friend, just like the kitty."

"Fower!" Holly squirmed, trying to grab the fronds.

"Flower, yes." Sort of. I slung her onto my hip. She rubbed her eyes and I knew it would be nap time soon.

From outside, I heard shouting. Raven and the goblit twins were bored. It was too wet to play soccer and there wasn't enough snow for winter sports. Princess added her voice to the argument in the back yard. Holly started screaming "Fower! Fower! Fower!" for no apparent reason and all the houseplants twitched and rustled as if a hurricane blew through the house.

Jacoby chose that moment to burst in through the back door with his arms full of his newest hobby. Princess trailed behind him. They tramped across the kitchen floor, leaving gobs of mud in their wake.

"Kyra-lady, looks! Looks!" Jacoby hollered to be heard over the shrieking toddler. "I collects them all!" He dumped a pile of muddy rocks on the kitchen floor and beamed at me. Princess squatted and piddled on the rocks.

The All-father had truly abandoned me.

Soolea suppressed a laugh. "I think I'll go put the baby down for a sleep." She made a stealthy retreat out the front door, leaving me alone with my cabin-fevered family.

THINGS DIDN'T GET BETTER that afternoon. Holly was restless. She didn't want to nap. She wanted her daddy. She shrieked his name until her face turned red. Tears cut streaks down her cheeks and her tiny fists were balled into nuggets of rage.

I could do nothing to console her. Daddy was still lost in his demon-induced sleep.

I finally crawled into bed with her, tucked her little body against me, and she slept fitfully.

I slept too, and my dreams were full of Terra.

"Find it! Find it!" Her voice cawed from the beak of the mountain devil, but it was unmistakably Terra's. Everywhere I turned in my dreams, she was there, and I found myself tossing in the bed as restless as Holly.

I finally rose, leaving her to sleep and went to check on Mason. He lay like a stone effigy in our bed. Not even his eyelids twitched. I smoothed back his hair. His beard grew slowly while he slept, but his chin was rough with stubble. It would be time to shave him again soon. I kissed his forehead and went into the kitchen where Dutch was preparing dinner.

Without asking, he poured coffee from the urn and handed it to me.

"Thanks."

He nodded and went back to chopping carrots. Dutch didn't talk much and today I found that soothing. With coffee rations still in place, it was hard to overdo it on the caffeine, but I felt like I'd drunk a potful. My legs were restless. My hands needed work, and my stomach ached with an emptiness that had nothing to do with hunger.

I decided to check in with everyone in my contact list. I texted Nori, asking her if she had any new leads on Mason's condition. She answered with a curt, "No." That was fair. I asked that question twice a day, as if I wouldn't be the first person she'd tell if she found something new.

Emil answered my call with a sleepy, "Hello?"

"Hey, just checking in." He grumbled something about everything being fine and hung up. I needed to give him some space. That last encounter with Gabe had really thrown him.

Next I dialed Oscar.

"What?" He sounded frazzled.

"Sorry. I was just wondering if you had any news from Hub."

"I told you I'd let you know as soon as I did."

Oscar was one of the few people who knew the truth about Mason's condition. He'd made excuses to the other ministers, telling them that Mason had gone on a last minute trip to Manhattan to tour the new industrial park that was being built beside the train station. Our contact in Manhattan, Kester Owens, was backing us up. But if Mason didn't wake up soon, we'd have to tell the Parliament the truth, or at least part of the truth.

"I shouldn't disturb you," I said. "I just wanted..." What did I want? Reassurance that everything was going to be fine? A kind word to know that I still had allies? A simple connection to the outside world?

Oscar must have heard the desperation in my silence.

"Geez, Kyra. I'm sorry. I didn't mean to be so gruff. I've just got a lot on my plate right now. But I'm sure you do too. I'll come over as soon as I can and we can discuss...things."

I nodded, even though he couldn't see me. By "things," Oscar meant we'd discuss what to do if Mason didn't recover. Nori was convinced that he'd wake up any day now. I didn't want to blow up his career by panicking too soon, but time was running out.

"I do have one bit of news," Oscar said. "Hold on. Let me find some privacy in this gods-forsaken office." I waited. A moment later, Oscar came back on the line.

"I found some info on your Nici friend," he said. I heard the sounds of traffic behind him. "She's pretty high up in the Vioska tribe. My source wasn't clear, but she's either Ichovidar's sister or his mate."

"Ichovidar?" I'd heard that name before. I wracked my brain to remember where. It had been during the briefings after the first vampire incursion. "He's the opji king, isn't he?"

"King, leader, chief. We're not sure what to call him, but yeah, he's in charge."

Interesting.

"And Kyra, Hub is aware of the opji raids. So don't hesitate to call them if there's a problem."

"Okay." That made me feel better. I hadn't heard a peep from Captain Lowe. "How're things going at the lab?"

Oscar hummed in that way he did when he was puzzling out a particularly difficult problem.

"I've figured out what Bauch was feeding the knucklebones, but they no longer seem to be responding to it. Still, it's a start."

I'd almost forgotten about the knucklebone infestation with all the opji problems.

"I'm sure you'll figure it out," I said. Oscar liked a good conundrum.

He grunted, then said, "Gotta go. Talk soon."

I hung up feeling even more agitated than I had before.

My widget buzzed with an incoming message from Avie.

Tracked down that info you wanted. A thrall can only be broken upon death of the master.

I noted that she omitted all references to the opji and the godlings. It was good news though. That meant we could free Gabe and the others by killing Nici.

I typed back.

Any info about coconuts?

Like Avie, I kept my references to the shar-lil vague. I didn't think my messages were being spied on, but an abundance of caution couldn't hurt.

None. Aunt Cece looking into it.

I texted back a quick thanks and put the widget away. I had no other contacts to bother, but my feeling of restlessness hadn't gone away. I sat at the kitchen table sipping my lukewarm coffee. The sound of my fingers drumming on the table was unnaturally loud in the quiet house. It felt like the calm before the storm, only I had no idea what shape the storm would take. I needed information, and I had no way to get it.

At times like these, I headed for the barn and some critter therapy.

28

'd been thinking of creating an enclosure off the side of the barn, a screened-in play area where some of the smaller critters could get fresh air. The ground had finally thawed, and I decided to stake out my new structure and draw up some plans.

I dressed for the cold—puffy jacket, toque, gloves, boots—and hurried across the mucky yard. The pressure had dropped and the sky felt like a dark pillow hovering overhead, ready to smother.

When I entered the barn, all thoughts of manual labor left me. It smelled so good, like fresh hay and animal musk. Yes, I'm one of those weirdos who even likes the smell of manure.

The goblins had already been and gone, leaving the cages cleaned and stocked and the floors swept. Gita poked her head from the old tack room where she nested.

"Just me." I gave her a little wave.

"Any news?" She sniffed, but that did nothing to stop the tears that continually leaked down her cheeks.

"He's still sleeping. I'll tell you as soon as he wakes."

Gita's frown deepened the lines around her mouth. She nodded and went back to her latest paperback romance.

It was the drowsy part of the afternoon, when the daytime creatures were full and content and the nocturnal creatures not yet awake.

I trailed my fingers in Hunter's tank. The little kraken wrapped a tentacle around my thumb and crawled up my arm until I wore him like a gelatinous bracelet. I knew he could stay out of the water for at least an hour, so he made the rounds with me as I peered into cage after cage.

Someone had given Kur a fresh bowl of ice, and he lay sprawled across it like a tiny, drunken yeti. Bijou, my multi-hued snail, had outgrown her original habitat, and I'd built her a new one last fall. She was now the size of a soccer ball. Part of me worried she'd outgrow the barn altogether one day.

I stuck my nose in the terrarium that housed the vampire slugs. Our recent hatchlings were getting big too. I scratched the troll bats under their furry chins. They like that. Hunter batted a tentacle at their fluttery wings.

Next, I scooped up Sweet Pea and Niblet and sat on the floor in a pile of clean straw to let the lizard-mice zoom up and down my legs. They seemed happy to see me. Hunter did his silly walk down to my knee and Sweet Pea nuzzled him with his nose.

I leaned my back against the horse stall. Gallivant nuzzled my hair before he went back to chomping hay.

This was nice. I needed this. The easy quiet, my sleepy critters, and time away from worrying about problems I couldn't solve. I could almost forget that my husband was in a coma and that an opji had my friend in a thrall.

Almost.

I gazed at my rescues, thankful that they didn't seem affected by the restlessness infecting the rest of the forest creatures.

That brought me back to Nici and her damned shar-lil again. It had to be the artifact disturbing the forest creatures. That would explain why I'd had to dose Princess with some pretty strong power words to keep her close when we rode to the Hewitt's. But then why hadn't Gallivant been affected? And Raol? He was more squirrel than man.

A tiny connection was sprouting in my mind. It had something to do with the level of sentience. The song of the shar-lil could only be heard by animals. Or those blessed with the keening.

So why weren't my rescues affected?

I could only surmise that our house ward protected them. Errol tuned it to keep out hostile magic. If I let the squamice loose outside the ward, would they run off too? Not something I wanted to chance.

Niblet ran up my arm, his claws scrabbling on my jacket. I cupped him in the palm of my hand and held him to my nose. His little rodent eyes peered up at me, while his lizard tail wrapped around my wrist for stability. He still wore the collar that Gabe had fashioned for him. The collar that could hold a small camera.

Or a tracking device. By the One-eyed Father. I had a way to find Nici.

I stood up and put the squamice back in their cage before dropping Hunter into his tank.

"Sorry, buddy. I've got work to do."

The kraken sank to the bottom and pressed his face against the glass, watching me as I pulled crates of supplies from the storage closet, until I found the one with the squamice gear.

Cables and electronics were jumbled in the crate. I sighed. Electronics weren't my strong suit. Not for the first time that week, I wished for Gabe's help. He'd have this all sorted in no time. But of course, Gabe wouldn't save me from my ineptitude this time. It was my turn to save him.

I finally found the tracking transmitters. They were powered by a tiny chip not unlike the Apex stones, so I had no need to recharge them. Eventually, I matched the cable to the hand-held tracker. Next came a frustrating ten minutes of struggling to attach the transmitters to Sweet Pea and Niblet's collars while they squirmed and tried to run away. All the while, I eyed the day outside the one barn window. It was hard to tell how much daylight I had left with the overcast sky, but it wasn't much.

When the boys were all harnessed, I scooped them under one arm and dumped them into a small animal carrier. I draped the strap with the tracking device around my neck. Then I tacked up Gallivant. He wasn't happy about leaving his pile of hay. He stamped and tossed his head, but I ignored his objections and strapped my sword across the back of the saddle. Finally, I grabbed the go-bag I kept in the barn, and banged on Gita's door.

"Can you check on Holly? She'll be awake soon. I've got an errand to run."

"Of course." She showed me her widget. I'd downloaded the baby monitor app onto it and she already had it open to show my sleeping angel. Nice to know Gita used the widget for something other than a flashlight.

"Thanks." I waved goodbye.

Outside the sun was slanting toward the west. I had about five hours of sunlight left.

I pulled Gallivant to the edge of the yard with the critter carrier banging against my leg. Errol's ward was strong, and I keened a tingle through my body as I stepped over it.

The squamice immediately started to thrash in their carrier.

"Okay, guys. Hang on." I pinched the latch to open the carrier door and the squamice shot out. They immediately disappeared into the forest. Two steady pings appeared on the tracking device. They were heading northeast and fast.

Now, I would find Nici. And maybe the shar-lil too. And maybe I would shut up the annoying god in my dreams.

29

Running headlong into the Inbetween with no backup wasn't my most brilliant plan. If Mason were in charge, he would have never done it. My style of leadership was less "delegate" and more "do it all on my own so no one else gets hurt."

At least I'd had the presence of mind to go at it on horseback, because those squamice could run. It was getting easier to sync my magic with Gallivant's. After only a minute or two of his prancing and pawing, my magic settled over him and our bond clicked into place. For the first time, I noticed another perk of that bond. Not only was I attuned to my magnificent steed, but I cued into his senses. I could hear every crackle of twig in the forest. Even my keening sharpened. And the song of the shar-lil that I'd sensed momentarily in the cottage seemed to fill the forest.

Wow. I thought my keening was good. Gallivant's was off the charts. And yet, he didn't seem drawn to the shar-lil's song. He was aware of it, sure, but more as a curiosity than an obsession.

With no prodding from me, he followed the squamice at a fast jog.

I held the reins with one hand and the tracking device in the other. Normally, the squamice ran like drunken toddlers, scurrying left and right, back and forth, wherever their noses took them. Now the two blips on the screen headed steadily northwest along the shore of the Ottaway River, with no rodent-like detours. If that wasn't the effect of a thrall, I'd eat my sword.

A new thought occurred to me. Vioska lay another hundred kilometers along that river.

I clearly hadn't thought this through. What if the squamice were headed all the way to the opji ward? My go-bag had enough food for a day, but I didn't want to spend a night alone in the Inbetween.

The collars that Gabe had fashioned for the squamice included a tiny shock device that would temporarily paralyze them. It was for emergencies only, like if they were about to run into a nest of pythons. Gabe insisted it was perfectly safe and only stunned the little guys, and we'd never had to use it, until now. I couldn't leave them alone in the Inbetween.

Critter wrangler rule number nineteen stated, if you love them, set them free. The second part of that rule was: if they return to you, you'll be forever cleaning up after them. But what was happening to the squamice right now wasn't freedom. It was enthrallment.

I'd set them up as bait. It was my responsibility to make sure they got home safely. I decided to let them run for an hour. If we hadn't found the shar-lil (and hopefully Nici) by then, I'd zap them.

Gallivant slowed to a walk when the squamice moved deeper into the forest. The tracker screen flashed steadily. They were less than a kilometer ahead. Gallivant balked at a low, brambly hedge. His wings flapped but we didn't lift off the ground. The whole flying thing was new to both of us, I reminded myself. We wasted precious minutes while I cajoled him into jumping the hedge. When we were finally on our way again, I glanced at the screen. The squamice weren't moving.

My heart lurched. That could only mean they'd found something. Or something had found them.

I kicked my heels into Gallivant's flanks. He puffed out a complaint, but picked up speed. I let him find his own route as long as we headed in the right direction. My eyes were glued to the screen. Five hundred meters and closing.

The afternoon was warm for March and I unzipped my jacket. Four hundred meters. Gallivant leapt over a fallen log. He'd picked up my anxiety and it put some pep in his step.

Three hundred meters. The squamice still weren't moving. Dear All-father, let them be all right.

Two hundred meters.

Cold snapped around me like a whip.

Gallivant stepped on a hard crust of snow. That was odd. We'd been slogging through mud until now. Gallivant whinnied as he lost his footing on ice. I jumped down before we both took a tumble.

He was puffing badly and his eyes showed white all around. I grabbed the reins and patted his neck.

"It's okay, buddy." I tried to sound calm, but he sensed my agitation and pranced on the spot.

"It's just a crisp. Nothing to worry about." My breath came in a puff of mist.

Tiny micro climates like this weren't unusual in the Inbetween. Pockets of rogue magic left over from the Flood Wars meant you could suddenly walk into a patch of wet, humid rainforest or smack into a blizzard-like wall of snow. I'd seen it before.

We'd walked into a crisp, a small zone of arctic weather. They happened in the city too, though not as often. The air wasn't just normal winter cold. This was the kind of cold that froze the snot in your nose. The kind that caused hypothermia within minutes of exposure.

I squinted into the setting sun. It looked like the crisp spread for hundreds of meters in every direction. We were smack in the middle and it. I re-zipped my jacket. I'd taken off my gloves some time ago and now my fingers were too cold to fumble in my saddlebags for them.

"Come on." My teeth chattered. I pulled on Gallivant's reins. We needed to leave the crisp immediately.

I found Sweet Pea and Niblet curled up together beside a frozen log. Even Nici's thrall couldn't overpower the absolute need for warmth.

Poor little guys. I scooped them up. They were so cold, they lay unmoving in my hands. I wrapped them in my scarf and tucked them inside my jacket.

It was time to go home. I'd have to find the opji another way. Rather than risk riding on the ice again, I pulled Gallivant forward. Steam puffed from his nostrils. My body tried to keep warm by shivering.

I could see mud ahead. Then as suddenly as we'd found it, we walked off the ice and out of the crisp. Warm, moist air hit me like a wet towel. Even though the March temperature was only just above freezing, it felt balmy after the magically induced cold.

I looked for a way around the crisp, pulling Gallivant over uneven ground. There was no path here and brambles tore at our legs.

Sweet Pea and Niblet woke up and started to fuss inside my jacket. I took a moment to punch up my personal wards, protecting them from the magic that called to them. They settled back down and I kept moving.

A ridge rose ahead of us. I looked back the way we'd come, wondering if we'd be better to turn around.

And that's when I keened them. Animals of all kinds. Hundreds. Thousands. They were close.

"Stay here," I said to Gallivant as I loosely tied his reins to a tree.

I crept up the ridge. My fingers hadn't warmed yet and they were clumsy as I tried to pull myself up on branches. My boot skidded on loose dirt and I went down on my knee, soaking my jeans.

I worried about startling some beast. All I needed was to disturb a coybear and get myself mauled.

I came upon them from behind. A ring of animals circling the ridge.

So many! A barricade of fur, feather, hoof and horn. A quivering wall as tails swished and feathers ruffled.

My first instinct was to reel in my keening and wrap my magic around me like armor, but I risked letting down my wards to taste the immense magic before me. They were unnaturally calm.

I stepped between the rumps of two deer-like creatures with short stubby antlers. One whickered. The other watched me with huge, dark eyes.

A tumble of gumberoos—creatures that look like hairless black bears— was next. I tip-toed around them. The cubs were sleeping. Mama gumberoo curled her lip as I passed, but made no move to stop me.

I stepped around hares, turtles, giant worms, sand drakes, badgers and moon frogs. Overhead, the branches were full of owls, birds and hanging bats. I even spotted an eldritch screech, a rare monkey-like creature covered in mucus instead of fur.

It was unfathomable that so many creatures had come together, that the lions could lie down peacefully next to the lambs. And still, my keening picked up nothing but low-key harmony.

It had to be the effect of the shar-lil. It was close.

I waded through the ring of animals to stand on the lip of a ridge overlooking a tiny niche of what had once been a forested valley.

I'd found the opji.

I wasn't surprised. I had been looking for them after all, and the call of the shar-lil was hard to miss. I *was* surprised by organization of the site. This wasn't a small camp like we'd raided last week. This was a near-permanent fortification. This was a base from which the opji could launch a war.

My knee-jerk desire to rush in and kill Nici faded. I needed backup. A lot of backup.

had no time for dinner, no time for anything but throwing weapons and gear into a bag. I could hear Holly crying in her room and Gita sniffling along with her between verses of Too-Ra-Loo-Ra. The mommy muscle in my gut urged me to go to her. I stopped packing and clenched my fists, taking a deep breath to calm my nerves.

Holly needed me. But if I didn't do something about the impending opji invasion…I didn't even want to think of what that would do to my child. If she was lucky, they'd kill her. But there were worse fates than death. It didn't even bear thinking about.

I shoved gear into my bag faster.

I'd already called Emil. A bit of luck was on my side and he was with Angus in the gatehouse. They'd been playing poker while Emil tried to forget his life.

A plan was forming in my head, and Emil would be vital to its success.

I filled a canteen and stuffed it into my bag along with a coil of rope. You could never have enough rope.

With one hand, I dialed Captain Lowe's private number and put it on speaker phone.

"This is Lowe. Leave a message. If this is an emergency contact Hub dispatch at…"

It seemed to take forever for the beep.

"Captain. I found the opji camp. It's a big one. They're planning an offensive. I'm going back there now. I could use backup." I left her the coordinates and rang off. I didn't know if she'd get the message in time, or if she'd believe me. Informing Hub was my duty, but I wouldn't hold out for their help.

A few minutes later, Angus stormed through the door, stamping snow off his boots. Emil followed closely behind him. His eyes looked bruised, like he hadn't slept in a week. I knew the feeling.

"Are we doing this?" he asked.

"Yes. There are weapons in the basement." I tossed him the keys to the locker and he gave me a grim smile before heading downstairs.

Dutch opened a map on the vid screen over the desk in the great room. Angus and I leaned in to mark the terrain. I pinpointed the area where I'd stumbled over the camp.

"There's a crisp here," I pointed to where I'd almost been trapped in the arctic zone.

"A crisp, you say." Angus rubbed his brambly beard. "Nothing worse than fighting while Jack Frost nips at your arse."

"Exactly. So we should come at the camp from the north or east. The crisp is less than a kilometer wide. We should be able to avoid it." I studied the map, wishing I knew more about the country north of the camp.

I told them about the gathering of animals and Angus's frown deepened.

"We should wait for the rest of the crew to come back from patrol," he said.

"There's no time. Nici is there." I jabbed the air where the camp was projected on the map. "The shar-lil is there. Tell them to meet us, but we're leaving now."

Emil returned swinging a light double-edged sword, rolling his wrist to loosen up. The anger in his eyes sparked as sharply as the blade. Another long knife hung from his belt, and I had no doubt that others were hidden in his boots and jacket.

I looked around the room. Angus, Emil and me. We weren't enough. Not to fight an entire camp of opji. A selfish part of me wished that Mason would wake up and even the odds. But the rational part of me knew that was a bad idea. Mason couldn't be allowed to face an opji army of that size. He'd be too tempted to use his magic, and Grim had warned me. There might be no coming back from that.

Where was Grim? I glanced around the big room and found him by the fire, but not curled up. He was alert, watching the vid screen.

I sat beside him. "Are you coming?" I asked. He tilted his chin in a curt nod. I felt some of my panic ease and couldn't resist the urge to stroke his back. His fur was so, so soft. He let me have 2.4 strokes before he hissed and jumped away.

Raven came down the hall from his bedroom, looking sleepy and rumpled. Had he even changed his clothes since yesterday? Gods, what a bad mother I was. I hadn't yet cracked the super-secret code to saving the world and being a parent at the same time.

Raven rubbed his eyes. He looked much younger than his fourteen years. "Are you going to fight? Can I come?"

"No! I need you to…" I almost said to "stay out of it," but checked myself in time. Raven needed to feel useful. "I need you to stay here. Protect Mason and Holly. This is our last defense. If things go bad, I'll fall back here. I need to know it's safe. Can you do that?"

Raven ground his jaw side to side. I could see him mulling my words, trying to decide if I was patronizing him.

"Listen to me." I grabbed his hand and pulled him close. "The animals of the forest are gathered in a mass by this camp. The shar-lil did that. Do you understand?"

"That coconut thingy you talked about?"

"Yes."

He still looked uncertain.

"It seems to call to animals. The opji think it's a weapon of some kind."

"They're going to use the animals to hurt someone?"

"Maybe. I don't know. But if Princess steps foot outside our ward, she'll fall under its sway too."

That seemed to convince him. He sucked in a breath and stood taller.

"All right. I'll stay. Can I have a blaster, just in case?"

Grrr. Bad mother and good mother warred over that one for a moment, then I nodded. Mason had been teaching him proper gun etiquette. I trusted him not to be foolish.

"Come on, laddie," Angus said. "I'll help you choose the baddest-ass gun in the locker before we go."

They went to the basement, and I took a moment to go over my preparations. My mind was scattering with all the possible what-if scenarios that could happen between now and the impending fight.

"Kyra-lady?" A tiny hand tugged on my shirt cuff.

"Not now, Jacoby." I pulled my hand away. Had I packed enough blades? They were my best defense against the opji. Should I ask Errol to go with us? I wasn't sure his brand of galvanic magic would have any effect on the vamps. No, better to leave him home where he'd be safe.

"Kyra-lady!" Jacoby's voice took on an urgent edge.

"What is it?" I barked and immediately regretted my harsh tone. "I'm sorry. What is it?" I said more softly. I brushed the frizzled fur from his eyes. He latched onto my fingers.

"It's Mister Mason."

I FLEW DOWN THE hall to our bedroom to find Mason sitting up with his legs over the edge of the bed. He swayed in place. I'd carefully shaven him that morning, and there was a sickly pallor under his usual swarthy complexion. A lock of hair stuck straight up from the back of his head where it had been mashed against the pillow for the last week.

He put his bare feet on the floor and tried to stand.

"You shouldn't be up!" I rushed over before he fell on his face.

"I'm fine."

"You're not."

He ran a hand through his hair, messing it even more.

"How long?"

"A week. You've been out for a week."

He made a growling noise in his throat, then nodded toward the knife sheath on my belt and the sword across my back.

"Where are you going?"

For the tiniest fraction of a nanosecond, I thought about lying. I almost told him that I was heading out on a Valkyrie Pest Control job. But Mason and I didn't play games. He'd find out about the opji camp soon enough and then about my lies.

"I found the opji. The forest animals have them surrounded so the shar-lil has to be there too."

"You're going to retrieve it." It wasn't a question. I nodded. "Because some god told you to in a dream."

Put like that, it sounded ridiculous.

"I'm going to destroy it because the opji have my friend in a thrall and they're planning to use it to attack Montreal. If there's even a chance that breaking it will free him, I'm going to take it."

He puffed out a breath and tilted his head side to side to crack his stiff neck.

"Fine. Give me five and I'll be ready."

"No." I kept my tone firm. "You're not coming." He turned away, and my tone escalated to exasperation. I didn't have time to argue with him.

"Mason, listen to me. I've been watching you sleep for seven days. Seven days where I didn't know if you'd even wake up. Only Nori's daily infusion of magic has kept you going. You can barely stand. If nothing else you need to eat and get your strength back."

"Get Dutch to pack food. I'll eat on the way." He was already tugging on his pants.

"No! I won't have it." I pulled at his hands, trying to stop him. I might as well have tried to stop a dam from bursting.

His eyes flashed with impatience that bordered on anger. "You won't have what?"

"I won't have you putting yourself in danger again. Not now."

"It's okay for you to run into danger, but not me?"

"I won't turn into a fucking demon as soon as things turn bad!" I crossed my arms over my chest and glared at him. There I'd said it. Mason slowly buttoned his pants and stood.

"I'm sorry that I'm such a burden to you, but I'm going."

By the One-eyed Father. "That's not what I meant and you know it. Grim says the demon is growing stronger, and next time he may not be able to pull you back from the brink."

"That cat should mind his own business." He was pulling socks and a shirt from his dresser now.

"Holly and Raven need you here."

"*Tabernak*," he swore as his fingers fumbled trying to unfold his socks.

"They need you just as much. Would you stay home and let the opji run wild over our city? No, you wouldn't. Now leave me be, woman!"

I stared at him in shock. His old world values were peeking through his fine veneer. He tried to hide it, but every once in a while, it was obvious that he'd been born in a different time, a time when men ruled the nations and the house.

I gritted my teeth to hold back a bitter retort that I would only regret later and spun on my heel.

I found Emil and Angus in the living room, pretending that they hadn't overheard our argument.

"We're leaving," I growled out. "Now."

31

I didn't want to take the horses. Just in case. I had to at least say it to myself. Just in case we didn't come back. We'd be leaving the horses to fend for themselves. We took Oscar's widgets, the ones that worked outside the ward and had mapping capabilities, and hoped to find a road that would get us close to the opji camp.

I stowed my gear in the back of the van and turned to find Jacoby standing under the drizzle. His fur drooped with rain. He wore his work belt over his shoulder and a look of brutal determination on his face.

"Kyra-lady needs 'prentice." It wasn't a question. It seemed that vacation time was over.

"Come on." I moved aside so he could hop into the van.

Mason arrived, walking as if his shoes were made of razor blades. He hadn't bothered to comb his hair and it still stuck up in the back. No matter, the rain would soon take care of that. He didn't look at me but took the passenger seat. By the time I got in and started the engine, he was perfecting his brooding. A sandwich lay untouched in his lap. His magic had a rank, unsettled tang to it.

In the back seat, Angus swore. "Get yer furry ass off me, cat!" Grim hissed before finding a comfortable spot between Angus and Emil, and then they fell silent too.

I sighed. It would be a long, tense drive with an unhappy crew.

I drove through the dark, avoiding pot holes when I could, gripping the steering wheel like a lifeline when I couldn't. The rain came and went but the night was damp, and mist curled up from the road in ghostly fingers. The headlights barely penetrated the gloom and we almost hit a tree that had fallen over the road. That made us lose time as we backtracked and took another road.

Mason navigated with Oscar's widget. I had the other one in my pocket so we'd be able to communicate once we found the opji camp.

"Pull over here." Mason's voice rasped. He sounded exhausted, and I bit back the urge to tell him he shouldn't be here. He knew that. Everyone knew that. And yet here he was. No amount of nagging would change it.

I parked the van as far off the road as I could without hitting trees. Mason tilted the widget toward me.

"There's your crisp." He pointed to a bluish glow on the screen. It looked to be about two kilometers west of us. That meant the opji camp wasn't far. We'd hike the rest of the way, looking for scouts and getting a feel for the land.

I pointed to the tip of the crisp. "We stick together until this point. We'll see the camp from there."

Mason nodded. "And decide the best attack once we get a better look."

I took a breath. He wasn't going to like this, but I'd done a lot of thinking while he slept.

"I already decided. You and Angus will head around the camp, taking out any guards you find. Emil and I will do the same in this direction." I ran my finger around the area we assumed was now opji territory. "Then we'll sneak in. Emil will pretend to be opji and I'll be his prisoner."

I'd already discussed this with Emil, and he was confident he could pull it off.

"And we should just bide our heels while you have all the fun?" Angus said from the backseat.

"You take out as many guards as you can. Once Emil and I have the shar-lil we'll make a run for it."

"That's the worst plan I've ever heard," Mason growled.

"You have a better one?" I snapped.

I could hear his teeth grinding and the muscles on his jaw bunched.

"No." He let out a deep sigh. "But I don't like it."

"Neither do I, but it's all we've got."

"We could wait for Hub."

I tried not to show my impatience. Calling Lowe had been an act of desperation. I wouldn't rely on Hub.

"No," I said. "If she even gets my message, Lowe will send half a dozen soldiers. The opji will wipe them out and disappear. This is our best chance to save Gabe and the others."

I cut off any other arguments by getting out of the van.

The misty rain had turned to sleet. Of course it had. That was just the icing on the shit cake we'd been given.

I pulled my jacket collar up around my ears.

Mason still had the widget out with the map displayed. He consulted it one last time and said, "This way." At least he'd dropped the argument.

We followed him into the damp, dark forest.

THE CAMP WASN'T HARD to find, surrounded as it was by the ring of creatures.

"Damnation and creepy-ass roses," Angus muttered.

"What are they doing?" Emil asked.

"I'm not sure." I turned in a circle to take in all the animals. There were even more than this afternoon. "My best guess is the shar-lil has some kind of sway over them."

"Like pilgrims come to pray at a holy shrine," Emil said.

It was exactly like that. The animals had come this far, but didn't try to get any closer.

I hadn't seen any opji that afternoon. They seemed to be taking advantage of the animals as protection, but with the sun down, we would likely run into guards too.

I motioned for everyone to be silent and pulled Mason aside. I turned on my widget and made sure my map was synced to his.

"Messages only from here on," I said. "No calls." Opji had impressive hearing, so radio-silence was a must. "I don't think the animals will attack, but don't take anything for granted. Grim go with Mason and Angus. Jacoby with me. Your job is to bring up the rear. Make sure nothing follows us—animal, human or opji."

Jacoby made a two-fingered salute. He'd been watching old movies again.

There was nothing left to say.

I turned to go, but Mason gripped my shoulder. Rain lashed down, plastering his hair to his head. I probably looked no better.

"I'm sorry." His eyes looked haunted.

I nodded. "I know."

"For before, but also…for everything."

I nodded again, not trusting my voice.

"Are you sure you want to do this?" His voice was deep and quiet and it dug under my armor.

"No, I don't want—" My voice cracked but I went on, the words tumbling out of me. "I want to be home with Holly, reading her a bedtime story. Or feeding the troll bats in the barn. Or doing any of the hundred other chores that need doing at home. But if we don't, we won't have a home, and I just can't…"

He pulled me in. His lips cut off my babble as they met mine. My shoulders were stiff, but his kiss melted me just enough. His tongue flashed like fire. I opened up to him. In that moment, nothing else mattered. Not the opji. Not the rain. Not the demon riding in his soul.

Angus coughed behind us, a polite way of saying we needed to get moving.

Mason pulled away just enough to look me in the eye. "I broke my promise to you once. I won't swear it again. I can't control the demon."

I nodded. There was something heavy and hot in my throat, holding back words.

"But I can control my rage that releases him. Let's get in there and get out. Clean and quick."

"Clean and quick."

I hugged him and felt him kiss the top of my wet head. He let me go and headed into the trees. I tried to keep the warmth of his embrace close as the cold rain battered me.

"Come on." Emil motioned for me to follow. We wound through the wet, enthralled animals. A wolf snarled as I stumbled over her tail.

"Sorry," I whispered automatically and rain dripped into my mouth. I wiped it away and rubbed my eyes. The chill was starting to settle into my bones. We kept moving forward, over paws and tails, around antlers. Their passivity was unnerving.

I glanced at Jacoby, who padded over and around various rodents. His tongue poked from the corner of his mouth as he concentrated hard not to step on anyone. At least he didn't seem affected by the shar-lil's call.

A few minutes later, we'd crept past what I was starting to think of as the ring of fur. Emil and I crouched on the ridge above the opji camp. Jacoby hunkered down behind me, close enough to be my shadow. To our right, the ridge fell away, meeting the camp at ground level. To our left, it became a craggy plateau of bare rock. It would have been a perfect spot for a lookout, but the opji didn't seem worried about posting guards. Maybe they thought anyone foolish enough to stumble upon their camp deserved their fate.

I'd already scouted the site that afternoon, but I let Emil and Jacoby get their fill. I studied the forest, looking for movement that would indicate an opji patrol. Beside me, a low branch hung thick with pine cones. The cones shivered and turned to face me. They had goggling eyes and little gaping mouths. So, not a pine tree then. Nothing was ever as it seemed in the Inbetween. I would do well to remember that.

Jacoby's small hand slipped into mine. I gave it a squeeze and turned my attention back to our target.

The opji had cleared the entire small valley. Cut logs were tossed haphazardly in a pile at the far end of the camp with a bonfire burning brightly nearby. There was something odd about that fire. Rain didn't seem to affect it, and the orange flames were shot through with flickers of green.

Mage fire. It burned hot enough to smelt iron and couldn't be put out with water. Why would the opji need mage fire?

Beyond the fire, tents were arrayed in neat rows. I counted them—over three dozen. They were dark and sagging in the rain. Hopefully, the opji would be huddled inside, trying to keep dry, and not watching the yard.

Near the tents stood a large barn, probably the remnants of an old homestead. A newer construction loomed in the middle of the cleared space. It was a pagoda with all sides open to the elements. This afternoon, it had been empty, but now an opji stood under its shelter, feeding a small fire pit. An altar had been hastily constructed from two barrels with boards laid over them. The shar-lil sat on this inside its hideous nest of thorns. The flickering firelight lit up black stains on the barrels—stains that could only be blood.

Around the pavilion, a dozen wojaks crouched in the mud. The pathetic creatures were nearly naked in the cold and rain. They didn't huddle together for warmth. Instead, they squatted with arms wrapped around their knees and heads bowed. In the dim light, they looked like giant cabbages growing from the mud, like that old sci-fi movie about pod people that had kept me awake for many nights when I was a teenager.

But that wasn't the worst sight in the camp. That honor went to the cattle pen where human captives were crowded together in a miserable group with no shelter from the rain. One or two paced the small enclosure, while others sat in the mud, seemingly lost.

Opji kept humans for three reasons—to eat, to breed or to turn into wojaks, but I suspected Nici had another fate in mind for these poor souls.

As if to confirm my thought, the blond opji burst through the door of the barn. The bonfire illuminated her hair like a halo as she strode toward the pavilion. A mask of rage twisted her otherwise striking features.

A dozen opji followed her like ducklings after their mama. I wondered if any of them were Ichovidar, the rumored leader of Vioska. But Oscar had said Nici was his sister or possibly his mate. Either way, he probably wouldn't follow meekly behind her.

Nici said something over her shoulder and jerked her head toward the humans. An opji duckling left the line and walked to the pen with a languished stride, like he was out for an evening stroll. He made some complicated sign over the pen's gate. There was a flash of light, and he opened the door.

Warded. That's why there were no guards on the pen. The opji grabbed a man from the huddled group and hauled him away. Someone screamed but the man let himself be dragged off.

The fire beside the shar-lil glowed brightly, and I could easily see the man's face as they led him toward the artifact. A dark mark—bruise, blood or dirt—colored his cheek and blended into his scruffy black beard. He'd already fought the opji and lost. Now he seemed resigned to his fate.

Nici tipped his head upward with one finger. I'd forgotten how tall she was. She stared into the man's eyes until his shoulders slumped. She'd enthralled him. I knew what was coming next. I tensed, ready to bolt down there and stop this abomination. Emil held me with a firm grip on my arm. He shook his head, warning me to caution.

I bristled, but he was right. We needed stealth and the element of surprise if we were to have any chance of success.

I bit my tongue and watched. My muscles had cooled as we waited. They were stiffening, but I didn't dare move.

Nici's underling held the thrall upright and cut away his shirt with a lethal looking knife. Nici intoned those power words I'd heard in the cottage and I shivered. The opji guard took the captive's wrist and rammed it onto the spike above the shar-lil. The captive didn't scream. Blood ran down his arm and dripped from his elbow onto the artifact.

The shar-lil's song rang out in the night. Emil didn't seem to notice, but Jacoby pressed himself against my thigh. He was trembling. Behind us, wolves howled, coyotes yipped and a gumberoo bellowed.

An itch began in my chest. My hand pressed against it, but there was no way to scratch something so deep inside.

Nici watched the shar-lil like it might blossom. I braced myself for an onslaught of magic, but it never came.

The bleeding man sagged as his knees gave out, and the opji guard propped him up, jostling him so the blood continued to spill over the shar-lil. Still nothing happened.

Minutes passed while the man slowly bled out. Finally, Nici growled something. She spoke to several of the waiting opji in their guttural language.

"Can you hear what she's saying?" I whispered. Emil shook his head. I couldn't see his eyes in the dim light. That was probably a good thing. Even through my ramped-up wards, I keened rage and despair coming off him.

The guard slung the dying thrall around the altar, and left him to hang there. Nici said something else, then turned on her heel and stormed back inside the barn.

Mother duck wasn't happy. She clearly expected the blood to do something. She'd been blooding the shar-lil for days or even weeks with her godling thralls and now she'd been escalating things by taking captives and draining them over the little coconut. Clearly, this strategy wasn't working either. If the shar-lil was truly a weapon, then Nici didn't know how to use it. I couldn't help feeling a spark of hope at that. I glanced at the pen of miserable captives. It was a small spark. How many would die before she either activated it or gave up?

We waited for Nici's opji flunkies to follow her into the barn. Instead, they lounged on benches under the pavilion. That put a damper on our plan. We'd have to steal the shar-lil right from under their noses.

I took out my widget and sent a message to Mason.

Regroup

"Seen enough?" I whispered.

Emil grunted. We backtracked through the ring of fur until we found Mason and Angus. Grim was nowhere in sight, but I knew he wouldn't stray too far from Mason.

"You still think you can sneak in there?" Mason growled. I keened dark magic coming off him in waves. It had the faint whiff of brimstone.

"I don't see how we have any choice."

"We could wait for Hub."

I shook my head. "We went over this already. We've finally got them cornered."

"Cornered, but not outnumbered," Mason countered.

"No."

He stared at me for a long moment. He knew what I was asking. We had to fight the opji without his demon magic. Just the thought of him going dark sent cold water rushing through my veins.

I had to trust him to keep it together. That didn't mean I had to poke the demon by making Mason worry unduly about me.

"Okay. We abandon the idea of me pretending to be Emil's captive." That had been a long shot anyway. The opji were bound to recognize Emil as a stranger. I rubbed a hand over my damp face. It had already been a long night and we hadn't even started the fight yet.

"But if we wait until dawn to attack, they'll be weaker," I said. "We might even get in and out without a fight."

Mason considered me, then nodded. "But only if the opji retreat inside."

I nodded. See? I could compromise.

"Well, that leaves me loose as a rolling stone," Angus said. "I'll head back to the van. Maybe hub cavalry will make it that far. I'll leave them a great big arrow drawn in the dirt. Even Hub couldn't miss that." He winked and took my hand, forcing me to meet his piercing gaze. "Don't let the bossman do anything stupid."

I nodded.

Angus disappeared into the trees as if he were one of them.

"If we're waiting until dawn, I'm going to look around," Emil said.

I shook my head. "Too dangerous."

"I'll be careful. Maybe I can steal a uniform."

The opji didn't wear uniforms exactly, but I knew what he meant. They had a certain look to them—dark jackets and nondescript black pants, all made from homespun wool.

I considered his offer for only a moment. No doubt, Emil hoped to find Gabe so he could play the white knight, but we needed to know how many opji were inside that barn before we made our move. And maybe we could still try to pass Emil off as one of them. It might give us that precious moment of surprise we needed.

"Okay." I agreed with a short nod. "Do it. But stay away from killing any of the guards. They'll be at their weakest and most distracted just after dawn. We'll come at them then."

Emil turned to leave, but I grabbed his arm. "And Emil, if you find Gabe, don't do anything foolish. Come back and get us first."

"Sure thing. I know you like to be in on all the foolish." There was a maniacal edge to his grin.

CHAPTER

32

We returned to watch over the camp—Mason, Jacoby and me. I could only hope Grim was nearby. The rain slowed to a fine mist. Nici came out once more. She ordered thrall's body removed. The opji plucked the victim from the spike and tossed him onto the bonfire. Now the mage fire made sense. The green flames were hotter than any crematorium.

The guards chose another victim, a woman this time. She screamed and cried as they dragged her from the pen. A second woman tried to hang onto her, but the guards beat her back. She fell into the mud and didn't move. The new victim stopped screaming as soon as Nici enthralled her. It was a small mercy.

The camp fell silent. The thrall's lifeblood drained from her. I keened the shar-lil's strange, itchy song again. I wanted desperately to storm in and free the dying woman—to free all the captives—but we didn't stand a chance against so many opji.

So we waited, watching Nici play out her macabre anointing.

When the sky started turning mauve, Nici gave up. She snapped out some order and returned to the barn. The others followed her inside, except for two guards who stayed to clean up. They hauled the latest thrall onto the bonfire and sluiced buckets of water over the shar-lil's altar to wash away the worst of the blood. The black stains on the barrels remained.

We waited while the sun crept over the horizon.

The wojaks still crouched like subdued cabbages in the mud, making me wonder again at how the opji controlled them. Would they awaken if we snuck into the camp? Or did they need some signal from the opji?

I made a mental growl. I hated going into a fight without all the pertinent information.

The brambles to my right rustled and my hand went to the knife at my belt, then I keened Emil's agitated magic and relaxed.

He was wearing the black homespun of an opji.

"There's a supply tent behind the barn. They've got guns too. Guns enough for an army."

That was odd. The opji didn't use guns. Emil saw my confusion.

"The guns are for the thralls," he said.

"How do you know?"

"I snuck inside that barn. Don't worry. No one saw me," he said quickly when he saw my expression. "Anyway, it's set up like a barracks. Rows of beds, half empty. The rest are filled with humans who just lie there and stare at the ceiling. It's super creepy."

I assumed he would tell me if he'd found Gabe.

"I heard Nici arguing with someone. They plan to arm the thralls once they break the shar-lil. But the other opji guy wasn't happy that they'd wasted so much blood on it already."

"Break the shar-lil? Is that what they're trying to do?" That didn't make sense. If the opji were going to break it, why was Terra so insistent that I destroy it?"

Emil shrugged. "You said it's a weapon, right? Maybe they mean break some curse on it? Crack its shell. I dunno. My opji isn't perfect." He made a sheepish gesture with his hands.

"That's okay. You did good. Were there more opji inside?"

"Nope. Just the ones we saw. But it looks like they're set up to receive more. Thralls and opji."

That was my thought too.

"They don't want to bring in the others until they're sure they can bring down the ward," Mason said.

"Maybe."

"That could mean that Nici is on her own, trying to prove something to the opji elders."

Now that was an interesting thought. It would explain why the opji weren't here in force. Nici was either an advance scout or she'd gone rogue. I mulled both ideas in my head, and decided that for the moment, it didn't matter which was true.

We needed to destroy the shar-lil and hope that would break the thrall on the creatures and the godlings. Hope that Terra wasn't playing me for reasons only a god would understand.

The two remaining guards had finished their grisly chores and now lounged under the pavilion. One smoked a pipe. The other appeared to be sleeping.

The sun was up, but thick clouds gave the morning sky a flat glow. I hoped Angus had made it back to the van. We waited a little longer, until even the human captives seemed to settle after a night of being tormented by the opji.

The only movement in the camp came from the flickering mage fire as it ate through the evidence of Nici's murders.

I'd been aware of my sword's intense hum for some time. It keened blood and wanted to come out to play. I unsheathed it. Mason and Emil took that as the signal to move. They went along the ridge, and snuck up on the guards.

I headed straight down. My heels skidded on the loose earth, but it was wet and didn't make a sound. Jacoby slid on his butt right behind me.

My sword whined when Mason and Emil took out the guards. Mason broke one neck, quick and silent. Emil was less efficient. He stabbed the sleeping guard in the chest. The opji gurgled out a cry before Emil smothered his nose and mouth with one hand. He wouldn't kill the opji that way. They were too strong. But he could incapacitate him. While he waited for the opji to stop thrashing. Emil motioned for me to hurry.

I'd been stalled beside the bonfire. I hadn't seen the full picture of Nici's obsession from above. Bones of humans, deer, wolves, and more littered the yard. There was not one bit of ground uncovered by bone shards. Jacoby let out a small pained cry.

By the One-eye God, how much blood had Nici spilled for the shar-lil? I gritted my teeth as my boots crunched on the bones of the dead. My sword shrieked. I could only hope that none of the opji had the keening to sense it.

And then the itch in my chest blossomed to an ache. My keening went into overload, and I staggered the last few paces to the pavilion.

Emil was still holding down the thrashing guard. Mason stood by the edge of the pavilion with a blaster trained on the barn. He saw me falter and made a move to come for me, but I waved him back.

I had eyes only for the shar-lil. I felt like a tractor beam had locked on me and was dragging me in. Everything else faded. I could hear Mason's voice, but his words were far away, lost in another place and time.

Was this what the forest creatures felt? Had the bloodings increased its call so that the shar-lil could now affect humans as well? Or was my keening making me particularly susceptible?

In that moment, only the shar-lil mattered. I wasn't there to free the thralls or because some dreaming god commanded me. I was there for the shar-lil. It *needed* me. I could feel that need the same way my breasts had ached when newborn Holly had woken in the middle of the night and cried for her mother.

It was scared. And alone. My fingers closed over the husk-like shell. I hefted it, passing it from hand to hand. It was much heavier than a coconut. I could feel the weight of life inside it. The shar-lil wasn't an artifact.

It was alive.

33

The shar-lil's song blossomed and it tore off my wards like they'd been paper chains, but instead of being overwhelming, its magic delighted me. How could a creature so anointed in blood and death be delightful? I heard its voice in my head, like the coo of a cosmic baby. It wanted to play.

"Mason!" My voice was ragged with emotion. "It's alive and I think…I think it's a baby?"

The roaring noise in my head died down. Mason was peering at me with that stern look that used to scare me. Now I knew it was his confounded face.

"A baby what?" He stepped closer, still keeping his gun trained on the barn.

"I don't know. Here, feel it." I grabbed his hand and placed it on the shell.

The crease between his brows deepened. "I don't feel anything."

It wasn't just me. My sword had gone silent as soon as I picked up the shar-lil, as if it listened too.

In my life, I'd experienced various forms of non-verbal communication, from dragon mind-speak to Errol's odd brand of gobbledygook language. I'd even spoken to the disembodied spirit of my late father once. The shar-lil was like none of these.

It spoke to me, but not in words. Not even in images or thoughts. I just *knew* what it was feeling. It filled me.

I felt its abuse by the opji. I felt its revulsion for the constant onslaught of blood poured over it like anointing oil. I felt its loneliness and the way it called to the only ones who could hear it, the creatures of the forest. And now, apparently me.

I found myself muttering nonsensical words of comfort, just like I did to Holly when she woke in the middle of the night and needed soothing.

"We don't have a lot of time," Mason said. I looked into his eyes and saw what he really wanted to say.

We had to kill it. Nici was using this creature—I could no longer think of it as an artifact—to enthrall the godlings. I didn't know what she ultimately hoped to accomplish, but baptisms in blood weren't meant to create fluffy bunnies.

We'd come here to destroy the shar-lil, but now that I held it in my hands and felt the burgeoning life inside it…I just couldn't.

"It's okay." Mason took my wrist, gently but firmly. "Let me have it."

Mason would do what my soft heart couldn't. He would kill the strange creature that had caused so much havoc. My grip tightened on the husk. His fingers inched under mine, trying to pry them loose.

"Kyra, let go. You know we have to. Think of Gabe."

"No. I can't." Tears made my words thick. "I can't let you hurt her."

"Her?"

Emil had finally subdued the opji guard and appeared at Mason's shoulder.

"What's going on? We need to leave."

"The artifact has some kind of hold on Kyra." Mason was still trying to pull it from my grasp.

"Not an artifact." My breath was labored. Terra had called it a seed, but as my mind reeled from its overwhelming beauty and importance, I knew it was so much more.

"It's a child. A child of light."

"I don't care what it is," Emil said. "Just smash it."

"No!" I shouted and clutched the little egg to my chest.

My raised voice didn't go unnoticed.

"Who's there?" came a voice from the human pen. The huddled group had moved as close to the warded fence as possible without touching it. They were watching us, and had determined that we weren't opji.

"Help us!" cried one woman. More pleading calls rose.

"We have to go now." Mason gave up trying to pry the shar-lil from my grip. "Take it with you. We'll sort it out later."

I nodded and hugged the egg against my chest, not even caring that it was sticky with blood.

We ran.

And made it only to the edge of the pavilion before the doors to the barn opened and the opji stormed out.

tucked the shar-lil into my jacket and made it a solemn promise that the vampires wouldn't hurt it anymore.

"Get behind me." Mason stepped between me and the opji who fanned out in front of the barn. The human captives had gone silent as soon as the opji appeared. I couldn't bring myself to be angry at them for giving us away.

"No magic," I warned Mason. "Blades only." He growled out a noncommittal response, and I felt like a nag for reminding him. I had to trust that he knew his limits. His left arm had already gone to stone. His right held a long blade.

Nici emerged from the hall, looking exactly the same. Did she sleep in her clothes? Or did she not sleep at all?

She spat out orders and the opji advanced on us.

"She said she wants us alive," Emil said. He held two blades, a sword in his right hand and a long knife in the left.

"Good." That gave us a chance to kill more opji.

There were twelve of them, plus Nici, but she seemed happy to let her minions do the fighting. That meant four for each of us. I picked out my targets on the right.

I didn't have to wait long. An opji lunged across the open space. He was uncannily fast and leapt like a pouncing cheetah. Mason clubbed him with his stone arm. The opji fell and Emil cut his throat.

That was the popping of the cork. The wojaks unfurled from their crouched sleep and fell on us like a swarm. They came from all angles and we were overrun within seconds.

I slashed and whirled, taking off limbs and spraying blood with every strike, but it wasn't enough. The weight of the shar-lil in my jacket kept me from any truly agile moves. Claws raked across my neck. I fell back and raised my sword like a shield as I tried to scuffle away in the mud, only to come up against the boots of an opji. He wrenched the sword from my grip. The blade sang out its glee and cut his wrist as he twisted it away from me.

I had only a moment to savor that small victory before he flung the blade aside. It skidded on wet gravel, too far to reach. But the Valkyrie magic had done its job and broken the zycha curse on the opji. His eyes widened as his heart began to pump like a human's again.

I didn't let him suffer long. I threw my knife and it struck him in the throat. His surprised expression at finding his blood pumping over his hands was worth losing the blade.

I scrambled backward, reaching for my fallen sword. A wojak leaped on my chest and pinned me in the mud. The vamp's once human face looked more like the muzzle of a rabid dog, flecked with foam and flaunting yellow fangs. It snarled inches from my face, lips trembling, saliva dripping.

It had me pinned. I couldn't move. Couldn't breathe. I'd fought as hard as I could but it wasn't enough. I would die here in the mud.

From somewhere nearby, Nici barked a command. The wojak at my throat froze. Another shout from the opji and the pressure on my chest eased. The wojak released me and scuttled away.

I sucked in a breath and tasted mud. I rolled and coughed into the earth. Nici gave me no time to recover. An opji grabbed my braids and hauled me upright. Someone bound my hands behind me with rough twine.

Nici pushed through the crowd of opji. The wojaks paced around the clearing, still riled up for a fight.

Mason had been captured and bound too. His lip was fat and bleeding and he wore an expression of murder, but when our eyes met, he nodded.

The fear I'd been holding in my heart eased. He hadn't gone demon. He'd kept his promise even when we'd been overwhelmed. That was a small mercy.

We were alive. We'd work the rest out. The All-father only knew how. Maybe we'd get lucky and Captain Lowe had taken my warning seriously. Maybe Hub soldiers were on their way right now.

I turned left and right, as much as my captor would allow, looking for

Emil. I spotted him lying under a dead wojak in the mud. His face was turned away, but his mop of brown curls was unmistakable even plastered to his head with dirt and blood. He wasn't moving. I watched, waiting for him to get up, but he didn't.

The opji jerked me forward to face Nici.

"Hold him." Nici barely flicked a glance at Mason. She thought I was the dangerous one because I'd thwarted her thrall magic once already. Big mistake. Mason didn't struggle against his bonds, but his dark eyes tracked Nici like she was prey.

She stalked across the yard like a graceful cat, untouched by the violence that had erupted here just moments before. Up close, I could see that she wasn't as young as I'd thought. Her blond hair hid gray streaks and the lines around her eyes were pronounced. She was still beautiful with her alabaster skin and eyes cut like blue diamonds. She dragged a finger under my chin, and I felt the bite of her nail. Then she looked at the dirt her finger had wiped off my face and made a moue of disgust.

"I won't bother trying to enthrall you again." She dropped her hand and glared at me. "Since you side-stepped that little trick last time."

I willed myself not to look to my sword still sitting in the mud. She couldn't know that the sword's strong will had shielded me.

An opji came up and reported to her. He had a cut from one eye down to his chin. It was already healing. Too bad.

Nici listened to his report then turned to me with a frown.

"Where is it?"

I kept my face blank.

"Search her."

Rough hands patted me down, finding my hunting knife, my belt kit and the shar-lil. The opji handed it over to Nici. She held the little coconut-egg on the tips of her fingers and sighed. It wasn't a happy sigh. It was the sigh of frustration. I was glad the shar-lil was a puzzle she couldn't solve. At least one thing wasn't going her way.

She moved so fast, I didn't see it until her fingers gripped my throat and her snarling face filled my vision. "Why did you come?" She tightened her grip on my throat. "Why do you want my shar-lil?"

My answer came out in a wheeze. "Fuck…you."

She thrust me backward. With my hands bound, I fell hard. Pain lanced through my chest as I tried to gulp in air.

In a blur of fur, Jacoby launched himself at Nici.

"Leaves Kyra-lady alone!" He kicked her in the shin. Nici reeled back in surprise. Jacoby bounced on the spot with fists raised. Smoke trailed from his ears. He looked like a bedraggled poodle, but no one would mistake the rage in his eyes.

Nici blinked. It was something.

"Is that a dervish? How extraordinary. Seize it." An opji moved to do her bidding. Jacoby ducked and bit the opji. It did him no good. The opji clamped his hands on Jacoby's arms and lifted him. The dervish kicked and smoked.

He was going nova.

Nici didn't let him get that far. While the opji held up the struggling dervish, Nici enthralled him. Jacoby sagged limply in the opji's grip.

She turned to me. "Thank you. His blood will make a lovely addition to the shar-lil's training."

By the One-eyed God, I should have left Jacoby at home. And Emil. And Mason, who stood like a statue with his hands bound. None of us should have come.

And then the shar-lil called out to me. Its song soothed and buoyed my spirits all at once. The shar-lil was the reason we'd come. Not to steal it, not to destroy it. To save it.

Nici circled me, as if sizing up a horse she planned to buy.

"You don't look so formidable. I'm not sure why Gabriel was so insistent that we should have you on our team. We should ask him, shall we?" She turned to one of the waiting opji. "Bring him."

I rose to my knees, then staggered to my feet. Mason watched me with fire in his eyes.

We didn't wait long. The door to the barn opened and Gabe emerged with the opji behind him. His hands weren't bound, but he looked awful. His clothes were stained and rumpled like he'd been wearing them for days. His hair was greasy and uncombed. Dark stubble covered his jaw. I couldn't remember ever seeing him unshaven.

"Hey, Kyra. How's it going?" He said it like we'd just met in a pub for drinks.

I felt broken in body and spirit. "I'm good. You?"

"Good." He shrugged. His eyes were vacant. "I'm glad they found you. I told Nici we needed you on our side."

"You did?"

"Yeah, I told her all about your sword." He leaned in and whispered. "But don't worry, I also told her that only a Valkyrie can use it. So now she can't kill you." He leaned back again and grinned, pleased with himself.

"Thank you." My voice wobbled. "I feel so much safer now."

"You shouldn't." Nici jerked Gabe away. He stumbled and smiled at her, like she'd done something silly.

Oh, Gabe! I wished I could reach him somehow. If I had my sword, maybe I could cut him. A cut by my blade would probably break the thrall. It would also be fatal to a human, but Gabe was a godling. I really had no idea how it would affect him. It was a risk I'd take, now that I had no more options.

I glanced at my blade. It lay in the mud about ten paces away. If I kicked out the knee of the opji holding my arms, I could lunge for it. But there was no way I could cut my bonds before the waiting wojaks fell on me.

Mason caught my gaze and shook his head slightly. He knew what I was thinking, and he knew it would be suicide.

"Actually, I could kill you." Nici flicked her nail across my chin again. I felt the stab of pain as she drew blood. "I don't need a Valkyrie blade to open Montreal's ward. The shar-lil will do it for me."

"And how's that working for you so far?"

Her smile lost a bit of its brilliance. She stepped away and fondled the shar-lil, caressing it like a favorite pet. Its song had gone silent, like it was trying to hide. My heart ached to hold it again, to keep it safe from these monsters.

"How much do you know about wojaks?" Nici said.

I dragged my attention back to her.

"Only that they were once human. They're more of your victims." I tossed my head toward the pen of humans who'd been silent since Nici arrived.

"Human, yes. They start that way. It takes a long time to lose that humanity. When it works we call it the *zerwa*, the breaking. Only then can a mind truly embrace the ritual that turns them undead. Which is why we treasure them so." She glanced fondly at the hideous wojaks who sat in the mud, waiting to do her bidding.

"We have different ways to achieve the *zerwa*. Starvation works well. But that should be done slowly for best effect. Sometimes we need to rush things. We need a little push to break a mind completely. So you see, your death might have some purpose after all. Gabriel," she turned and cupped his chin like she might kiss him. "You love your Valkyrie friend, don't you?"

Gabe nodded, a witless smile on his face.

Nici patted his cheek. "Be a good boy. Kill her."

ici put a blade in Gabe's hand. "Don't waste any blood." She held the shar-lil under my chin. A flicker of uncertainty flashed in Gabe's eyes, there and gone so fast I could have imagined it.

The opji holding me tightened his grip. From the corner of my eye, I saw Mason struggle against his captor.

The sun finally broke through the clouds and glinted off the blade in Gabe's hand. His eyes were glazed and the line of his jaw tight.

Did he know what Nici was doing? Somewhere under the sway of Nici's magic, did he understand that she not only wanted me dead, but that my death would be his first step in turning wojak?

"Gabe, you don't have to do this." My voice sounded like it came from someone else, someone who wasn't terrified.

His gaze suddenly focused on me and his eyes narrowed.

"I know you're in there. Fight it. Please, Gabe. Fight her!"

Nici didn't intervene. She didn't have to. She watched our little drama with an amused smile. Sweat beaded on Gabe's forehead even though the day was cool. He twisted the knife side to side and pressed the flat edge to my throat. I swallowed hard and felt the pressure of the blade against my larynx. I licked my lips and tasted tears.

"Gabe, please! Look at me. It's Kyra. You don't want to do this!"

Sometimes, a moment can change your world, a speck of time, a nanosecond like all the other nanoseconds of your existence, but this one twists and morphs, then explodes into a synchronous and stupefying flow that can't ever be undone.

What happened next was a blur that I would only parse together later. Mason broke free of the opji and screamed in a shrill demon voice.

A third eye opened on Gabe's forehead.

It blinked at me.

Gabe swiped the blade across his own throat.

"I'm sorry," he mouthed as his blood sprayed my face.

Mason, thinking my death was imminent, let the darkness take over.

He swept aside his captors and his bonds, jumped on Nici and broke her neck with one sharp jerk. As easy as wringing a chicken neck.

A dozen wojaks fell on him.

Gabe's eyes turned glassy. The third eye—the eye of his god—winked out, and he toppled over Nici's body.

I leaped for my sword. My hands were cold and clumsy, but I had to get to Mason before the wojaks tore him to pieces. The blade felt heavy in my hand. I slashed at an opji that got in my way.

Before I took two steps across the yard, the pile of slathering wojaks erupted.

Mason burst through them and roared. The sound tore at the very fabric of the day. It was the sound of neither man nor beast, but something primal and really, really pissed off.

One after another, opji and wojak made a *wfft* sound and their heads exploded in a starburst of red mist.

Bodies toppled into the mud.

The day fell utterly silent.

And then a human in the pen began to wail.

Mason turned black eyes on the woman. He seemed taller, bigger around the shoulders and his face was full of hard angles.

A man shushed the blubbering woman and her cries turned to pitiful whimpers.

Mason raised a hand and the dead, headless wojaks rose from the mud. He sent them to the pen of human captives and the screaming began again as the wojaks attacked.

Grim burst from the trees and loped across the open ground. He was no longer my grimalkin, but the night jaguar—a massive, black beast with red glowing eyes. Paws the size of a bear's splashed through puddles, tearing up the ground. Muscles rippled across his shoulders as he bunched for one final leap. He flew through the air, claws and teeth primed to take Mason down.

The demon swatted him aside like a fly.

Grim yelped when Mason's hand connected to the side of his head. He fell with a solid thump and didn't move again.

"Stop it!" I screamed. Tears blurred my eyes and snot dribbled from my nose. I wiped both away with my sleeve and shouted again. My voice was raspy. I'd run out of steam. Only fear and fury drove me now.

The wojaks continued their slaughter.

Mason didn't move. I grabbed his arm and tried to jerk him around to face me. It was like pulling on stone.

The pitiful cries from the pen finally fell silent. Mason made a downward motion with his hand, and the wojaks collapsed on top of the corpses they'd just made.

Mason turned to face me. His eyes were entirely black. Charcoal tattoos inked up his neck and spread across his cheek.

"Mason?"

"Mason is dead." The flat voice coming from his mouth was not Mason's. It wasn't even human.

My husband, the only man who ever knew me, truly knew me, who saw past the dirt on my jeans and my utilitarian braids was gone.

I needed to kill him. I'd promised.

My sword bristled in my grip. I couldn't raise it. I couldn't.

Mason's lip curled into a snarl. No, it wasn't Mason. The demon scrutinized me with such utter contempt that my heart went cold.

He growled like a rabid dog, his face only inches from mine, so close, I could feel the heat of his breath.

He jerked his arm from my grasp and ran into the forest.

I stood in the weak morning light for…I don't know how long. An eternity or maybe seconds. Finally, I dragged my gaze to the scene around me.

The carnage was unimaginable. And yet, there it was, all its bloody glory on display for my imagination to replay again and again in future sleepless nights.

I watched crows descend into the yard, drawn by the scent of death and the promise of an easy meal.

And still I didn't move.

Didn't feel.

Didn't think.

Because if I let thought in, there would be Mason.

And how Mason had killed innocents.

And how Mason was a demon.

And how Mason was lost to me.

My heart was ice. My chest ached and I realized I'd been holding my breath. I let it out and it came with a wheezing cry.

Something bumped against my hand, the one still holding the sword that I hadn't plunged into Mason's heart.

Grim, back in his cat form, butted me with his head. Looking down at him brought Gabe into my view.

Oh, Gabe!

The sight of him finally broke the shell of ice around me. I crumpled to the ground and grabbed his hand, rubbing it over and over as if I could rub warmth and life back into it. His sightless eyes, his beautiful brown eyes, stared into the white sky.

He'd saved me. And he'd saved himself from becoming a wojak—a fate worse than death.

Then I remembered Emil, fallen during the attack. Great gobbing sobs tore at my chest and burned my throat. I couldn't even bring myself to go to him, couldn't bear the thought of looking into the face of another dead friend.

The shar-lil had fallen from Nici's hands when she died and landed in a puddle. I picked it up and ran my fingers over the rough husk. The puddle had washed away most of the blood. I cradled it in my hands, waiting for that feeling of light and life to wash over me again.

There was nothing. The shar-lil had gone dark. Was it dead? Maybe Mason's flare of dark magic had only stunned it. I had no way of knowing.

"Kyra-lady?" The small voice startled me. Jacoby reached out and hesitated with his hand raised. I grabbed it and pulled him into a hug.

Nici's thrall had ended with her death. It was the only bright bit in dark day. Jacoby squirmed and I let him go.

"Kyra-lady is hurts?"

What a question. Yes, I hurt in my very soul.

"I'm okay. Are you?"

He nodded. Mud had dried to a crust in the fur around his eyes. His vest was torn and he'd lost his work belt, but he seemed unharmed.

Someone shouted from on the ridge. The sound was so unexpected, it took me a moment to understand.

Hub had arrived. We had only moments. The soldiers would seize us and sort out the mess later.

"Here. Take this." I wrapped Jacoby's long fingers around the shar-lil. "I need you to go now. Take it and run. Run all the way home if you have to. Understand?"

He licked his dirt-crusted lips. "Understands."

"Good. Go." I gave him a little shove. He looked back at me once. "Go!" And the dervish ran, using his fire for a new purpose. To save the shar-lil.

He ran toward the tents away from the incoming soldiers.

In minutes, I was overwhelmed. They found me still crouched over Gabe's body. My legs had gone numb under me.

They questioned me for hours. More Hub soldiers arrived, along with Captain Lowe. Nobody touched any of the bodies until she saw the site and a forensic team documented everything.

While soldiers pulled bodies to the bonfire, Lowe found me at the makeshift control center that had been set up under the pavilion. She offered me tea. I accepted it, and wrapped stiff fingers around the hot mug.

"Tell me from the beginning, what happened." Her face was neutral, neither angry nor pitying. I was grateful for that.

"I told the other officer already."

"Tell me."

I sighed and went through the story I'd concocted again. I told her how I had found the opji den by accident yesterday. I left out all mention of the shar-lil. At best, Hub would want to study it in a lab. At worst, they'd destroy it. I wouldn't let them have it.

I also left out any mention of Mason. I let her think he was still at home in bed. The truth would come out soon enough. He was Prime Minister, after all. But I couldn't voice the words. Not yet. So, I told her that I'd been knocked out during the attack and didn't know how the opji, the wojaks or the humans had died.

Lowe eyed me with one eyebrow raised. "That's your story? You don't remember?"

"No. I didn't *see* anything. I *remember* being hit on the head." I was covered in enough blood for this to be plausible. I certainly didn't have to feign the headache that was grinding at my temples. "There are more humans inside that building." She nodded to the barn. "Do you know anything about them? They're very confused too."

"The godlings. That's who we came looking for. Our friend Gabe was with them. Nici, that blond opji, she had them in a thrall." Now that Nici's thrall had evaporated, the godlings would be confused and nauseous for some time, as if coming down from a high.

"Look, I told you everything I know. I need to get home to my family."

I rubbed my eyes and Lowe took pity on me.

"Fine, but we'll have more questions in a day or two."

I nodded and rose. Grim wound around my legs.

"Cute kitty," Lowe said. She reached out a hand for Grim to sniff. He looked as if her fingers were made of rotten eggs. Lowe didn't know that Grim was anything more than a cat and hadn't tried to question him. Grim had wisely kept silent.

"Captain!" A soldier called out. "We have a live one over here."

We ran to where the soldiers were helping Emil sit up. Blood from a gash on his cheek had dried like war paint. It was already healing though, thanks to his vampire blood. I hoped it didn't heal too quickly, or Lowe would have some very pointed questions for him.

"I suppose you're going to tell me you don't remember anything either," Captain Lowe said.

Emil looked at me and I shook my head, ever so slightly.

"I remember fighting the vamps. That's about all…Ow!" He yelped as a soldier tried to pull him upright. "I think my arm is broken."

"Captain, he's obviously hurt. Let me take him home. We have a healer staying with us. We'll both come into the station tomorrow to give a formal statement. I promise."

Lowe glared at me, but nodded.

I hurried Emil away before he saw the soldiers tossing Gabe's body into the mage fire.

EPILOGUE

Holly cried. Gita made shushing noises from the other room and sang an old sea shanty that always made Holly laugh. Neither crying nor song penetrated the bubble of despair I'd packed around me.

From outside, Princess barked. It wasn't a warning, just a play bark as she chased Raven and the goblits.

I ignored them too. And the ticking clock that told me I'd been sitting in my unwashed state, in my pajamas, for a whole day. And the sounds of cutlery clinking together as Dutch prepared supper in the kitchen. And the hundreds of other tiny sounds in the quiet house.

I ignored it all.

None of it mattered. Gabe was dead. Emil had gone home and wouldn't return my calls. Mason was gone. No, worse than gone. Gone would mean he was dead or he'd left me. Either way, I would have been able to mourn and move on. This was worse. He was still out there somewhere, unreachable, unforgettable.

Were possessed souls aware of their possession? Was Mason trapped inside his mind with the demon at the steering wheel?

Oh, gods. I pressed a hand to my stomach. The thought made me physically ill.

I went over and over those last moments with the opji. I knew what I'd seen—the demon staring at me through Mason's eyes. And I knew that if Mason was strong enough to defeat it, he'd come home.

But he hadn't. He was under a thrall worse than anything the opji could conjure.

My widget pinged. Oscar's face appeared on the screen, but I didn't answer it. Captain Lowe had been calling too. They both wanted me to make a formal statement at Hub Station. I couldn't muster the energy to drive into town.

Nori was gone, now that Soolea no longer needed her. Soolea would be leaving in a few weeks too, as soon as the baby was strong enough to travel to her parents' homestead in the north.

Angus and the Guardians felt Mason's disappearance as much as I did. They patrolled the Inbetween looking for him. I didn't know what they expected to do if they found him.

I glanced at the shar-lil. I'd left it in a basket by the fire, in case it needed warmth. It seemed dead. The spark of life I'd felt was gone. The ring of fur had been gone too, and the animals hadn't followed us home, a sure indicator that the shar-lil no longer held the forest creatures in its sway.

Gita emerged from the hallway that led to the bedrooms. Holly clung to her fingers with one hand and clutched a ragged toy giraffe in the other.

"She needs some Mama time." Tears stained Gita's cheeks and the collar of her shirt. Holly ran through the living room toward me and tripped on the edge of the rug. Before she sprawled on the floor, Grim was there. He slunk underneath her in time to catch the fall.

"Kitty!" Holly grabbed his ear in her little fist. Grim endured it with a pained expression.

"Gentle with the kitty," Gita said. That should be my job to teach her the proper way to treat animals. But I was so tired. It all seemed like too much work.

Grim gently extracted himself from the baby fists and escaped to the kitchen.

"I'll send Suzt down later to get her put to bed," Gita said. I only nodded. Bedtime should be my job too. Mine or Mason's. He loved reading her stories before bed.

I deliberately breathed in and out as the rush of pain washed over me in a wave. I squeezed Holly to me. She protested and squirmed from my arms.

Gita watched us with a pinched expression. She wanted to say something, but didn't.

There was nothing left to say.

Mason was gone. Holly would grow up never remembering her father.

Gita let herself out the back door. Alone with my daughter, fresh tears streamed down my face. I didn't even bother trying to hold them in anymore. Holly, who was so used to Gita's tears, didn't even notice. She petted her giraffe and picked up my hand to make me pet it too.

Because I'd become so good at wallowing in my misery and ignoring the world around me, I didn't hear the car pull into the driveway.

"Visitors," Dutch said, as he hurried from the kitchen.

"Tell them I'm not here." I didn't want a visit from Oscar or Nori or anyone else.

Dutch hesitated with one hand on the door, perhaps wondering how he could make excuses when I sat in plain view of the front door.

Then the door burst open.

Lisobet, my dryad grandmother strode in, followed by Kester Owens.

Holly took one look at the tall lady with white hair and the shadowy, imposing man behind her, and she started to wail.

I just stared, dumbfounded. Her wails turned into shrieks.

"None of that," Lisobet snapped. She picked up the screaming baby, kissed her on the forehead and handed her to Dutch. "I'll take care of you later, little lady. But first, I must speak to your mother."

Dutch held Holly in his outstretched hands like she was a live grenade. Luckily, Suzt had seen the visitors and came running in at that moment.

"I'll just take her up to the cottage for a bit, while you visit with your… um…friends." She eyed Kester. He smiled at her, but since he looked like a skeleton at the best of times, that did little to comfort her.

Once Holly, Suzt and Dutch were gone, Lisobet rounded on me.

"You look like a badger turd rolled in dirt."

"Thank you, Grandmother. I'm happy to see you too."

"Don't give me your snark, young lady. I'm here to help."

That was debatable.

Her expression softened. She sat on the edge of the couch. Grim, who had been perched there, hissed at her.

Lisobet gave him a stern look and he stalked off.

Kester had been left standing in the foyer. He looked a little lost as he squeezed a knitted cap in his hands.

"How did she manage to drag you here?" I asked.

He shrugged. "Oscar called me. I called the lady."

So that's how they found out. I'd have to have a little chat with Oscar about the meaning of top secret.

"I'll…uh, go for a little walk. Let you ladies chat. It's good to see you, Kyra." Kester smiled and went out.

Lisobet sat beside me. She didn't speak, but I could feel the weight of her frown as she studied me. Finally, I couldn't stand it any longer and I looked up.

"That's better." Lisobet folded her hands in her lap. "Now tell me all of it."

I'd like to say she compelled me in some way, but there was no magic to the verbal deluge that came out of my mouth. I'd been holding it all in and the release, if not good, was at least cleansing.

Lisobet was a good listener. She didn't interrupt me until I'd finished.

"Well, I see two roads forward." Her delicate eyebrow arched high.

"You do?" I couldn't see past the end of the couch.

"We find a way to cure Mason. Or we kill him."

I snorted. "You think I'm strong enough for either of those? You're wrong. Mason was the strong one."

Lisobet grabbed my hands. Her skin was rough as bark.

"You are dryad." She waved a hand at my protest. "You are. You were raised human and forged into a Valkyrie, but you are more dryad than either of those. Your magic is strong. And it's the magic of life. That is how you defeat a demon."

She sounded so sure.

"Come on, now." She pulled me off the couch. "You smell worse than you look. Time for a shower. And then we'll get some food in you. You'll see. Things always look brighter after food."

I wasn't so sure about that, but I let her drag me away.

I SAT ON THE garden swing that Mason had made for me with the shar-lil in my lap. The afternoon had been warm for the beginning of April, and even though the fading sun brought a chill, I didn't want to go in yet. Princess snoozed in a warm patch by my feet.

Two weeks had passed since the fight with the opji. Two weeks since I'd seen Mason.

Few people knew what really happened. Oscar knew the truth and he'd concocted a story about Mason contracting the flu and needing weeks to recover. It wasn't a bad story. The disease had decimated the shanty towns outside the gates, and hospitals within the ward were already overfull. Having the Prime Minister of the Alchemists contract it was big news, but thankfully few reporters dared to make the trek outside the ward to investigate. Those who did brave the Inbetween for the story were met by either the Guardians or a scary-looking hell hound. They went away pretty quickly.

Oscar had insisted that I tell Captain Lowe the truth.

"She's spearheading the committee that's looking into the opji movements in our area. She needs to know everything," he'd said on the day after the attack. I'd reluctantly agreed. The following day, Emil and I had driven to Hub Station to give our statements in private. Lowe had agreed that Mason's disappearance should be confidential for the time being, but we wouldn't be able to hide it forever.

I kept hoping he'd come home, that he'd remember who he was and come striding down the gravel driveway, tired and disheveled, but wholly Mason. That's why I'd taken to sitting on the swing when the weather permitted. I had a clear view of the driveway.

But he hadn't returned. He was out there somewhere in the Inbetween, living off the land. The demon was smart enough not to try to enter the city. He'd be recognized immediately.

No, he was out there.

I kept that thought close to my heart. It was both painful and reassuring.

Twice, I saw the flaming wings of the mountain devil. Terra's watch dog lurked in the trees, but it was too magical to come through our ward. And I barely slept, leaving Terra no way to communicate with me.

Good. I didn't care to hear her pleas right now. In time, I would decide what to do with the shar-lil, and I wouldn't be swayed by the demands of anyone, not even a god.

My widget vibrated in my pocket. I took it out and saw an incoming call from Avie. I almost let it go to voice mail, but that would only make her worry.

"Hey," I said, putting her on speaker.

"Hey." She hesitated. "How are you doing?"

I was already sick of that question, but there was no point taking my ill-temper out on Avie. "I'm okay."

"Good. That's good." She paused again and I could hear dishes clanking, and then the tone of background noise changed as if she'd moved to another room, probably the bathroom. It was the only door she could lock and guarantee a few moments of kid-free solitude.

"Listen, I have some news from Aunt Cece. About the shar-lil. She found only one reference to it, and it's kind of concerning." Her hand muffled the widget's mic while she yelled at someone to stop banging on the door. "Sorry about that. I can't get a minute to myself. Anyway, Cece said she found a reference in an ancient book of fables that are retellings of even older stories. She thinks the originals might even be Sumerian."

"Avie, just tell me what she found." I tried to keep the impatience from my tone, but my sunshine and roses filter was turned off.

"Oh, right. She said," another pause. I gritted my teeth. "She said it's a world killer."

"A what?" I glanced at the strange little coconut in my lap.

Avie rushed on. "It's just a preliminary translation, of course. Aunt Cece says these things are really hard to translate because it could have gone through several languages before the current one."

She paused for a breath and the line went silent. Then, "Kyra, I'm really sorry."

We both new she was talking about more than the translation. I nodded, even though she couldn't see me. I didn't trust my voice.

I wiped at my eyes. Part of me was amazed that I still had tears to shed. My eye sockets should have been dried out husks by now.

"S'okay. Just let me know if she finds out more."

"I will, and you let me know if…well, if things change."

"Thanks, Avie." I ended the call and took a moment to calm my breathing. By the One-eyed Father, I was tired of nearly imploding every time I thought of him.

I sniffled back the rest of my tears and turned the shar-lil over in my hands. A world killer, eh? That still didn't tell me much.

Her husk had started to peel like hairy burlap. I couldn't remember when I had started thinking of it as "her" but it felt right.

Another piece came off in my hands. At first, I'd thought that meant she was truly dead, but three days ago, the shar-lil had awakened. The magic aura I'd first keened inside the egg returned, slowly at first, then growing brighter like a psychic lamp turned on high. And now it hummed with life again.

Since her awakening, the critters in my barn had been unsettled. Today, Princess wouldn't leave my side. She'd snuffled at the shar-lil until I told her to leave off. The ward around our homestead kept the forest animals at bay so far, and Errol was working on a ward just for the shar-lil, to mask her song. Apart from the effect on my animals, I didn't know if the opji had a way to track her.

The shar-lil jumped in my hands. I nearly dropped it. She wobbled and rocked, and I gripped her shell more firmly. A crack formed in the husk.

Princess raised her muzzle from her paws and whined. The shar-lil jerked again. The hound's eyes widened. She woofed and scuttled backward.

"It's okay. She won't hurt you." I patted the shar-lil, hoping I spoke the truth. Despite the ill-treatment by the opji, I didn't sense anything malevolent in the little egg or seed or…whatever she was.

The crack in the shell grew into a round chip that suddenly popped away from the rest of the pod. The chip landed on the ground. Princess snuffled it, then pawed it and whined. I peered into the hole it made.

A foot kicked me on the nose.

Huh. So definitely an egg.

The foot waggled.

It was the shape of a bear paw, but as small as a cat's and covered in coarse brown hair with liver-colored toe-pads. The toes flexed and I stuck my finger between them. It gripped me with a firm squeeze.

I waited for the rest of the shell to break away, but the creature inside seemed exhausted from this first foray outside her shell. The magic calmed. I put my ear to the husk and heard a very faint snore.

Princess watched the egg with her ears at high alert.

"No doubt she'll come out when she's ready." I scratched the hound behind the ears to show her I wasn't concerned.

It was time to go in anyway, time to eat food that tasted like ash in my mouth, then lie awake for hours in the dark.

I rose and headed over to Gallivant's paddock before going in. He ran to the fence rail and sniffed the shar-lil. His tail rose straight up in the air. Yep, the shar-lil needed a ward. I'd check on Errol's progress tonight.

"And you need a good run, don't you, buddy." I patted Gallivant's neck. "Maybe tomorrow."

His attention shifted to the forest. We were at the edge of the property. Behind the paddock, the forest loomed, full of menacing shadows.

Gallivant whinnied.

Princess felt it too. She put one paw forward. Her haunches were bunched, ready to leap. A growl rumbled in her chest. Her eyes fixed on a point just outside the ward, where the shadows lay thick in the fading light.

A man stood there.

A bark erupted from Princess. She bared her teeth.

Mason broke from the shadows to stand in the light.

He looked like the hell his demon came from. His hair was matted, beard overgrown and face gaunt. Tattoos covered his left cheek from chin to forehead. He'd lost his jacket and his shirt was tattered and dirty.

I guess demons don't feel the cold.

Black eyes watched me.

Princess dashed to the end of the fence.

"Princess, hael!" I snapped her back before she ran through the ward. She stopped at the edge of the paddock. Every hair on her back bristled.

Mason watched us with a small smile nearly hidden under his bushman beard. He held out his hands as if testing the heat from a fire.

"You don't think this flimsy ward will hold me back, do you? Not for long, anyway." Now he full on smiled. It was gross. It was Mason's smile, and yet not—a twisted parody of the face I loved.

I didn't say anything. In the silence, Mason prowled along the ward's perimeter. I called Princess back and dug my fingers into her scruff.

Mason pushed at the ward. I felt its magic tug at me. He moved on, slowly, testing the ward as he went.

"You know, your god is very accommodating," he said. "So much life around here. Life is good. It means there's also death. And I breathe death."

Again with the grin. My stomach churned with emotions I couldn't identify.

"Give me a few weeks, lover, and I'll be able to come home to you for good."

"You talk too much." My Mason never spoke five words when three would do.

He winked and blew me a kiss. Then he stepped back into the shadows and was gone.

I slumped against the fence post. Princess whined and licked my hand.

I stood straight, fury giving me new energy. I was done with nameless despair. Lisobet was right. I needed to step up. I'd never been good at making the tough decisions when it came to my family. Mason made those. He'd always had my back. And now I had to have his. He wouldn't want to live like this. He wouldn't want his daughter's last sight to be her daddy's face, twisted by demon magic.

My anger had a focal point now. The demon who'd taken my husband from me would come for the rest of us. I wouldn't let that happen. I'd see him dead before he stepped a foot over that ward.

"Come on, Princess." I whistled for the hound. "It's time for dinner."

And after dinner, it would be time to make plans.

Dear Reader,

There are more adventures in the Inbetween coming! Book 8 of the Valkyrie Bestiary Series is already in the works. Be sure to sign up for the Readers' Group at KimMcDougall.com to get updates on new releases. When you subscribe, you'll get a free eBook, *Tales from the Inbetween*, that includes deleted scenes from Valkyrie Bestiary books, including one from book 7 where Gabe and Emil fight the mammoth rat-eater. You'll also get a short story from everyone's favorite dervish, Jacoby. This story won't be available anywhere else, so be sure to join the Readers' Group to claim your copy.

You probably know that authors love reviews, but do you know why? Reviews are important because they help other readers know what to expect from the book, they let me know how my books are received by readers, and they help booksellers decide which books to show to new readers.

If you enjoyed this book I would be grateful for your honest review. It can be as short as you like. Even a few positive words will go a long way. And I'll try to make it as painless as possible. Use this link, https://kimmcdougall.com/Review-Devils-Don-t-Lie to find the review site of your choice.

Thank you for reading *Devils Don't Lie* and I hope to see you in the Inbetween again soon!

Kim McDougall

Want to find out more about Kyra's world?

- Learn more about the Valkyrie Bestiary series and other books by Kim McDougall at https://kimmcdougall.com.

- Poke around at Kyra's blog at http://valkyriebestiary.com.

- Find all the Valkyrie Bestiary books (including prequels and novellas) along with deleted scenes and series FAQ at https://kimmcdougall.com/valkyrie-bestiary.

Other places you can follow Kim McDougall Books:

- Facebook: https://www.facebook.com/KimMcDougallBooks

- Instagram: https://www.instagram.com/kimmcdougallbook

- Amazon: https://www.amazon.com/-/e/B002C7CI2M

- Bookbub: https://www.bookbub.com/authors/kim-mcdougall

- Goodreads: https://www.goodreads.com/author/show/1432797.Kim_McDougall

Also By Kim McDougall

Valkyrie Bestiary Novels
Dragons Don't Eat Meat
Dervishes Don't Dance
Hell Hounds Don't Heel
Grimalkins Don't Purr
Kelpies Don't Fly
Ghouls Don't Scamper
Devils Don't Lie
Unicorns Don't Cry

Valkyrie Bestiary Novellas
The Last Door to Underhill
The Girl Who Cried Banshee
Three Half Goats Gruff
Oh, Come All Ye Dragons

The Hidden Coven Series
Inborn Magic
Soothed by Magic
Trigger Magic
Bellwether Magic
Gone Magic

Writing as Eliza Crowe
The Shifted Dreams Series
Pick Your Monster
Lost Rogues

About the Author

If Kim McDougall could have one magical superpower, it would be to talk to animals. Or maybe to shift into animal form. Definitely, fantastical critters and magic often feature in her stories. So until she can change into a griffin and fly away, she writes dark paranormal action and romance tales, from her home in Central Ontario.

Visit Kim Online at KimMcDougall.com.